Also By Dr. Cecil H.H. Mills

Ghost Hunters Adventure Club
and the Secret of the Grande Chateau

Ghost Hunters Adventure Club
and THE EXPRESS
TRAIN to NOWHERE

Ghost Hunters Adventure Club

AND THE EXPRESS TRAIN TO NOWHERE

DR. CECIL H.H. MILLS

PERMUTED
PRESS

A PERMUTED PRESS BOOK

Ghost Hunters Adventure Club and the Express Train to Nowhere
© 2022 by Game Grumps
All Rights Reserved

ISBN: 978-1-63758-184-1
ISBN (eBook): 978-1-63758-185-8

Cover illustration by Paul Mann
Cover typography by Cody Corcoran
Illustrations by Rachel L. Allen
Interior design and composition by Greg Johnson, Textbook Perfect
"Siobhan's Waltz for Revenge" written by Jesse Cale and Dr. Cecil H.H. Mills

PERMUTED PRESS

Permuted Press, LLC
New York • Nashville
permutedpress.com

Published in the United States of America

Introduction

L isten kid, there's a way we can both make money off of this. I'll tell you all about it in a second, but first let me make some introductions.

Hello, dear reader! It's your old friend, Dr. Cecil H.H. Mills: accomplished and sometimes controversial wordsmith and author of many intellectual adult novels that you might not have heard of, considering that you're reading this book.

You see, I used to be an author of serious novels. Adult novels. Novels meant to challenge the reader to look deep within their soul and examine their deepest, darkest thoughts. They required of a reader the reading comprehension skills necessary to parse the art that I created. For instance, *My Travels Abroad and Within* was a book that featured me traveling the American Heartland, interviewing the people who form the soul of this great nation, and then challenging each and every one of them to a fistfight.

But as Fortuna would have it, I was sent on a very downward spiral. It started with every known copy of my last adult novel, *Cerberus, From On High*, being destroyed in a mysterious warehouse fire that I'm legally bound to not discuss any further.[1]

From there I was unjustly exiled from the literary world, lost what wealth I had left in a dice game/challenge of physical strength gone awry, and soon realized that I had some pretty hefty financial arrears coming due.

---

[1] Other than to say that my former publishing company Bradford & Bradford can eat dirt, as is my court-appointed right.

So, faced with a crowbar-shaped problem and trying to avoid a knee-cap-shaped solution, I did what any reasonable person would do: I wrote a Young Adult mystery novel.

And then all this happened, I say, gesturing to the train station around us. Right now, you and I are standing on a platform in Harborville Union Station, a bustling transport hub located in the hometown of the Ghost Hunters Adventure Club. Footsteps echo over the crowd's chatter in the concrete tunnels leading to platforms. The train we're waiting for is right behind us. I'll address that in a bit.

Now, I figure you must be confused. Never mind the setting, that's artistic fluff. Why, you ask, standing on a platform with me, would a man of my repute compromise his artistic integrity and, on purpose, write a story for people who have not yet formed their prefrontal cortex?

Because that's the only thing the publishers would buy from me. Listen, I don't have the time or patience to explain to you the intricacies of the literary publishing world, but rest assured that it is completely devoid of any artistic merit whatsoever and any person thinking of delving into such an industry deserves to be hunted.

The long and short of it was that I wrote *Ghost Hunters Adventure Club and the Secret of the Grande Chateau*, a completely serviceable story in which two detective brothers, J.J. and Valentine Watts, traveled up to a snowy chateau in the mountains to solve a mystery with their new friend, Trudi de la Rosa. They overcame some obstacles or whatever, and at the end of the book they decided to stick together. This was for the specific purpose of me being able to write a sequel, if the first book was a hit and on the off chance any debt collectors figured out that I was no longer residing in international waters.

* * *

KID, THE REASON WE'RE HERE is because the last book *was* a hit and I *did* get a sequel. You're inside of it right now. Smell that diesel exhaust in the air? That's the smell of a seven-book franchise in the making. Who knows; if we play our cards right, maybe we can squeeze a feature film out of it!

Now, I don't personally doubt that the public at large would fall for such meaningless mass-market slop, turning what is, I wholeheartedly assure you, a derisive commentary on the frivolities of youth into my most popular book to date. Which I'm fine with, I guess.

Maybe I should have less faith in humanity, I don't know. But audience analysis and existential crises aside, I see something here. And I hope you see it too. What is it?

Opportunity.

As you know, I've never done or plan to do any research on what exactly constitutes a "Young Adult" reader. I can only make the inference that they lack the mental fortitude to understand my much more intellectual adult novels, and thus are susceptible to confidence scams. But here's where you come in and here's how you and I can get rich quick before we all disappear without leaving a paper trail: I'll keep punching out these schlocky Young Adult mystery novels if you keep upholding the cottage industry of bootleg *Ghost Hunters Adventure Club* merchandise that seemingly sprung up overnight.

It's that easy! Look at it this way: there exists a market yearning to drop coin on the things we create, heretofore known as Content, and we both have the ability to feed into the same burgeoning market. The more people who know about Ghost Hunters Adventure Club, the more people buy the book. The more people buy the book, the more they become fans. The more they become fans, the more they flood secondary markets looking for Content to the degree of fan art, trinkets, posters, and T-shirts. All things that you, yourself, can produce and sell at a profitable markup.

I know what you must be thinking right now: "But Dr. Cecil, why would you just go out and tell everyone your plan? Isn't that counterproductive to the plan's success?" To which I counter with this: Who do you think actually reads these introductions?

Let's face it, dear reader, you've cleared the admittedly very low bar of a Young Adult readership. In fact, I'd argue that if you're still reading then you're smart enough to know a cushy deal when you see one. I don't know why you're reading this filth, which is a cruel showcase of teenage bravado and wish fulfillment *at best*. Maybe you fished it out of a river that this book was thrown into out of disgust. Maybe your idiot nephew asked you to read it and you're just being polite. Maybe a copy of this book has existed into the near future and you've found the clues hidden within these pages to help you lead a rebellion against your robot over-lords.[2] But whatever the case, good on you. Glad to have you here, glad to have you on my side. Welcome to the grift.

* * *

So WHAT'S THE DEAL with the train? That diesel electric behemoth you see looming over us is the Harborville Express. Don't let its brand-new paint job fool you; it's been around for a while. This right here is the setting of *Ghost Hunters Adventure Club and the Express Train to Nowhere*. It'll be leaving the station soon.

But where's the Ghost Hunters Adventure Club, you ask? As per usual, J.J., Valentine, and Trudi are running late. This is probably through some fault of J.J.'s, but more honestly it's because I wanted the chapter to be snappier and feel a little more kinetic.

They'll come running around the corner and down the steps to the plat-form soon, huffing and puffing as they make it onto the train at the last possible moment before it pulls out of the station. However, with this brief moment before our titular heroes arrive, let's discuss something important.

Kid, I firmly believe with my whole heart that each and every person on earth—no matter how young or old—should have a plan that will one day lead to them owning and piloting their own yacht. My dear reader, this novel you hold in your hands is my Yacht Plan, and I hope you will

---

[2] z dvoo grnvw vnk yozhg rm z wzgz xvmgvi dlfow trev blfi ivhrhgzmxv grnv gl nzmvfevi

make it yours. If we keep this transactional relationship going for long enough, you and me are gonna be racing luxury boats off the coast of some undisclosed equatorial nation very soon.

To that end, I say, leaning in close to inspire confidence, I promise you that I will do anything, absolutely anything, to make as much profit off of this intellectual property as possible.

These protagonists, the Ghost Hunters Adventure Club, they mean nothing to me. Their actions are abhorrent, ill-advised, half-baked, and above all, illegal in most jurisdictions of law. If this story were to happen in real life, I can guarantee you that not only would J.J., Valentine, and Trudi be arrested for their reckless vigilantism, but they would also be held up by many as a portent of doom for the upcoming generation of morally bankrupt youths.

And, obviously, these dumb idiot mystery-solving children do not exist. They are a figment of my imagination. And while I will concede that of all the imaginations that Ghost Hunters Adventure Club could have come from, they're coming from the best; I will also freely admit that even I can't make them real. There is nothing I can do to turn these characters made of paper and ink into actual flesh and blood, so I urge you to treat them as such. I will put these characters into whatever dangerous situation that I deem will make the most profit. And that's fine, because they are not real.

So, with all that said and done, I think it's finally time to switch over to past tense and start the tale of the Watts brothers, their friend Trudi de la Rosa, the business entity known as Ghost Hunters Adventure Club, and the Express Train to Nowhere.

The train's whistle blows, indicating last call for passengers. This means I can leave you with my one last surprise.

Just before the train departs, I step on board.

CHAPTER 1

The Harborville Express

"We're late!" Valentine Watts yelled as he zipped past a marble pillar just inside of Harborville Union Station. He slid to a stop on the concrete floor in front of a set of stairs leading down to the train platform below. Readjusting his rucksack and pushing up the sleeves of his baby blue sweater, he looked behind him.

J.J. Watts and Trudi de la Rosa were trailing close behind. In addition to the rucksacks the two were carrying, J.J. had the added weight of his leather satchel slung around his neck. He also had a large soft-serve ice cream cone in each hand.

"I don't know how many different ways I can say sorry for that!" J.J. yelled back.

"How late?" asked Trudi as she arrived at the top of the stairs.

Valentine looked down toward the platform and spotted their train: the Harborville Express. It had already begun moving.

"We should run," he said.

The three of them bolted down the stairs at an all-out dash toward the train. Now on the platform, Trudi could see an open door near one of the cars toward the front.

"I think we can make it!" she shouted, as she led the charge forward. Beating the pace of the slow-moving Harborville Express, she removed her rucksack and tossed it through the door of the train car before jumping on herself. "Come on!" she yelled at Valentine just behind her.

Valentine didn't bother removing his own baggage before he made his entry attempt. He snagged a hand onto the steel railing alongside the door before using it to swing himself up into the car, catching his horn-rimmed glasses before they fell off of his face. He and Trudi stuck their heads out of the door to lend their support to J.J. By now the speed of the train was picking up.

J.J. bounced along the edge of the platform, barely holding on with the acceleration of the Harborville Express. He ran carefully, so as not to further disturb the two ice cream cones dripping down the sleeves of his red sweater.

"You gotta drop the soft serve!" Valentine shouted at his brother.

"No!" J.J. yelled back. "I've grown emotionally attached to them!"

Trudi looked to the other end of the train. Her eyes widened. "You're running out of platform!" she called out.

J.J., by now losing pace with the train, looked down at his ice cream cones. He remembered haggling with the clerk at the ice cream parlor. He remembered being offered a 20 percent discount if he stopped trying to haggle. He remembered being just about to enjoy the two ice cream cones he had legally purchased at a discount before Valentine pointed at a clock.

And then he saw the edge of the platform fast approaching.

"I'm sorry, fellas," he said with great sorrow to his ice creams as he cast them aside on the Harborville Union Station platform. Now unencumbered, J.J. turned up the heat and made his way within striking distance of Valentine and Trudi's outstretched arms.

J.J. yelled mightily as he hurled himself onto the train, bowling over both Valentine and Trudi in the process. The three crashed to the floor of the train compartment they were now safely aboard.

"I'm gonna miss those guys," J.J. said. He stood up, offering an elbow of support to both Valentine and Trudi in turn. He then reached into his satchel and pulled out a moist towelette from its Ghost Hunters Adventure Club-branded packaging. "And you guys said this would be a useless mechanism for advertising," he said, wiping ice cream from his hands.

Trudi found her glasses that had been knocked off in the initial jump attempt. She reaffixed them to her face and smoothed out the ruffles of her business casual blazer. The three of them cased the joint.

"Would you look at this opulence?" asked J.J. as he marveled at the tasteful art deco interior design aesthetic surrounding them. The mahogany hallway ran along the side of the train, with several doors leading to several travel quarters unknown.

"This must be the passenger compartment," said Valentine. "Where's ours?"

"Just hold on a second," J.J. held up a friendly hand to interrupt him. "I had a speech prepared and I've been waiting all morning to deliver it."

He took a step forward and turned in a practiced way to face his two friends. Clasping his hands together, he spoke as if he were lecturing in an auditorium. "Good morning, everyone. As you all know, Ghost Hunters Adventure Club has seen a fifty percent increase in hiring in the past few months." He nodded at Trudi. "We're growing as a company, and now more than ever it's important that we truly learn the meaning of teamwork. So with that I would like to say the following."

He swept his hands open in a grand gesture. "Welcome to the First Inaugural Ghost Hunters Adventure Club L—"

"Tickets, please," came a voice from behind them. J.J. paused his speech and the three turned to see a man in an ill-fitting, dark blue uniform with a matching cap. A badge on his coat pocket read, "Conductor."

"Just a moment," J.J. said to the man. "I was in the middle of a speech."

"Tickets, please," the conductor repeated in a firmer tone. He scratched at the five o'clock shadow on his face, looking as if he hadn't slept in days.

"Fine, fine," J.J. grumbled. He reached into his satchel and produced three tickets. "Which one of these are ours?"

"None of them," the conductor said after a cursory glance. He shot his thumb toward the back of the train. "Second class is just past the lounge."

"Second class?" J.J. demanded. "That isn't right." He grabbed the tickets back from the conductor and reexamined them.

"Whoa!" yelled the conductor. Where once there was an aloof gaze, he now looked as if someone had lit a fire under him. "The snatching of tickets out of my hands is in direct violation of train law. Don't do that again."

A phrase got caught in Trudi's ear. "Train law?" she asked.

The conductor sighed impatiently. "See that out there?" he said, pointing out of the window to the view of the rolling hills and sporadic commercial buildings passing lazily by. "Not train law. This here?" he gestured broadly within the confines of the train. "Train law."

"Well that makes sense, I suppose," said Valentine.

"They're laws as old as trains themselves. Sometimes cryptic, but always resolute; they were created and are now followed to make sure you arrive to your destination safely and on time. I'm duty-bound to throw you off of this train in as comical of a fashion as possible if you try something like that again."

The conductor pulled out a hole punch from his coat pocket and clicked it on the three tickets in J.J.'s hand. "Second class is back behind the lounge," he repeated. He then stalked past them and continued his duties, knocking on doors and checking tickets.

The three of them looked at each other. J.J. took another look at the tickets in his hand.

"Whoops! I guess we *are* in coach."

Valentine and Trudi groaned. The three walked to the end of the hallway and through an adjoining corridor. Opening the next set of doors, they found themselves in a dining room with finely upholstered chairs and booths. Clinking silverware and soft conversation accentuated the soft rumblings of the train's movement.

"I don't mean to be the guy asking the hardball questions so early in the morning," started Valentine, as the three sidled past a waiter taking breakfast orders, "but how much planning did you do for this trip?"

"Plenty!" replied J.J. "Despite the admittedly rough beginning, I promise you guys that we're all in for a treat this weekend."

They walked through to the end of the dining car and into another adjoining corridor. Standing in the space between train cars, J.J. turned to the team again. "Let's start over."

He spoke faster this time. Clasped hands, proper posture, auditorium voice. "Good morning, everyone. As you all know, Ghost Hunters Adventure Club has seen a fifty percent increase in hiring in the past few months." Nod to Trudi. "We're growing as a company, and now more than ever it's important that we truly learn the meaning of teamwork. So with that I would like to say the following."

Big sweeping gesture.

"Welcome to the First Inaugural Ghost Hunters Adventure Club Leadership—"

The door to the other end of the adjoining corridor burst open and a small person wearing a red baseball uniform and cap marched through, seemingly steamed about something. Across his chest read the word "Elks."

He collided with J.J.'s shoulder, checking him into the walls of the gangway.

"Watch where you're going!" J.J. shouted. "I've got a speech going on!"

"Die alone, boner," the baseball player replied, before marching in the opposite direction as the team, pushing past Valentine and Trudi.

"I get weird vibes from this train," said J.J. as he opened the door to the next carriage. They were immediately met by a cacophony of hooting and hollering. Before them was an entire baseball team dressed in the same uniform as the person who knocked into J.J.

Trudi noted the plush carpeting and variety of comfortable-looking chairs. While it felt like she was entering a speakeasy, this, apparently, was the lounge car. The sun shone through a copse of trees into the window, making shadows flicker across the small cocktail bar up against the wall in the middle of the room. Baseball players happily chatted with each other in dotted groups around the train car. There was a baby grand piano at the far end of the lounge. A baseball player sat on it.

"Howdy," the three members of the Ghost Hunters Adventure Club heard. A man sitting at the bar next to them swiveled in his chair to face them. Chewing a stick of gum, he wore a blue polo shirt, cowboy hat, and the highest-up pair of gym shorts any of them had ever seen.

"Sorry about Smalls," he said. "Heard his catchphrase all the way back here. Kid's got a fire in his belly but he never made it through all those etiquette classes. Great left-handed shortstop."

He extended a friendly hand out toward them. "Coach Hank."

Always being one to seek new avenues of business, J.J. stepped into center stage. He produced a business card, offering it to the man.

"How do you do," he started. "My name is J.J. Watts and these are my two compatriots: Valentine Watts, brother; and Trudi de la Rosa, newest inductee. Together we make up the business entity of the Ghost Hunters Adventure Club. Harborville's foremost crime-fighting and mystery-solving team."

Coach Hank paused for a moment, looking back and forth between the blonde hair and blue eyes of Valentine and the dark hair and brown eyes of J.J.

"Wait, are you two actually brothers?"

J.J. ignored the question. "Feel free to contact us if you ever need anything. Ghost hunting or otherwise."

The three members of the Ghost Hunters Adventure Club each took turns shaking the man's hand.

"Pleased to have y'all on board," he said. "Hope you don't mind sharing a ride with the team."

"You guys play baseball, right?" asked Valentine.

"Minor League American Baseball," Coach Hank replied. "We're the Harborville Elks. Got a game with the New Troutstead Skipjacks this evening."

"Oh!" Trudi's eyes brightened. "I don't follow the minor league, I'm sorry to say. How's the season going so far?"

"Best OBP in the league," Coach Hank replied. "We got a tight team this year due to budget cuts, but they're all playing like their lives depend on it."

Valentine looked at the coach quizzically. "Oh-bee-pee?"

"On base percentage," Trudi replied. "It's a stats measurement of the amount of times a batter reaches base. It's like a batting average, but it also takes into account the batter getting walked."

J.J. and Valentine shot each other a glance. Neither of them had ever heard Trudi speak like this before.

"That's the one," the coach said. He tipped his cowboy hat to the three members of the Ghost Hunters Adventure Club, who took that as a social cue to formally disengage from that conversation and continue on their journey.

"That was an interesting bit of Trudi lore," Valentine remarked at the other end of the train car.

"Yeah," said J.J. "I remember you telling us multiple times that you were the least athletic person you knew."

"There's a big difference between *playing* baseball and *knowing* baseball," Trudi replied. "But you can thank my Uncle Berting for getting me into a sport so obsessed with numbers and statistics."

Exiting the lounge, the three finally found themselves in the second-class passenger car. It was a far cry away from first class. The mahogany walls were, instead, aluminum. The carpeting gave a distinct aura of municipal transit.

What they saw in this train car, strangely, was nerds. Many of them. Groups of nerds—dressed in a variety of button-down dress shirts, slacks, and pocket protectors—hung around and chatted in the hallway and among the economy-class train compartments.

"I'm doing my speech in our room," J.J. said. The three of them quietly slipped past the intellectual conversations occurring around them and found their compartment at the back of the car. They opened the door and walked inside.

"This is...cozy," Valentine said.

Before them was a very small train compartment without much room to move around. Most of the space was taken up by two upholstered benches that faced each other. They looked as if they could be converted into sleeper beds—with the right knowledge. There was another door near the seats that appeared to lead to the next berth. Against the wall was a window, out of which they could see Harborville disappearing slowly into the distance.

The three stowed their baggage away in a compartment above their seats. Not to be outdone by a small stage, J.J. hopped up on one of the seats and readdressed his compatriots. "Here we go."

He spoke even faster this time. Clasped hands authoritative voice, "Good morning, everyone. As you all know, Ghost Hunters Adventure Club has seen a fifty percent increase in hiring in the past few months." Sidelong glance at Trudi. "We're growing as a company, and now more than ever it's important that we truly learn the meaning of teamwork. So with that I would like to say the following..."

Sweeping gesture, "Welcome to the First Inaugural Ghost Hunters Adventure Club Leadership S—"

The door that seemed to lead to the next compartment burst open to reveal a man with a pristine, tucked-in, white dress shirt. His slacks were neatly pressed. If Trudi had to guess, she would have easily placed him with that crew of nerds outside.

"Hiya!" he said, waving enthusiastically.

"Oh, come on!" J.J. yelled in frustration.

The young man walked into their compartment without their inviting him to do so, shaking each of their hands vigorously.

"Oliver Path," he exclaimed. "Co-founder and current standing president of the Harborville Train Appreciation Society."

"Do they have boundaries in your appreciation society?" Valentine asked.

"You may have seen some of my colleagues out in the hallway. You see, we're here to take the famous Harborville Express to learn about its storied history and marvel at its wondrous engineering."

He shook everyone's hand once again. "Anyway, I just wanted to make a friendly introduction to the neighbors. I'll have to run now. Got official Train Appreciation Society business to take care of."

And with that, the train nerd disappeared through the door as quickly as he had appeared through it.

"Why'd he smell like rubbing alcohol?" Valentine asked.

J.J. massaged the scar running horizontally across his nose that he continued to not like talking about. "Weird train."

"Weird train," echoed Trudi. She turned the lock on both of the doors inside their compartment.

J.J. paused for a moment, wary of whatever unexpected interruption might come his way. Then he addressed Valentine and Trudi.

"Welcome..." he looked around, confirmed it was safe, then continued.

"To the First Inaugural..." another pause; everything was still in order.

"Ghost Hunters Adventure Club Leadership Summit!" he exclaimed. The words came out like a waterfall. He exhaled in equal parts relief and triumph for having finished a sentence.

Then he went on, more confident now.

"After a short and delightful trip on this beauty of a luxury liner, we'll be checking in at the New Troutstead Inn and Suites and utilizing their conference ballroom for an extended weekend of seminars, trust-building exercises, and, most important of all, the development of our mission statement."

Valentine and Trudi nodded in support.

"Now, if you'll all open your binders to page one."

"Binders?" Valentine asked.

"I'm getting ahead of myself," J.J. replied. He reached into his stowed-away satchel and pulled out three identical white binders, handing one to each member of the team and keeping one for himself. Across the three of them and along the spines were the names of each binder's owner: J.J., Valentine, and Trudi.

They all opened their folders to reveal the logo of the First Inaugural Ghost Hunters Adventure Club Leadership Summit.

"All right everyone, shall we get started?" asked J.J.

Then there was a knock on the door to the hallway.

"At least they let you finish your sentence this time," Valentine said. He turned to the hallway door, opened it, then immediately slammed the door shut before throwing his back against it. On his face was an expression of unbridled terror.

He looked helplessly to Trudi and J.J. "Guys, we've got trouble."

CHAPTER 2

Old Friends

"What is it?" asked J.J.

Valentine remained glued to the door. "Not what, who."

He looked to J.J. and Trudi. Each of them was standing with a perplexed look on their face in their compartment on the Harborville Express. The soft, rhythmic thunking of train travel filled in the silence.

"It's Siobhan," he said.

"Siobhan?" asked Trudi.

"Siobhan," J.J. replied, grimly.

"Still don't know who Siobhan is," said Trudi.

Valentine took a deep gulp. "Remember back at the Grande Chateau how I had to pitch a book idea to Thad to keep him occupied? *Boob Quest?*"

"Didn't you secure an advance on that?" J.J. asked.

"I'm halfway through the first draft. But that's not important right now. You see, when I pitched the story, I sort of did that thing where you draw upon your own world and life experiences."

"Did you write this Siobhan into your tit novel?" asked Trudi.

Valentine was visibly sweating by this point. "A woman who's chasing after our protagonists so that she can drag them back into a life of

13

lying, cheating, and stealing? Yes. She doesn't have three boobs in real life, though."

"So what's the big deal?" asked Trudi. "This is just someone from your past you don't want to deal with."

"I suppose I should jump in here," J.J. said in a grave tone. "I'm very aware that I talk a big game about my leadership abilities, my good looks, and my natural talent for solving mysteries. And while I like to think I can back up many of those claims, I'll readily admit that I'm still a work in progress. Siobhan, though? Siobhan is something else. She's got me beat in all categories. She's smarter, she's more charming, deadly with a knife at a distance, and, most importantly, she's more nefarious than I could ever be."

He hopped down from his standing position on the seat and began pacing with what little floor space he had. He seemed lost in thought. Pausing momentarily, he gazed out the window at the landscape gently parallaxing by. The fields surrounding Harborville were slowly transitioning into woodland.

"Except for movie trivia," he finally said. "I got her beat on that. She thinks they're too long."

"What are?" asked Trudi.

"Movies. But listen, my point is that Siobhan could convince the devil himself that he should give up on the fiddle. She is evil incarnate, a malevolent harvester of sorrow. Don't fall for whatever she's slinging."

He looked over to Valentine, who by this point was drenched in sweat. "All right gumshoe, we might as well get it over with."

Valentine shook his head. "Even if I were to agree with you, which I don't, I need you to know that my knees have locked into place as a form of subconscious protest. I cannot be moved. So I'm gonna use my once daily veto to cut that order and suggest that we just pretend like we're not here."

"You know I can hear you, right?" came a voice from the other side of the door.

Valentine crumpled with a fear-induced slump to the floor, knees in proper working order after all. "I don't wanna," he whispered weakly.

J.J. sighed. He sat down on the floor with his brother and spoke in an encouraging tone. "Valentine, ordinarily I'd say that it's your god-given right as a human being to have a mental breakdown wherever and whenever you want. That's inalienable. But buddy, we're at the First Inaugural Ghost Hunters Adventure Club Leadership Summit. We're here to tackle our problems. What I see right now is a challenge. A challenge that can be overcome."

"I can still hear you," came the voice again. "These compartment walls are pretty thin."

Valentine felt another wave of anxiety wash over him, but fought against it. He shot up to his original position with his back against the train compartment door.

"Okay," he said, appearing to psych himself up. "Okay, okay, okay, okay…"

J.J. stood up as well. "This is for your own good, buddy. By the end of the summit you'll be amazed at how much you've grown."

Valentine nodded. "Okay."

"Okay?"

"Okay."

J.J. placed his hand on the entryway handle.

"I changed my mind!" Valentine shrieked, batting J.J.'s hand away.

"Sorry pal." J.J. went for the door again. "You'll thank me later."

Valentine grabbed his brother's arm and the two fought for custody of the door handle. J.J. managed to secure a pretty ironclad half nelson on his brother, who responded tactically by flailing around like a recently caught fish. It was a brief scuffle that ended with the door open and the two fighting on the floor of their compartment.

J.J. tapped out when they saw that there was a figure standing in the center of the now-open door.

"Hey Siobhan," he said, looking up from the floor. "Long time, no see!"

It was then that Trudi saw who the boys were talking about.

Standing in the doorway was a woman about their age, maybe a little older. She was tiny, her face dotted with freckles around her nose. Her dark, curly hair fell down to her shoulders. She wore a jean jacket over a floral print dress.

That was not what Trudi had expected.

"J.J., Valentine, I'm so glad you're here!" she said in her soft voice.

The two scrambled to their feet. Siobhan crossed over to them as if she were gliding on air. She embraced a flabbergasted J.J., sighing deeply as she hugged him. She did the same for a shell-shocked Valentine.

Taking a small step back, she held Valentine's face in her hands as if he were a prized work of art. A warm smile crossed her face.

"Look at you, Valentine. As handsome as ever."

Valentine attempted a cordial smile. He did not succeed.

J.J. began to talk. "Hey, so, um…"

"And who's this?" Siobhan interrupted, looking over toward Trudi.

"Trudi de la Rosa," Trudi responded with an air of suspicion.

Siobhan extended a delicate hand toward Trudi. "Siobhan Sweeney, pleased to meet you."

Trudi cautiously accepted her hand.

"You know, I used to work with the boys back in the day. Is J.J. as irascible as ever?"

"What'd you call me?" J.J. demanded.

"Irascible means to have a hot temper and be easily provoked into anger," Trudi said.

"Ah, it would seem that you're filling the role I used to play," Siobhan smiled. "I hope you enjoy it as much as I did."

"So you're not mad at us?" Valentine blurted out. This was the most that he could manage to say. It came out at a high pitch and fast velocity, but at the very least it was a complete sentence.

Siobhan let out a light laugh. "Valentine, I had hoped you'd grown up a little more since I last saw you. But oh, darling." She put a hand on his shoulder. He flinched. "Of course I'm not mad at you. Any anger or resentment has been long lost to the sands of time. What could I hold against you two for some of the most fun years of my life?"

"Were you in the mystery business as well?" Trudi asked.

"Not quite, but close. It's a long story. I'd love to tell you all about it sometime."

"So what are you doing on this train, Siobhan?" J.J. asked.

"Isn't it such a coincidence?" Siobhan replied. "I'm out here on some new work and someone mentioned that there was a mystery-solving team aboard the train. I had read about your success at the Grande Chateau, so I figured it must be you. It's so amazing to see you two again."

"And who's your friend?" Trudi asked, motioning to the end of their compartment. Leaning in the doorway was a man who nobody on the Ghost Hunters Adventure Club team had seen before. He was dressed smartly in a dark blazer, a turtleneck sweater, and tailored pants. His face, while stern, made no expression toward the positive or the negative.

"This is my new business partner, Luther Adedeji."

Luther nodded toward everyone. There was a moment of silence while everyone waited for him to elaborate.

"Not a very talkative fellow, is he?" remarked J.J.

"I try not to speak unless I have something to say," Luther said.

"He tries not to speak unless he has something to say," Siobhan repeated.

"That's strange," said J.J., who couldn't imagine a fresher hell.

"It's such a departure from the usual company I keep, but we work well together. Don't we, Luther?"

Luther did not respond. He gave another respectful nod.

Siobhan sighed contentedly. "Well, I'd hate to take up any more of your time. I'm just so glad to see you both. Like an old Dr. Cecil H.H. Mills paperback, you two haven't lost your charm."

Siobhan joined Luther in the doorway, then turned back to the team. "They'll be serving brunch in the dining car in a small while. I do hope you'll all join us. There's so much we have to catch up on and I'd love to tell you more about what I'm working on next. Until next time, friends."

And with that, Siobhan left the three with an impressive final display of grace and poise. Luther followed closely behind.

As soon as they were gone, Valentine rushed to the door and slammed it shut, throwing his entire body against it in a vain attempt to barricade the team safely within their compartment.

"There is absolutely no way I'm going to willingly see that woman for the rest of my life, let alone the remainder of this train trip."

"I don't get it," said Trudi. "She seemed perfectly nice."

"That's what she wants you to think!" Valentine cried. He scrambled from the door to the train window, clawing at it. "Why is it so warm in here? Are you guys warm?"

J.J. thought the situation over for a second, which was usually all the time he needed to form a plan. He spoke as if a light bulb went off in his head. "This is a great thing!"

Valentine paused his clawing at the window for a small moment. "What?"

J.J. popped up to make another speech, squeezing between Valentine and Trudi to make as much of a dramatic effect as possible. "Of all the times we could've run into Siobhan, we ran into her during the First Inaugural Ghost Hunters Adventure Club Leadership Summit!"

Every word that J.J. said seemed to drive a stake further into Valentine's heart.

"What better time to learn about leadership and teamwork than in a moment where we're placed outside of our comfort zone? These are optimal conditions for cementing our working relationships and becoming the best team we possibly can."

Valentine thought over what J.J. was saying. He made sure to take the proper time to chew on the words and weigh the pros and cons of what his brother was trying to say. Then, he looked over to J.J.

"Absolutely not." He went back to trying to open the window of their train compartment. "If I can get this thing open I can hurl myself out into this lush woodland area and be back in Harborville by lunch."

J.J. and Trudi allowed Valentine to tire himself out. Eventually, he gave up.

"This thing is sealed, isn't it?" he said.

"Valentine," said Trudi. "Take a couple deep breaths. You're hyperventilating."

Valentine sat back down in his seat. He buried his head in his hands, feeling a great sense of despair. "Of all the trains in all of Harborville, we had to get stuck on the one with Siobhan Sweeney."

"Hey now," said J.J. "We don't *have* to do this…"

Valentine looked up. "Really?"

"…is something I would say if we weren't trying to help you become the absolute best version of yourself. Valentine, you can't be afraid of someone like this for the rest of your life. You're gonna have to grow up."

Valentine groaned. "I am convinced that that woman is going to kill me."

"Look at it this way," started J.J., "this is a short day trip to New Troutstead. We've got a packed schedule of seminars and team building exercises that I've planned out for us even while we're on our way to the retreat, and once we leave the train you're not gonna have to deal with her again. You'll be so busy that you'll barely even notice her."

"Plus you've got us here with you," Trudi added. "You're not going through this alone."

Valentine took a few more deep breaths, his heart rate slowly returning to somewhere around the realm of normal. "Okay," he said. "Okay. I see what you're saying. As long as we don't have to deal with her and especially if we stay away from this brunch thing she wants us to come to, I think I can do it."

"That's great!" J.J. said enthusiastically.

"So what's next on the schedule?"

J.J. opened his binder to the tabbed section labeled "Itinerary." He looked up at Trudi and Valentine.

"Brunch."

CHAPTER 3

Brunch

"I feel like we should start this off with introductions," said J.J. between bites of his steak and eggs. "While I recognize that it's a bit redundant being that we all already know each other, I wanna go into this weekend with fresh eyes."

The three members of the Ghost Hunters Adventure Club were seated at a far-off corner table in the dining car of the Harborville Express. A majority of the space was taken by tables set with white cloths and ornate cutlery. Plenty of light shone in rays through the dense forest that the train was traveling through. Waiters walked up and down the aisle, taking brunch orders from a variety of baseball players and train nerds, among the other passengers.

"My name is J.J. Watts. My favorite color is red and here's two truths and a lie about me."

J.J. looked over to his captive audience. Trudi seemed as if she was trying her hardest to seem enthusiastic about the introduction/fun facts block of the summit. Valentine, on the other hand, looked as if he were a fighter pilot pulling a high g-force maneuver.

"I know how to pick locks, I know how to drive a stick shift, I truly believe that I could be pushed to kill if circumstances were dire enough. Valentine, you there?"

As if an eject lever were pulled, Valentine was rocket-propelled through a glass canopy and back into the conversation at a high velocity. "I'm sorry, who killed who?"

J.J. finished his plate and pulled his auxiliary order of steak and eggs in front of him, pausing to take a sip of coffee. "Communication is key to a well-oiled mystery solving team. As someone who's known you for a while I feel as if I can tell when something's bothering you. Do you have anything you want to share with us in confidence?"

The reason why Valentine was pinned to the back of his seat, eyes wide and bulging, looking as if he had aged ten years, was because Siobhan Sweeney was sitting at the other end of the dining car. She was sharing a laugh with Luther Adedeji, who wasn't looking all that animated, and an elderly woman he didn't recognize.

"I promise I'm trying my hardest to be a team player here," he said. "But...*she's* over there."

"Who?" J.J. asked. He turned around very conspicuously and locked eyes with Siobhan. She raised a glass of orange juice to him as a toast and flashed a demure smile.

"Oh right, her," J.J. said as he turned back to the table. "Truthfully she wasn't on my mind at all. We've got much more important things to deal with."

Valentine gulped. "I have been in fight-or-flight mode for the past thirty minutes, so if you don't mind I'm just going to vibrate silently in my chair, hoping that the nervous energy burns off."

J.J. sighed, leveling a sympathetic look at his brother. "You're right; I'm scared of her too. I just felt as if I should project confidence to help improve the morale of my team. I have no idea why she's here or what she has planned. Trudi, what qualities do you think good leaders embody?"

"I still don't get it," Trudi said. "Why are you guys so afraid of her?"

J.J. looked over to his brother, who—to keep the metaphor going—seemed as if he wasn't sure if his ejection seat came with a parachute or not. "Should I tell her?"

"She should know."

Taking a deep breath, J.J. leaned forward onto the table, speaking so as not to be overheard. "Trudi, there's something you should know about us. We...weren't always the co-founders of Harborville's foremost ghost hunting and mystery solving team."

Trudi raised her eyebrows. "I thought that was obvious."

"The thing is, we were a part of something that was sort of the opposite of our current organization." He massaged the scar across his nose before speaking. "Technically, I guess you could say that we were the ones who created the mysteries that needed to be solved."

"You guys were crooks?" Trudi leaned into the table as well. Her expression was hard to gauge.

"Mostly box jobs. Safe crackings. Henchman-type work. There were a few more elaborate heists in there."

"And we were Siobhan's direct reports," Valentine cut in. He carried a heavy look of regret on his face. "We had issues with her leadership philosophy."

"Saying we were ruled over with an iron fist would be an insult to Siobhan's clearly superior titanium fists," agreed J.J. "But we saw an opportunity to get out of that life and we took it, and Siobhan's taken it personally ever since. We thought we finally made a clean break when our juvenile records were sealed on our eighteenth birthdays, but here she is."

"I'm sorry we kept that from you," said Valentine. "It's something we thought we had put behind us."

Trudi sat back. She felt a confluence of emotions, and she knew she'd be lying to herself if one of those emotions wasn't suspicion. But when she thought about it further, searching for the feeling of betrayal she thought she would hold, she couldn't find it.

"I had sort of figured. No one else I know has that many speech-binding non-disclosure agreements on one another."

"You don't have to be cool with our past," said J.J.

"I'm still on the team," Trudi replied. "Valentine, is there anything we can do to help you out right now?"

"If everyone could just let me sit silently and vibrate in place for a while, I would super appreciate it."

The team was distracted momentarily by the familiar squawk of a PA system. "Next stop, Maple Bay," came the conductor's voice.

The train came to a slow stop outside of a train platform beside a small, oceanside town. Trudi looked out of her window at the platform: It was completely empty except for a short, bespectacled man with a bushy beard. He tucked his umbrella under his arm and straightened out his overcoat before stepping onto the train a car ahead of them.

Turning her attention back to the dining car, Trudi saw that the room had settled into a comfortable chatter, and both the baseball team members and the train nerds seemed to be getting along cordially. Examining the car further, she spotted several black and white pictures hung in frames along the walls, presumably suggesting a lush locomotive history.

"What's the deal with this train?" she asked.

"A phenomenal question!" came a voice from across the aisle.

The three of them turned to the table next to them to see none other than Oliver Path, the president of the Harborville Train Appreciation Society that they'd talked to earlier, leaning toward them. He was sitting with a few other train nerds, all of whom seemed to be locked in animated conversation with one another, presumably about trains.

He went right into a speech. "Built in the early 1920s, the Harborville Express was a connecting throughway between the large city hub of Harborville and its neighboring sister city, New Troutstead. Along the way, it made a stop at the Lake Nowhere mine, a long-since deserted salt mine surrounding an eons-ago-dried-up sea bed."

J.J. groaned as politely as he could. "This is all really interesting information, I guess."

Oliver continued on. "Switching from steam engine to diesel to diesel-electric, and no longer providing its main duty of hauling cargo loads of salt between Harborville and New Troutstead, the Harborville Express now functions as a luxury commuter train operating daily to connect the two cities."

"Valentine!"

Valentine heard his name called above the chatter, across the busy brunch crowd, and from Siobhan Sweeney and her table of friends. They were all looking at him.

He felt a lump grow in his throat as his skin tingled in preparation to perspire. She was waving him over.

"Valentine! Won't you come have a chat with us?" Siobhan's words whizzed past his head like bullets. He turned to J.J. and Trudi, looking for any supporting cover fire he could find.

"And that's how the Harborville Express went from steam to diesel, but if you want a really wild story, you should hear about the switch from diesel to diesel-electric!" Oliver went on. J.J. and Trudi were locked into polite conversation, as happened sometimes in modern society.

"Um, guys…" Valentine's voice came out in a whisper. The lump in his throat had only continued to grow in size. He attempted a throat clearing maneuver, but that wasn't enough to pull his teammates' attention away from the train nerd.

"Valentine! Yoohoo!" Siobhan called once again.

Against every alarm bell ringing inside of his head at this moment, Valentine was still bound by the modern social politics of his era. He was required to respond. Slowly rising from his seat, he willed himself forward, step by excruciating step, until he arrived at his destination with a certain rigidity that betrayed whatever confidence he was trying to project. Siobhan was seated next to Luther. Across from him was the elderly woman Valentine didn't recognize. She was dressed in a sensible purple dress and wore coke-bottle-thick eyeglasses.

"Valentine!" Siobhan's voice rang out again. "Won't you sit with us for a spell? I have someone I want to introduce you to."

Siobhan motioned toward the empty seat across from her. Valentine made the laborious, robotic movement to sit down, his heart rate increasing as he stared directly at Siobhan, who smiled politely back at him.

"Valentine, allow me to introduce you to Rudith. Rudith, this is my dear old friend Valentine."

"Rudith Espiritu." The woman extended a frail hand toward Valentine, who shook it politely. She had a warm smile that unfortunately didn't help Valentine feel any better.

"Rudith here is the curator of the Harborville Museum of Fine Art," Siobhan said. "She's hired us for our services, and that's why you and I have met so serendipitously on this train. You know, Rudith, Valentine and I go way back. We even worked together, for a time."

"Oh!" Rudith squeaked gleefully. "Do you work in the security industry as well?"

"The...security industry?" Valentine asked.

"Oh, no no no," said Siobhan. "He and I worked in a separate but adjacent industry." She flashed a look at Valentine. "But I can vouch for this man's trustworthiness and dogged loyalty to his work colleagues."

Valentine felt those words carve into him. "It's...good to see you thriving in the...security industry? These days?" Valentine stammered in a way that could just barely be understood.

"Isn't it so useful?" asked Rudith. "I was at a complete loss as to how I was going to transport these jewels from our museum to the New Troutstead Museum of Contemporary Art. Then these two came along and offered their services! And at a steep discount, no less, since they're trying to get their fledgling business off of the ground."

Valentine's mind finally found a path through the fog of terror. "Wait. What services do they offer?"

"Why, security detail," Rudith said matter-of-factly. She raised her left hand above the table, revealing handcuffs around her wrist. The hand kept rising and eventually revealed what she was tethered to: a small, black leather briefcase.

"I thought these two youngsters were being silly at first," said Rudith, as she gestured to Siobhan and Luther. "Who would rob a little old lady on the Harborville Express of all places? But still, they convinced me, and I must say I'm feeling quite safe in their care. Although I do wish this one talked a little more," she said, gesturing to Luther. "It's okay if you're a little shy on your first security detail, young man."

"I try to only speak when I have something to say," said Luther.

"He tries to only speak when he has something to say," echoed Siobhan. "But in any case, the security is going quite nicely. Certainly easier than the sort of trouble we used to get into back in the day. Isn't that right, Valentine?"

Valentine was perplexed. Siobhan's previous line of work had nothing to do with security. In fact, he would argue that it was the exact opposite. With what little cognitive ability his brain had left, he searched his surroundings for answers. It was then that he spotted something he hadn't noticed Siobhan wearing earlier. Hanging around her neck, fashioned into a necklace, was a small key.

"What's the key for?" he asked, pointing to Siobhan's neckline.

"My! Aren't you perceptive?" Rudith interjected. "You should watch out for this one, Siobhan." She said it kiddingly, but we all know exactly how Valentine took it.

"I just may have to," Siobhan replied, once again making and maintaining intense eye contact with Valentine.

"Say, Valentine." Rudith leaned toward him. "Would you like to see it?"

"See what?" he asked.

Rudith placed the small, black leather suitcase on the table. "Siobhan, may I?"

Siobhan removed the key from her neck and handed it to Rudith. "It's a classic security industry maneuver," she remarked. "I hold onto the key while Rudith holds onto the briefcase. If you wanted to steal it, you'd have to get past me first."

Rudith placed the key into its keyhole at the top of the briefcase. She opened the case toward Valentine, revealing a sparkling ruby necklace set in fine gold. For a moment, Valentine was taken aback by its brilliant luster.

After a short time, Rudith closed the briefcase, smiling sheepishly. "I know I'm not supposed to be doing that. Don't want to be constantly broadcasting that I have invaluable jewels to the entire train. It's just so interesting, isn't it? There's so much history behind the ruby jewels of the duchess of Cordelia."

"They're beautiful," Valentine said.

"Oh, you should have seen Princess Annalise wearing them at her cordiality ball when she was a baby. It was just priceless!"

"Priceless?" A scary realization instantly appeared in Valentine's mind. He grabbed a glass of water as casually as he could, which was not very casually at all, and raised it mechanically to his lips, gulping down the entirety of it. "It was very pleasing to meet you all. I must be getting back to my friends."

"Toodaloo!" Siobhan said cheerfully as Valentine got out of his chair and began shuffling back to his compatriots. "Oh, Valentine!" Siobhan shouted after him.

He stopped dead in his tracks as if he had stepped on a landmine. He turned to address Siobhan once more.

"They have a piano next door in the lounge. We were thinking about doing a little recital in a bit after brunch."

Rudith's face lit up. "Oh, what fun!" she said. "Security *and* a show! I used to be a jazz singer back in my heyday, you know."

"You should join us," Siobhan said. Her lips curled into a smile that only Valentine was convinced was malicious.

And yet he was still bound by the cruel constraints of modern social politics. He had to give a response.

"I'll…see if I can make it."

* * *

"But what does it all mean?" J.J. asked. He and the two other Ghost Hunters Adventure Club members were in their second-class compartment in the back portion of the Harborville Express. The train continued its rhythmic back and forth rocking motion. The landscape, once lush with forest, was now slowly turning into an arid desert.

"It means I could've used your help with the whole Siobhan situation back there," said Valentine. He kept his head buried in his hands, pausing only momentarily to rub his aching temples. "What happened there? I thought we were supposed to be a team?"

"That's a great question, Valentine," replied J.J. "And a phenomenal segue into our next seminar. If you'll all turn to page thirty-three in your work binders and find the page labeled 'Surviving Alone Together: When to Split Up for Maximum Efficiency.'"

Trudi interjected while J.J. found the page. "We got stuck in that conversation with that Oliver Path fellow and couldn't get out of it, Valentine. I'm sorry."

"And I'm sorry for the extra thirty minutes we had to endure of that conversation after you flew the coop," said J.J. "Why does he smell like rubbing alcohol? I truly do not trust anyone this enthusiastic about railway steel tempering."

"Wait," said Valentine. "How long has it been since I ran out of the dining room in a sweating huff?"

J.J. looked at his watch. "It's been an hour. I spent a lot of time not-so-furtively glancing at this watch to hopefully give that Oliver kid a clue that we had a seminar to get to."

"Oh no, it's almost time." Valentine shot out of his chair, switching places with J.J. so that he could pace.

"Almost time for what?" Trudi asked.

"Siobhan's got a recital in the lounge in a couple of minutes."

"How about we go ahead and skip that," J.J. suggested, "and get back to the seminar at hand. This hour was supposed to be dedicated to developing our mission statement."

"We can't do that!" Valentine cried out.

"Of course we can. It's just a matter of thinking up and declaring a goal for our organization. Businesses do it all the time."

"Listen, something's gonna go down at the recital and I think I know what."

"What is it?" asked Trudi.

Valentine stared forlornly out of the window. He saw a lonely cloud floating alone in the air. "Isn't it obvious? Siobhan's going to steal the ruby jewels of the duchess of Cordelia."

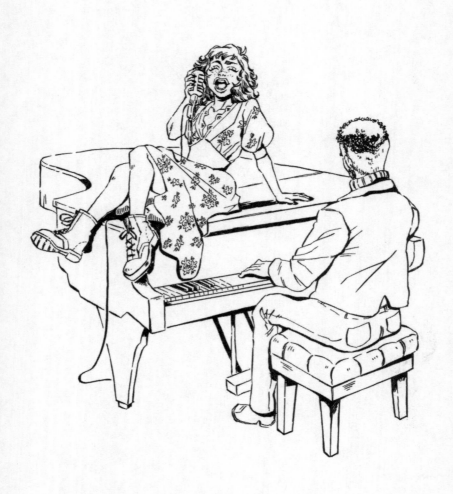

CHAPTER 4

The Recital

V alentine hunched in the furthest back corner of the furthest back booth in the lounge car of the Harborville Express. He sipped coffee nervously as his eyes darted around the room, looking for any sign of Siobhan, or any indication about her upcoming plan.

"So I think we all know that we're on the heels of a potential job right now, what with a now-formally declared enemy of the team in our midst," started J.J., as he and Trudi joined Valentine at the table. "And I'm sorry to say that if we keep doing things as well as we're doing them, we'll be getting so many jobs that we're always gonna be fighting for time to re-hone our skills and develop strong team bonds."

He plopped his First Inaugural Ghost Hunters Adventure Club Leadership Summit work binder in the middle of the table and flipped it open. "So even while we're in the field performing our duties, we should also constantly be working on ourselves. Trudi, any ideas on our mission statement?"

Trudi, like Valentine, was scanning the crowd for any possibilities of danger—of which there did not seem to be any. Just baseball team members and train nerds cohabitating peacefully.

35

"Valentine," she asked, "could you go over the facts one more time? I want to be of use here but it all sounds like conspiracy theory right now."

Valentine dragged his face back to attention on his two teammates. "Okay, so we end up on this train and an old acquaintance from our past is here. She's running *security* for this Rudith lady, who's transporting these ruby jewels of the duchess of Cordelia."

"So, what makes you think Siobhan's gonna nab it?" asked Trudi.

"Because Siobhan always has a plan," said Valentine. "Think of how perfect it would be. Siobhan's got the key to Rudith's briefcase right there on her neck. She has complete control of the Cordelian jewels. If this isn't a con then I don't know what is."

J.J. interjected. "All right, that's maybe the fifth time you've used that word. What does it mean?"

"What?" asked Valentine. "Cordelia?" He put his coffee down and looked at his brother quizzically. "Are you serious?"

"This is a bit, right?"

"You know, Cordelia. The postage-stamp-sized European country whose government we all had to study in middle school?"

"What?"

"I truly cannot believe you don't know this," said Valentine. "Didn't they make you construct a diorama of Cordelian parliament in the eighth grade?"

"I was Cordelia in model U.N.," Trudi remarked.

"What…?" asked J.J.

Just then, Siobhan entered the lounge from the dining car. Following closely behind her was the stone-faced Luther Adedeji, along with Rudith Espiritu, who had a big smile running across her face.

"Movement," announced Valentine. He once again felt his knees lock in place when he spotted the trio greeting some guests at the opposite end of the room. He saw them shake hands in turn with the short, bearded, bespectacled man who had boarded the train earlier. Valentine sank deeper into his chair.

"If you guys are that convinced that Siobhan's gonna pull something, then we need to figure out her scheme," said Trudi.

J.J. got up out of his chair. The sudden movement startled Valentine.

"J.J., for the love of everything good and holy what are you doing?" he demanded.

"There's time for talk and there's time for action," J.J. said. "Leaders lead from the front, and if I'm going to embody that ideal here at the summit then I need to show you all how it's done."

To Valentine's dismay, J.J. began walking to the other end of the room, right where Siobhan was sitting. "Watch and learn, students," he said, looking back at them.

He squeezed past a group of train nerds excitedly admiring the train's craftmanship to arrive at Siobhan's table. The moment he got there, he realized that he had been focusing all of his brain energy on crafting a dramatic display of leadership. He opened his mouth...and nothing came out.

Luckily, Siobhan initiated conversation immediately. "J.J.! I'm so glad you joined us!" She looked over to Luther and Rudith. "Would you mind if my dear old colleague steals me for a moment? We've so much to catch up on. Luther, maybe you could take Rudith to her seat near the piano. I have a surprise for her that I think she'll really enjoy."

Luther nodded and rose, gesturing for Rudith to follow him.

"Hey pal," J.J. said to Luther. "I was wondering if you could say more than two sentences to me."

Luther made a slow, mechanical turn toward J.J. He locked eyes with him for a moment and then turned back to continue with Rudith.

J.J. looked to Siobhan. "These the sort of charismatic henchmen you're surrounding yourself with these days?"

"Oh, hush now," Siobhan said as she rose from her chair. "Luther is a phenomenal business partner. Real ambitious. We can't all have your gift of gab."

She wrapped a hand around J.J.'s arm and led him to the bar area of the lounge car, next to a boisterous conversation about baseball's relationship to train travel between Coach Hank and Oliver Path. "Plus, most importantly of all, he's loyal."

J.J. winced. He turned to her. "Okay Shiv, you can drop the act now. It's just you and me."

Siobhan tilted her head at him. "Act? What do you mean?"

"I've been around the block enough times to see a confidence scam when I come across one in the wild. What's the deal with the key around the neck? What's with you and this Luther guy offering security services to a little old lady? Come on, pal. Don't take me for a mark."

"J.J., I'm hurt," she started. "I'm trying my hardest to clean up my act just as you and Valentine have. The hand-to-heart truth is that I'm walking the straight and narrow now."

"Yeah, right," J.J. replied. "And you also consider yourself a cinephile, huh."

"Movies are just so long," she groaned playfully. She accepted two cups of black coffee from the bartender and offered one to J.J. "Remembered how you took your coffee."

J.J. leaned in toward Siobhan. Using calm, clear language as an efficient communicator would, he spoke. "Listen, this weekend is really important to me and my team, and I just super need you to not pull anything wacky."

Siobhan took a sip of her coffee before leaning in as well. "Well, what's so important about this weekend?"

"It's the Ghost Hunters Adventure Club Leadership Summit, so we really need to be focusing on teamwork and goal setting."

Siobhan raised her eyebrows. "You're holding a leadership summit? Who's helping you run it?"

"Actually," J.J. replied, a little surprised at the question, "I'm running the whole thing myself."

Siobhan set down her coffee. "Very impressive. I'd always seen you as a leader, but to be this dedicated to your team and its success shows profound dedication."

J.J. let forth a self-conscious smile. "It's really nothing."

"So, what are you teaching your team members at this leadership summit?" She rested her chin on her hands, giving J.J. her undivided attention.

"Well, it's actually super interesting. We're spending the first day covering all of the basics of team building and leadership, then the following days I have discussions set up to start building upon these basic skills. By the end of it—and after the hand-to-hand combat section—I think we'll all have really congealed into something we can be proud of."

"You know," said Siobhan as she took another sip from her cup of coffee, "Warren Bennis once said that leadership is the capacity to translate vision into reality. How do you feel about that statement?"

J.J. was talking excitedly now. "I'd have to say that I strongly agree with that, and that the true leaders are the ones who see this translation as an iterative process."

"Well spoken," said Siobhan. "I hope you remember these maxims while you're helping your friends to see the true meaning of leadership."

"Oh, I'm very sure I will."

Siobhan looked at her watch, "And wouldn't you know it, it's almost time to start!" She set her coffee down on the bar and gave J.J. a warm hug. She pulled back a little so that they could meet eye to eye. "I'm so proud of you." She gave his hand one last squeeze, then turned on her heels and walked over to where Luther and Rudith were sitting. Rudith appeared to be giddy with excitement.

It took J.J.'s brain a little bit to catch up to the ruse.

"That woman is a pro," he said as he sat back down at the table with his teammates. "At least I got free coffee out of it."

"What'd you find out?" asked Trudi.

"Apparently that I have a weak spot for people who pay attention to me."

Valentine groaned. "Something's going down, right? This is all too perfect with Siobhan on the train, in a new security job, with a harmless little old lady. What are the odds that we would be on the exact same train on the exact same day that Siobhan would?"

Valentine got caught up in his last few words as they were coming out of his mouth. He wiped his face, looking toward his brother. "J.J., how did you book this train trip?"

"Oh, it was pretty simple. I received a letter in the mail that told me I had accrued enough mileage points for a free train trip for me and two others. The blackout dates were a little restrictive, but I was able to find us something that worked for our summit."

"J.J., what were the blackout dates?" asked Trudi.

"Literally every other date and time except for this exact train," replied J.J.

The table exploded in a chorus of groans from Trudi and Valentine. "So you're telling me," Valentine started, "that we're exactly where Siobhan wants us to be at the exact moment she wants us to be here?"

J.J. frowned. "Well, when you just lay it out like that it makes me sound real dumb. I apologize for searching for the absolute best deals I could get so that Ghost Hunters Adventure Club, Incorporated, can stay above water."

"So, what happens next?" asked Trudi.

They all turned as they heard silverware clinking against a champagne glass. At the other end of the room, standing in front of a microphone by the baby grand piano, was Siobhan. Behind her, Luther opened the piano stool and pulled out some sheet music before he sat down. Rudith was sitting excitedly at a table nearby.

"Excuse me, everyone," Siobhan said. The once-boisterous room quickly quieted to a low chatter. "I'd like to thank you all for stopping by our little impromptu recital. We've had such a fun time here already with our new friend, Rudith Espiritu of the Harborville Museum of Fine Art."

"For running security detail," said Trudi, "they sure do love being in the spotlight."

"So, thank you to the Harborville Express for allowing us to do this. We certainly hope you enjoy it."

There was polite applause.

"The first song I'd like to do is an original," Siobhan said, as she removed her jean jacket to reveal the elegant, floral print dress beneath. "About some dear old friends who I hadn't seen in a long while."

Luther began playing a tune on the piano, which Siobhan sang along to. Perhaps the best way to show this would be to simply just include the sheet music and lyrics. So here you go. There are a couple spots in there left open for improvisation, so feel free to get a little creative with it.

Siobahn's Waltz for Revenge

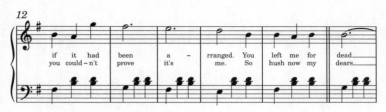

3

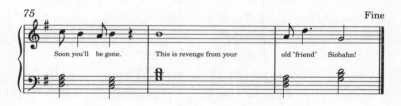

Siobhan finished her song to applause from the patrons of the lounge car. "Thank you, everyone," she said. "Thank you."

"Wait that wasn't about us, was it?" J.J. asked. "It just felt a little over the top with the 'left me for dead' bit."

Valentine felt a crushing pressure against his whole entire being. "I can't take it anymore. What's her plan?"

"Um, guys," said Trudi. "I think this might be something." Trudi pointed out the window of the train while it made a slow turn cresting a hill. Far off in the distance, at the base of a mountain, the three spotted a tunnel.

"We've actually got one more surprise for you in store," said Siobhan. "Apparently our new client and now friend, Rudith Espiritu, used to be a jazz singer back in her heyday."

Rudith's face flushed. She gave an elaborate gesture to suggest, *Who, me? Oh, do go on.*

"With the audience's permission, we'd love to have Rudith come up here to sing us her rendition of the Cole Porter classic, 'I Get a Kick Out of You.' Whaddaya say, fellas?'" Siobhan whipped the crowd of baseball players and train nerds into a raucous applause.

Rudith, grinning madly, graciously rose out of her seat and joined Siobhan and Luther by the piano. J.J., Valentine, and Trudi could all see the briefcase that remained handcuffed to her left wrist.

"It's the perfect show tune-based crime," J.J. said in realization.

"What is?" asked Valentine.

"There's a sustain note in 'I Get a Kick Out of You' at the end of the song. I bet Siobhan's timed it with the tunnel. Rudith's gonna be occupied when the train car goes dark."

"So we need a plan to stop her," Trudi said.

"That's the thing," replied Valentine. "Siobhan's too smart for us. She's got everything planned out. Every plan has a counterplan. Those counterplans are backed up by a variety of contingency plans. We can't beat her there."

Valentine furrowed his brows, thinking hard to find a way out of this jam. "What we need is chaos."

"I can do chaos," said J.J.

"No fire," Valentine replied.

J.J. seemed to deflate a little in disappointment.

Trudi scanned the room, looking for options. She saw the small groups of baseball players listening politely at their tables, the train nerds doing the same. She spotted the short, bearded, bespectacled man sitting down at a table by the other end of the room. He was lifting a brandy snifter to his lips.

Then, she saw what she needed: Coach Hank and Oliver Path maintaining their conversation at the lounge bar. But what were the odds on this idea forming in her head? She had heard them discussing baseball from all the way at their table, so that was good. Oliver seemed like a man of statistics. That worked in her favor. She gave herself 2:1 odds that this would backfire. It was as good a bet as any.

She got up from the table.

"What are you doing?" asked Valentine.

"I've got a plan for chaos," Trudi responded.

"What's the plan?"

"I know baseball."

Trudi left the table and approached the two men at the bar. She waited for the right moment to interject.

* * *

Dr. Cecil H.H. Mills here, popping in to explain the inherent humor within this following joke. I usually don't like explaining my nuanced sense of humor as I find the discussion of comedy mechanics to be one of the absolute unfunniest things you can do. However, considering the Young Adult nature of our readership, I will allow myself this one indulgence to aid those who might be ignorant to the great sport of baseball.

You see, there exists two governing bodies within major league baseball: the National League and the American League. In a bid to make the game more interesting due to pitchers' notoriously poor batting averages, the American League decided in the 1970s that instead of sending the pitcher up to bat while their team was playing offense, they would instead designate a hitter to bat in that pitcher's stead. This is called the "Designated Hitter Rule." The National League flatly voted against the rule change in the 1980s, leaving the two leagues at diametrically opposed stances on the matter.

Now, there is an endless amount of debate over which version of the game is the "true" version of the game. I will not give my opinion on the matter, so as not to spoil the spirit of debate with my opinion which, frankly, is the correct one. However, I would direct the reader to look up archival footage of the Mets's legendary pitcher Bartolo Colón's at-bats. Within that footage is all the argument you need for deciding one way or the other.

What's important to know for the following gag is that this has been a hotly contested debate since even before the rule change was implemented. Articles and opinion columns arguing for or against this rule date back as far as 1887. Blood has been shed over the historical lifetime of this debate, because of this debate.

Now, with that said, you may proceed forward in this book with the knowledge you now carry to properly understand and appreciate the following joke.

* * *

"WHAT DO YOU THINK ABOUT the Designated Hitter Rule in baseball?" Trudi asked.

Coach Hank chuckled. "Well, obviously, the Designated Hitter Rule is an affront to the very concept of American baseball." He made sure to keep his voice at a reasonable volume so as not to interrupt the performance currently underway.

"With respect," said Oliver next to the coach, "I think the Designated Hitter Rule can make games more interesting, shifting the focus to an offensive-play style instead of focusing on filling gaps within a batting lineup."

It wasn't long before they were full-volume screaming at each other. Luther played the piano diligently against the rising volume of the two men at the bar. Heads slowly turned to examine the commotion.

Trudi sat back down at the table with J.J. and Valentine, each of whom were at a loss for words.

"If that doesn't create chaos, I don't know what will," she said.

"When you allow designated hitters into the lineup, you're taking a key strategic element out of the game!" shouted Coach Hank. There was a small group of Harborville Elks attempting to assuage Coach Hank's impassioned anger, but they weren't getting very far.

Rudith, for her part, didn't notice the commotion. She was in the show tune zone. And she was nearing the big finish at the end.

Valentine looked out of the window by their table again. The tunnel was just moments away. "Well, if something is gonna happen, it'll happen in a couple seconds," he said. He looked over to Siobhan, whose focus seemed to be shifting over to the rising conflict between the train nerds and baseball players.

"The Designated Hitter Rule elongates the careers of historic sluggers who wouldn't be able to keep up on the defensive field!" Oliver shouted. By this time there were train nerds in the fray trying to quell the argument. Oliver attempted to punctuate his sentences by stuffing a finger into Coach Hank's face. The two tumbled backward in a mess of baseball players and train enthusiasts.

Just as Rudith reached the high note in 'I Get a Kick Out of You,' she was knocked over by the quarreling Coach Hank and Oliver Path.

Then, the entire train car plunged into darkness. All J.J., Valentine, and Trudi could perceive was the crashing of plates and yelling of patrons. The rumbling of the train echoed in the tight spaces of the tunnel.

It was only a short few seconds before the train was through the tunnel and the Ghost Hunters Adventure Club could take stock of their surroundings. Rudith, Coach Hank, and Oliver Path were on the floor of the lounge car, as was Siobhan. Many of the people sitting down at tables immediately stood up to help those on the floor.

"Something's happened," said Trudi.

All of a sudden, Siobhan's hand shot up to her neck. "My key! Someone's stolen my key!" she gasped.

Rudith, regaining her senses on the floor of the train, looked over to the briefcase handcuffed to her left hand. It lay there on the ground, open. She gasped. It was empty.

The short, bearded, bespectacled man shot out of his chair and stood bolt upright. "Nobody move!" he shouted. "A crime has been committed!"

CHAPTER 5

The Ruby Jewels of the Duchess of Cordelia

The passengers of the Harborville Express sat silently in the dining car as it continued its journey toward New Troutstead. The mood was palpably tense; barely anybody spoke and a malingering feeling of confusion hung in the air. Everyone's eyes were directed at the train conductor in his ill-fitting uniform and five o'clock shadow. Next to him was the short, bearded, bespectacled man who had stopped the scene unfolding in the lounge car.

J.J., Valentine, and Trudi were seated at a table near Coach Hank and Oliver Path at the front. All of them seemed to shrink down in their chairs to arouse as little suspicion as possible.

The conductor cleared his throat and the room fell into a quick silence. He stepped to the center of the aisle. "Good morning," he started. "Um, this is your conductor. I know a lot of you must be wondering why we're all sitting here in the dining car—especially if you weren't in the lounge car just a few minutes ago. And since I usually do these sorts of announcements over the intercom, this must be a pretty big thing, right?"

The crowd, eager to find out what was happening, was hanging onto his every word.

He let out a big yawn.

"Wow, weird time to yawn, huh?" he said. "Anyway, there's been a high-profile robbery aboard this train."

Quiet murmurs erupted at tables up and down the train car. Valentine looked over to Siobhan's table. She was sitting, innocently, next to Luther near the front of the car. Rudith was right next to them. Her arms were folded, and she had a very distressed look on her face. She apparently did not like being robbed.

The conductor waited until the room quieted down a bit before he spoke again. "Now, we here at the Harborville Express take great pride in your safety and security. And luckily we have a passenger who's able to help us conduct a proper investigation under the jurisdiction of federal train law. So, to that end, I'd like to have him come up here to say a few words."

The short, bearded, bespectacled man stood up from his chair, his impressive pair of dress shoes leading him in a pronounced saunter. Valentine felt a great wave of terror wash over him. This felt like it was leading somewhere bad.

The bespectacled man walked around his table and went to the center of the aisle, nodding his thanks to the conductor. He adjusted the tiny, circular glasses at the very tip of his nose.

"Just minutes ago, an unknown party utilized a boisterous argument and the cover of darkness to steal something of great interest to me." He paused, drawing the crowd in like he had caught them in a net. "What they stole was...the ruby jewels of the duchess of Cordelia!"

The crowd gasped at an admittedly fancy-named thing that sounded like it cost a lot of money.

"Now, some may argue that this jewelry is priceless, but let me assure you," said the man as he walked down the aisle, the occupants of the dining car watching as he stroked his impeccably manicured beard, "a price will be paid." He paused once again for effect. "This assailant, or assailants, did not account for the fact that Neutral Moldevik's premier detective was also riding the train."

"What's Neutral Moldevik?" J.J. whispered to his two team members.

"Are you serious?" asked Trudi. "The equally small bordering country to Cordelia that's been at a tenuous peace with them for centuries?"

Valentine leaned in as well. "Do you remember any social studies classes you've ever taken?"

"No," said J.J.

"Allow me to introduce myself," the short man went on. "My name is Inspector Sandor Horvath, at your service."

J.J. still didn't seem to understand. He leaned over to a table of train enthusiasts. They all seemed to resemble Oliver in some way, shape, or form.

"Hey man, you ever heard of a place called Neutral Moldevik?"

The train enthusiast looked offended. "I used to organize Neutral Moldevik and Cordelia peace rallies when I was in high school."

J.J. leaned back into his chair. "Huh."

"Now, some time ago in my world travels, while I was solving another high-profile case of ingenious design, I received a letter."

Inspector Horvath reached into his coat pocket and revealed a small, black envelope. "This letter, from a mysterious benefactor, suggested that it would behoove me and my skills to be on this exact train, on this exact date, at this exact time. I can now see why."

Valentine's mind was racing. More puzzle pieces falling into place. This, too, had to be a part of Siobhan's plan.

The inspector reached the other end of the dining car and turned around. "Now far be it from me to ever help a Cordelian in their time of need, which is what I assume this may look like. Far from it. I am here, today, to serve Neutral Moldevickian justice!" He slammed his fist on the nearest table for dramatic punctuation.

"I, Inspector Sandor Horvath, am going to interview each passenger of the train, establish a timeline of events, and utilize my superior intellect to identify who stole the ruby jewels of the duchess of Cordelia, and to deduce exactly how they did it."

One of the baseball players, the one Valentine recognized as Smalls, stood up. He looked as heated as when they'd first met him earlier in the day. "But we got a game today."

Coach Hank spoke up. "And come to think of it, what gives you the jurisdiction to practice law enforcement here in the United States of America?"

"I had a feeling that someone, quite rightfully, might challenge my right to lead this case," said the inspector. "I spoke with the conductor just before this meeting of ours and he assured me that this was within the jurisdiction of American train law. He even gave me something to illustrate my authority."

Inspector Horvath reached into his coat. Although one would expect him to pull out a badge or any other signifier of dominion, he instead produced a revolver from his pocket, waving it over the heads of the crowd. Everyone in the train car instinctively ducked. A few screamed.

Oliver Path, clearly bothered by this, shouted. "This is outrageous and dangerous! Is he even allowed to do this?"

Everyone looked over to the Harborville Express's train conductor. He folded his arms and leaned against the wall of the train. Then he realized that somebody had asked him a question.

"I'm sorry, what?"

Then, "Oh right, federal train law dictates that I, as the conductor, may deputize anyone I deem may be helpful to the apprehension of a train criminal."

He performed the most lackadaisical shrug that J.J. or anyone on his team had ever seen. "I dunno man, if you have a problem with it you can take it up with the Federal Train Governance Commission."

The inspector readdressed the crowd. "I will be holding interviews with all passengers here in the dining car. With luck we will keep the train running and will still arrive at our destination of New Troutstead on time and with a suspect in custody.

With a flourish of his pistol, he placed it safely back into his coat pocket. "We will begin the interviews in earnest immediately. That is all."

J.J. looked at Trudi and Valentine. "I've got a bad feeling about this."

"Me too," Trudi and Valentine echoed alongside each other.

"Oh! One last thing," the inspector said. "With the size and breadth of the investigation, I will be assisted by my two new compatriots."

"No," said Valentine, almost loud enough for Inspector Horvath to hear.

"Allow me to introduce Siobhan Sweeney and Luther Adedeji, two young startups in the security industry." He motioned over to the table he was initially sitting at. By this time Luther was standing and Siobhan had sat down atop the table, her boots hanging off the edge and swaying back and forth. She had a clipboard.

"No, no no no..." Valentine went on, coming to another horrifying conclusion in his mind. He looked desperately to Trudi and Valentine. "Guys, her plan wasn't just to steal the jewels."

"Miss Sweeney," said Inspector Horvath, "Who is first on our interview docket?"

With a deep look of sorrow on his face, Valentine spoke again. "She's going to steal the jewels *and* frame us for it."

The inspector's newly ordained assistant looked up from her clipboard, an unashamed smile crossing her face. She looked directly at Valentine.

"The Ghost Hunters Adventure Club."

CHAPTER 6

Neutral Moldevik's Premier Investigator

The Ghost Hunters Adventure Club sat, rather nervously, squished together on the same side of a booth in the dining car of the Harborville Express. The other half of the booth in front of them remained empty.

Valentine surveyed the room once more; Inspector Sandor Horvath was nowhere to be seen. Neither was Luther Adedeji. Siobhan Sweeney, however, was there a few tables down, thumbing through some paperwork and doing a good job at what Valentine assumed was acting like an impartial assistant. The door toward the front of the train opened and Inspector Horvath entered the room. Walking, as he did, with a leisurely gait that indicated his veteran status in the crime-solving world.

"The Ghost Hunters Adventure Club!" Inspector Horvath said as he sat down at the table across from the team. He spent a moment examining their documents, I.D.s, and a business card that J.J. had snuck in there. After a while, he looked up at them.

"Are you two actually brothers?"

Normally this would be the moment where J.J. would shirk the question by giving the hard pitch on his business entity. But right now he was currently occupied with getting himself and his team out of the predicament they were currently in: seemingly set up for the fall by their old friend Siobhan.

To reason, he instead wanted to focus on putting forth a stonewall defense toward potential inquest; citing their inalienable right to remain silent, the protections against illegal search and seizure granted to them by the fourth amendment, and every other trick in his playbook to skip out of a sweat session with a deputized officer of the law.

But there was one other thing on his mind.

"Are you all being for real about this Cordelia and Neutral Moldevik stuff? Because right now I feel like a targeted individual in a disinformation campaign meant to make me question my own sanity."

Inspector Horvath stared quizzically at J.J. "Did the American education system fail you or have you been living under a rock this entire time?"

"The two aren't mutually exclusive," J.J. replied.

"Let me back up," said Inspector Horvath, as he ran his fingers through his beard and went back to examining the documents. "J.J. and Valentine Watts and Trudi de la Rosa, correct? The three of you form the crime-fighting and mystery-solving team known as the Ghost Hunters Adventure Club?"

The version of J.J. that didn't trust authority figures sprang back into action. "Listen man, I make a point of not speaking to any officers of the law without my lawyer present, so for the purpose of this thinly veiled interrogation I'd like to say for the record that I don't know what you're talking about."

"Your name or the name of your group?" the inspector replied.

"I don't recall."

Valentine had seen J.J. respond like this in similar situations and knew from experience just how effective J.J.'s nonresponses could be. If

J.J. could maintain the stone wall for long enough, it would give them enough time to think of an escape plan from all of this Siobhan business.

That was unless the inspector exploited the one weakness of J.J.'s armor.

"The Ghost Hunters Adventure Club," he said. "That name rings familiar. Were you all in the news recently?"

There it was.

J.J.'s eyes lit up. "Why yes, now that you mention it, we were featured recently for our work in solving a crime and apprehending a criminal."

"Was that the Grande Chateau case?" the inspector asked.

"That's the one!" said J.J. excitedly. "You know, I wasn't sure that that TV interview was gonna drum up any business, so I'm glad to see us making waves in the mystery-solving world."

"I was highly impressed with your work. You'll all have very prominent careers if you continue the momentum of crime solving that you're currently keeping."

"One can only hope so, sir," said J.J. in a tone of reverence that made Valentine side-eye him.

"In that case, maybe you could help me out with this case," Inspector Horvath went on. He spun some documents toward the team, who all leaned forward to read it. "This is a manifest of all the passengers on the train."

Scanning the document further, Trudi recognized some names on it, from Coach Hank and his baseball team to Oliver Path and his group of train enthusiasts, to even Siobhan, Luther, and Rudith.

"One of these people—or peoples—stole the ruby jewels of the duchess of Cordelia. My intention is to understand the timeline of events, eliminate those who couldn't have stolen the jewels, and then identify the motives of those who remain on the list, eventually narrowing it down and accusing the correct perpetrator of this heist."

"We're aware of how crime investigations work," Valentine said defiantly, taking up the now-vacant slot of "person who doesn't trust authority figures."

"Well, the first thing I would do in this situation," J.J. volunteered, "would be to find a clear motive that could lead to this thing being stolen."

"Very astute," Inspector Horvath said, encouraging J.J. to leak information uncontrollably. "Let's go over what we know. The stolen jewels were a priceless Neutral Moldevickian artifact."

"Wait," Trudi interrupted. "It's a Neutral Moldevickian artifact? I thought they were the duchess of Cordelia's."

"They were," Inspector Horvath said excitedly. "It's a wonderful piece of Neutral Moldevickian history, actually. You see, the royal jewels were originally in the ownership of the Cordelians, yes, but after a series of misfortunately-timed business deals a decade ago, they fell into the ownership of the Neutral Moldevickians. The Neutral Moldevickian government now parades these jewels around from museum to museum as a petty display of cultural victory over those Cordelians."

"Okay, stop right there," J.J. said, confused. "I'm really going to need you to explain this warring postage stamp-sized European countries thing you keep throwing at me. Blame the American education system or whatever, but why do your two nations hate each other so much?"

"It's quite simple, really," said Inspector Horvath. "Neutral Moldevik and Cordelia couldn't be more different from one another. For example, Neutral Moldevickians take pride in honor, truth, and courage, whereas Cordelians value virtue, honesty, and steadfastness."

J.J. took a moment to compute this. "Is there, like, a language barrier here? Because I'm pretty sure those were synonyms."

"You wouldn't understand," said Inspector Horvath with a tone of finality.

Trudi spoke up. "So, are you suggesting that a Cordelian could have attempted to steal the jewels back?"

"I'm suggesting that it's one motivation out of many that exist," replied Inspector Horvath. "We must examine any possibility that comes our way."

"I have an idea," Siobhan piped up over the inspector. Valentine could feel his blood turn to ice at the very sound of her voice. Everyone turned to see her sitting in her booth, with perfect posture as if it were picture day at school. "Well, maybe it's all so much more simple than international intrigue. Maybe this could be something as simple as a greed-motivated crime."

"And how come we haven't ruled out Siobhan and her friend as possible suspects?" asked Valentine. The words came out of him faster than he could stop them. He stifled his instinct to throw his hands over his mouth.

Siobhan gasped. "How could I ever betray the trust of my client and jeopardize my burgeoning career in the security industry?"

"Will you stop calling it the 'security industry?'" Valentine responded with the last bit of adrenaline in his fight or flight response. "You're a con artist who exploits the naivetes of the weak for personal gain."

"And not even in a fun way," added J.J. "Normal con artists prey on greed rather than naivete."

"Is there…history between you all?" asked Inspector Horvath.

"We ran into each other from time to time in a past life," Siobhan said. "Once you lose my trust, it's hard to get it back."

"Hmm," said Inspector Horvath. He adjusted his impossibly tiny spectacles at the bridge of his nose. "It's probably not important to the current investigation. But to answer your question, Mr. Watts, I've already deduced through my own personal investigative methods that neither Siobhan nor Luther were culprits."

This was the first time that Trudi felt like something might be off with Inspector Horvath, other than the moment where he pulled a gun on a crowd of train patrons. She had assumed that Horvath's renown as the greatest detective in Neutral Moldevik meant she was working with some grand intelligence that would prevent her and her friends from unjustly being framed. But his line of reasoning was making less and less sense.

But then again, she thought, *wasn't that one of the oldest tricks in the book? To feign ignorance and lure your suspect into a trap?* It's what Trudi would do if the situation were reversed, for sure. She decided to remain on guard.

"Please, Miss Sweeney, continue with your line of reasoning," said the inspector.

"Well, I understand that everyone was in the lounge car at the time of the heist." She pulled out a pocketknife and picked at one of her manicured fingernails, seemingly aloof of her very serious accusation. "But not everybody knew that Mrs. Espiritu had the jewels. That is, except for Valentine here."

Valentine could see the puzzle pieces falling into place in real time. He was too afraid to object.

She went on. "I think one of the most important clues is that the key around my neck was stolen. So, it would stand to reason that whoever has that key is the likely culprit."

The door to the dining car, the one leading in from the lounge, swung open. Standing in the doorway was Luther Adedeji. He had a small plastic bag in his hand.

"Ah, just who we were waiting for," said Inspector Horvath. "Please, please, come here."

Luther strode over to the inspector, placing the plastic bag into the inspector's hand.

Inside of the bag was a key. One exactly similar to the one that Siobhan was wearing earlier in the day.

"This was found during a search of your room," said the inspector.

"What!?" chorused the three members of the Ghost Hunters Adventure Club.

"Anyone could've planted that there!" J.J. exclaimed, gesticulating wildly.

"We've spent plenty of time outside of our rooms, and anyone could have put it there when we were unaware," offered Trudi.

The inspector's stern gaze split time between each of his three interviewees. It was as if he were staring into their souls to judge their guilt on an ethereal plane. Then he spoke. "I don't believe you."

"Oh come on!" shouted J.J. "Can you even do this? Legally?"

Inspector Horvath pulled out the revolver from his coat pocket, examining it for some time. He checked the cylinder, confirming the existence of six bullets seated within their chambers. Placing it back within his coat, he looked to J.J., shrugging. "Train law."

J.J. massaged the scar across his nose. "You've got to be kidding me."

"Well, it's time for the moment of truth," said Inspector Horvath. "Siobhan, would you please bring me the briefcase?"

Siobhan reached under her table and produced the small briefcase that they had all seen Mrs. Espiritu carrying. The latch on it was now broken from the scuffle in the train's lounge, but the keyhole remained intact. She placed it on the table in front of everybody.

"Oh, like that would prove anything," said J.J. defiantly. "How do we know that was the original briefcase? Anyone with half a brain, a pair of scissors, and a can of soda could have made a shim and gotten the handcuffs off the original briefcase's handle *twice* in the time it took to go through that dark tunnel. Then they could replace it with a new, empty briefcase."

Inspector Horvath paused to address J.J. "Do you spend a lot of time thinking about how to secretively remove handcuffs?"

Valentine finally summoned the will to speak. "Can't you see? We're being set up for a fall by your assistant, Siobhan! She greeted us in our room when we were first aboard, so she could've dropped the key there intentionally. She sang a catchy song about getting revenge on us! Don't you think this is coming together a little too perfectly?"

Inspector Horvath ignored him. He slipped the key into the brief-case's keyhole. It fit perfectly. He paused again to look at the three members of the Ghost Hunters Adventure Club. "Interesting."

"No," said Valentine.

"Yes," said Siobhan, who had crowded up to the table. Her elation was hard to hide now.

The inspector looked back at the briefcase. He turned the key.

It didn't budge.

"What?" demanded Siobhan.

Inspector Horvath jiggled the key a few more times for good measure. Nothing opened.

"Hmm," said the inspector. He stroked his impeccable beard and spent a few moments lost in critical thought. "Well, I suppose it's not illegal to have a key in your room. Back to the drawing board!"

"What?" demanded Siobhan again. No matter how good of an actor she was, both J.J. and Valentine could tell that Siobhan was actually shocked.

"Oh, don't worry, Miss Sweeney," said Inspector Horvath. "That's how investigations work. You form hypotheses and you test them until you find the right one."

"Oh," replied Siobhan. She quickly regained her sense of composure. "Well, it looks like we'll have to interview a couple more people to get a better idea of just what happened today." She could have damned Valentine's soul with how demonically she was staring at him.

"I suppose we will," said the inspector. "This does lend credence to my theory that this could have been an act performed as revenge by Cordelian partisans."

"Or it could be anyone," Siobhan added. "The real thieves could be staring you in the face right now, after having narrowly avoided an initial accusation."

He ignored her, going on. "That's the interesting difference between Cordelians and Neutral Moldevickians, you know. A Cordelian can't resist a good puzzle."

The statement hung in the air for a little. Trudi ventured a response. "And Neutral Moldevickians?"

"They aren't *just* puzzles to us."

Inspector Horvath readdressed his interviewees. "I have no further questions for you at this moment, although I may have some later. We will find you if we need you again, but for now you're all free to leave."

A great sense of relief washed over the Ghost Hunters Adventure Club. The three got up.

"Well, it was very nice talking to you all," said J.J. "Best of luck finding your culprit. C'mon team, let's peel out."

Getting up, Trudi couldn't help but think more about Inspector Horvath. This didn't seem like the methods of a great investigator. Was she missing something? This had to be a trick.

"Just one second," said Inspector Horvath. "That second-class cabin sure is a little tiny to accommodate three, don't you think? Trudi, the manifest the conductor gave me says there's an unclaimed compartment in the first-class car. Why don't you take that room?"

"I, uh..." Trudi stammered, trying to process why he would request something like this. "I'd prefer to stay with my friends."

"Please, I insist," said the inspector.

Trudi stammered some more. She did not like the idea of being stranded away from her teammates.

"I really must insist. And I simply won't take no for an answer." Inspector Horvath's expression became stern.

She got the message.

Trudi got up from the table and made a slow walk toward the first-class car. The last thing she saw as she turned around to close the train door behind her were the two helpless faces of J.J. and Valentine.

CHAPTER 7

Alliances

"Well that didn't go all so well," said J.J., closing the door to the Ghost Hunters Adventure Club's second-class berth. With the removal of Trudi de la Rosa and her placement in the first-class car, there was a little bit more room to gesticulate wildly. Valentine, however, stood facing an empty wall of the compartment as if he were an anxious kitten.

"This is a predicament," J.J. went on. He took off his red sweater and wrung the sweat out of it before placing it back on to preserve brand recognition. "How are we gonna run the summit when one of our team members is stuck on the other side of the train?"

Silently staring at a blank wall became too much for Valentine. "J.J., will you quit it with the leadership seminar stuff? We don't have time for that."

"Normally I'd have a solid comeback," said J.J. He could feel himself begin to calm down. "But I spent a really long time making all of these teaching materials, and I worked really hard, and I refuse to stop this until the Ghost Hunters Adventure Club at least has a mission statement."

Valentine let out a long, heavy sigh. "Did you have to tell the inspector how to make a handcuff shim?" He disengaged from the wall and walked across the room to take up a moody, contemplative position staring out of the window at the landscape drifting by. The train traveled onward, now through an increasingly desolate desert landscape.

It was serene.

"I don't think it mattered what I told him," replied J.J. "Putting a man like that on the case is the justice equivalent of sending a toddler into a room with a loaded gun. Which, coincidently, is a pretty solid description since he was carrying that iron."

He looked to his brother, who seemed stuck in a pretty deep rabbit hole of anxiety. "Let's break down what happened back there and maybe we can figure out our next move."

Valentine took a moment to respond as he collected his thoughts. "Siobhan has been meticulously planning and executing a scheme to frame us for the theft of priceless jewelry, presumably to get away with the loot herself, in addition to seeing us locked up. What's impressive is that she designed her plan in such a way that she was able to craft a really poetic mixture of unbridled fear and telling us that we're bad at our jobs."

"She framed us and she wants us to know," replied J.J.

"And she wanted to see us humiliated as detectives while she was at it."

"But we're still here."

"Then something went wrong," Valentine went on. "Her plan failed. I don't know if you caught a look at her face when the key didn't open the lock, but for a moment I thought she could be human. That if you cut her, she would bleed."

"So that must mean that she's on the back foot," J.J. said.

"But you and I both know that won't last for long. Every one of Siobhan's plans comes with a secondary backup plan and a tertiary backup-backup plan, so we gotta figure out what we're gonna do before she puts the final nail in our coffins."

"I feel bad for saying this," said J.J., "since I want every member of the team to feel a certain agency in their ability to affect the outcome of a mission. But there's no way we can outsmart Siobhan if it's just the two of us. Trudi was the only reason why we survived the last hour or so with the move she pulled in the lounge."

"What was the inspector's angle with separating us?" asked Valentine.

"It's a classic prisoner's dilemma," replied J.J.

"A what?"

"You know, the prisoner's dilemma. It's...uh..." J.J. searched his mind. "It's a theory thing where a detective will separate two parties and then he...does something...to get them to rat on each other?"

"Man, I wish Trudi were here," Valentine sighed. "She would know what that is."

Something happened in this moment that neither of the brothers were expecting. At about the exact same time, the two detected the pungent smell of rubbing alcohol.

J.J. thought fast. "I was thinking that we'd need to break out the grappling hook for this one." As he spoke, he slowly and silently rose from his chair and began moving toward the source of the smell: the door to the adjoining room.

"What?" asked Valentine.

The Watts brothers, who had known each other for a long while, had long since developed a complicated and nuanced hand-signaling system to communicate freely in moments of subterfuge. J.J. made a gesture that suggested, "I need you to remember that one time we both took an improv comedy class and 'yes-and' with me here."

"...are we gonna do with a grappling hook? We're on a train," responded Valentine.

"I was thinking we could use it to get to the train's roof." J.J. continued his slow and steady march, reaching the door.

"Yes, and then what will we do?" asked Valentine, offering a paltry setup for J.J. to riff off of, but at the very least showcasing that he had a base-level understanding of improvisational comedy.

"I was thinking we could find a way to get to Trudi's room on the other side of the train without Inspector Horvath noticing." As he spoke, he held three fingers up and counted down. "And hopefully we can combine info and find a clue."

J.J.'s fingers reached zero. He pulled the door as swiftly as he could. Oliver Path, who had been listening attentively against the door, fell straight to the ground at the feet of Valentine and J.J.

"Or a rat," concluded J.J. as he looked down at the train nerd.

J.J. and Valentine grabbed their suspicious neighbor by the shoulders, picked him up, and set him down in one of the train seats. The room was now back to its more comfortable, "there are too many people here" quality of charm.

"Listen," started Oliver, "I can explain!"

"Then explain," J.J. replied.

"I…um…I heard everything you two said."

The two Watts brothers remained silent, allowing the sound of the rumbling train to grow almost deafening to the train nerd. They were entering a rough section of track.

As modern social politics dictated, the train nerd was compelled to speak further, lest he suffer the social disgrace of dead air in a conversation.

"Something's off about this whole investigation. The Neutral Moldevickian inspector, the missing jewels…. My guys are worried that they might catch a stray accusation from whatever that Horvath fellow is trying to pull. They're all very anxious people."

"So then you feel like you can solve things by spying on your neighbors?" asked J.J. "We're good, thanks. I suggest you leave this compartment because once my brother figures out how to open these sealed train windows, we're throwing you out of it."

"But…" Oliver stammered.

"But what?"

Oliver looked back and forth between two apparently menacing young adventurers. His voice came out like he was flipping losing cards onto a poker table. "You guys are cool! Okay? My club looks at trains all day, talks about trains all day. We're all just obsessed with trains, which is okay I guess, but I get how everyone can make fun of us. *Your* club solves mysteries. *Your* club gets into action, into adventure, into intrigue. And I…just want to help."

J.J.'s features softened a bit. "You…think we're cool?" Then he snapped back to his senses. "Valentine, Ghost Hunters Adventure Club official sidebar conversation?"

The two present members of the Ghost Hunters Adventure Club turned their backs to the train nerd. They didn't have much room in the cramped cabin, so they spoke in whispers.

"An important part of leadership is recognizing your previous mistakes and growing from them," started J.J. "Right now I'm telling you that I'm feeling flattered, and I don't want to fall for that again. I don't trust this nerd as far as I can throw him. Which is more a commentary on our comparative size rather than my strength."

"You probably couldn't get a proper windup with him in your arms, no," replied Valentine. "But what else have we got? We need help. Siobhan's probably thought up three separate contingency plans since we left the dining car. There's a Neutral Moldevickian investigator between us and Trudi, and I don't see a way that we can get around him."

"Actually," Oliver butted into their conversation with a feeble raise of his hand. It was a very small compartment. "I can help there."

J.J. and Valentine broke from their Ghost Hunters Adventure Club official sidebar conversation to address Oliver Path, sitting right next to them.

"I can help you execute your plan to rendezvous with Miss de la Rosa," said Oliver. Saying this seemed to fill him with an air of confidence.

J.J. scoffed. "What are you gonna do, challenge Inspector Horvath to a debate?"

"I know the complete blueprint diagram of this train by memory," replied Oliver. "I can get you around the dining car undetected."

J.J. and Valentine looked at each other and did some silent consideration. Then J.J. reached into the storage compartment of their berth and pulled out his beat-up copy of the Ghost Hunters Adventure Club Field Manual. He handed it to Oliver.

"All right," J.J. started. "We would like to extend to you the offer of a provisional membership to the Ghost Hunters Adventure Club. We're in the middle of our leadership summit, so you'll have to catch up as we go. Do you have any opinions about teamwork or leadership you'd like to share with us right n—"

As happens on rough train tracks sometimes, the train jerked ever so slightly. J.J.'s speech was cut off when the three of them heard a commotion in the hallway. It sounded like someone being jostled off balance, knocking almost imperceptibly against the door to their compartment. Looking toward the source of the noise, they could all see the shadow of two feet cutting the light at the base of the door.

"Tell him a little bit more about the leadership summit," said J.J. as he got up from his seat.

Valentine's improvisational comedy engine had spun up to full speed by this time. "Generally there's a nominal entrance fee to joining the club but we'll waive that. Also, it's really important that you put some thought into those leadership and mission statement questions. J.J. won't drop it."

J.J. continued gliding toward the entrance to their cabin. His footsteps were masked by the soft rumbling of the train.

"Wait. Didn't anyone else hear that knocking sound?" asked Oliver Path.

"Oliver!" J.J. groaned at their new companion. He turned and dashed the rest of the short distance to the door and swung it open.

No one was there. J.J. stuck his head out of their berth and looked up and down the hallway. Empty. Waiting there for a moment to see if any eavesdropper would materialize, J.J. eventually closed the door and returned to his conversation with the other two.

"There's a whole section in the manual on improv comedy and its applicable uses in real life situations. Oliver, I suggest you start there. Read quick. We've got some work to do."

It was only a short time after, when the three were no longer paying attention to the goings-on outside of their compartment, that a figure hopped down from their hiding place lodged up near the ceiling of the second-class passenger car, above the team's door.

They scampered off without retribution.

CHAPTER 8

The Other Half of the Train

"Listen Mrs. Espiritu, I think it's all going to turn out for the best," said Trudi. She was sitting in a plush seat across from Rudith Espiritu in the woman's first-class cabin. It was significantly larger than the second-class berth that Trudi was previously squeezed into, with room enough for a small bed and a doorway that led to a private washroom.

Trudi had been in here for some time, consoling Mrs. Espiritu over the robbery that had recently transpired.

"Oh man," said Rudith, "if I don't get those jewels to New Troutstead then I'm in trouble. The Harborville Museum of Fine Art won't be happy about me losing a prized relic on loan from a European nation."

"I'm sure it will be fine," said Trudi. She had long since run out of ammunition for reasons why Rudith shouldn't feel down.

"It sure is a good thing I had my security detail with me, and that that nice Neutral Moldevickian inspector just happened to be on board at the exact right time."

"It certainly is all very coincidental," Trudi remarked, with the slightest hint of disingenuity. "How did you go about finding this Siobhan and Luther character to hire them?"

"Oh, well, that's sort of funny," replied Rudith. "They actually found me."

"You don't say."

"They reached out to me and told me they were brand new to the security industry but were willing to work hard and at a discounted rate to prove their worth in a no-doubt competitive business space. I really liked their enthusiasm, so I said heck, why not? Beats what I'd usually do."

"What would you usually do?" Trudi asked.

"Oh, normally I would have just stuck the jewels in my purse and ridden the train all the way to New Troutstead. Nobody really bothers an old lady riding the train. We do it all the time."

Trudi looked out of the window of the first-class cabin to the landscape that was drifting past. By this point the scenery had fully transitioned to desert. Cracked dirt within the sand created fissures spanning far off into the horizon, meeting a cloudy, gray, and foreboding sky. She figured now was as good a time as any to lead a horse to water, but she already had sincere doubts as to whether or not she could make it drink.

"So," Trudi started, "Don't you think it's a little funny that the one time you do get a security detail, something like this happened?"

Rudith paused, seeming lost in thought. "You know what? You're right. It *is* kind of funny."

"And these people who reached out to be your security detail, isn't it a little strange that they reached out to you out of nowhere, offering you a really specific service that you needed?"

Mrs. Espiritu furrowed her brows. "That *is* a little peculiar, isn't it?"

"And so, do you think, maybe, that the most likely people to have stolen the jewelry are the people who had the easiest access to it in the first place?"

"Wow," said Rudith. Her gaze floated through her glasses and around the cabin in thought. "You actually might be on to something here."

Trudi paused expectantly, tacitly urging Mrs. Espiritu without words to take the next logical step on her own.

"...but...I'd have no reason to steal the jewels. I'm just trying to deliver them to the New Troutstead Museum of Contemporary Art! Oh, do you think they would suspect me? Oh no, if I thought I was in trouble before just for losing the jewels, how much worse off would I be if they were convinced I took them as well? It's all so dreadfully terrifying!"

Trudi let out a very soft and very subdued groan of frustration. She crossed out "Rudith saves the day" from a list she kept in her mind. "I'm...sure you'll be fine."

Rudith sighed. "It's a terrifically interesting subject, you know? The Cordelians, the Neutral Moldevickians, and the ruby jewels."

"How so?" Trudi asked. "When we were interviewed by Inspector Horvath, he mentioned that the Neutral Moldevickians actually owned the Cordelian jewels. That they were showcasing it in museums throughout the world as an act of pettiness."

"Isn't it romantic?" asked Rudith.

"I'm not sure what about that makes it romantic."

"Well, look at it this way. The Cordelians and Neutral Moldevickians have been at each other's throats for hundreds and hundreds of years, pockmarked with petty grievance after petty grievance."

"I still don't see how that's romantic," replied Trudi.

"That's the thing," Rudith said with a smile. "For those hundreds and hundreds of years that these two small nations have been like this, they have never once had an armed conflict between the two of them. The pettiness, while, yes, petty, has led to years and years of technical peace between the two nations. It's a tenuous peace, but it's peace nonetheless. It's almost as if the people of these two nations would rather tease each other than fight each other."

"Peace out of pettiness," said Trudi thoughtfully. It was a strange concept, but she could understand why someone would consider it a fascinating thing to study.

A thought popped into Rudith's head. "Say, do you want to see an old Cordelian riddle?" She pulled out her purse from a storage compartment and fished around inside of it, eventually producing two identical pieces of dice.

"There's only two things I can tell you about this riddle: the name of the game is Ring Around the Rose and the name of the game is important."

She threw the dice onto a small table between the two of them. They came up like this:

"What does that total up to?" asked Rudith.

Trudi stared at the dice for a moment. She figured the only answer she had to give was the correct one.

"Six."

"Four," Rudith responded. She picked up the dice and readdressed Trudi. "The name of the game is Ring Around the Rose and the name of the game is important."

She threw the dice again. They came up like this:

"What does that total up to?" she asked once again.

Trudi thought harder this time. If it wasn't the number at the top, then there had to be a different way to interpret it. If two threes made four, then what did six and one make?

"Four," was her best guess.

"Zero," Rudith responded. "Wanna try it one more time?"

Trudi exhaled. She was getting frustrated, and she knew she didn't think as well when she was frustrated.

"Go ahead," she said.

For a third time, Rudith picked up the dice and threw them down on the table. They came up looking like this:

"The name of the game is Ring Around the Rose and the name of the game is important," she said. "What does that total up to?"

Trudi spent some time lost in thought here. If three and three was four and six and one was zero, what would five and three make? She ran through math equations in her head but couldn't extrapolate what the five meant, since she had never seen it before.

She thought a lot about numbers, but very disappointedly couldn't come up with any workable theories.

Then she thought about the name of the game.

"I've got it!" she shouted. "It's six!"

Rudith smiled. "That's correct! How'd you figure it out?"

"The name of the game is Ring Around the Rose and the name of the game is important. I thought so hard about the numbers the dice came up with, but I didn't actually look to see how the numbers were arranged on each die." She pointed to the five and three dice. "If you see the center dot as a rose, then the number you get is how many 'petals' surround each flower."

"Very good!" Rudith exclaimed excitedly. "It's an old Cordelian proverb told in the form of a puzzle: If one doesn't understand something, then maybe one is looking at it the wrong way."

Rudith collected the dice and put them back into her purse. "Thanks for taking the time to console me, dear. It was very sweet of you."

"I'm happy to do it," Trudi replied. She got up from her seat and walked to the compartment door. "Let me know if you need anything or come to any realizations about the sort of company you keep."

The frail old lady looked at Trudi quizzically. Trudi shrugged, then walked out of the door. She stepped out into the hallway and surveyed the first-class passenger car.

Along the hallway there were doors to other first-class compartments. Trudi knew that Siobhan, Luther, Rudith, and Inspector Horvath each had rooms in this car, and that she now had one herself. One of the concierge staff was nice enough to bring her her luggage from the second-class car. She had not had any contact with either of the Watts brothers since their collective interview with Inspector Horvath earlier.

She looked down toward the rear of the train. Beyond that was the dining car, where Inspector Horvath was performing interviews. Then it was the lounge car, where the crime had taken place. Inspector Horvath had made a point to assign the conductor to oversee the lounge to make sure that the crime scene wasn't disturbed. Then it was the second-class car, where J.J. and Valentine were, then it was the luggage car.

J.J. and Valentine. She already missed having their help. They were doofuses, yes, but for all his strange peculiarities J.J. was a good leader, and Valentine would have been level-headed enough to help her come up with a plan. Maybe. Valentine was having a tough time. That Siobhan lady seemed to know exactly how to get under his skin.

Still, though, she'd rather have them than not have them.

She did not know what was in the other direction, toward the front of the train. Without much else to do other than wait, she decided her time would be best spent finding out what else there was. Walking through to the adjoining corridor that connected the two train cars, she came to an abrupt stop.

In front of her was a door. But something felt different about this place. The air felt electric. Each step that brought Trudi closer to that entryway felt, for whatever reason, like it could be her last.

The torment was almost unbearable as she reached for the handle. Pausing momentarily to catch her breath and steel her nerves, she read the words printed across the door in front of her.

PRESIDENTIAL SUITE

She took a deep breath, opened the door and walked in.

HOLD ON.

I got up from my writing desk and looked to the other end of the room, toward the door. There was Trudi, standing there.

"Are you kidding me? Did I forget to write in a hallway?"

She stood there for a moment, perplexed.

"I wanted a larger footprint for my presidential suite," I said, walking toward her. "So I had it take up this whole car. But it's fine. None of the story takes place up here, anyway."

Trudi's initial confusion wore off. "Dr. Cecil, what are you doing here?"

"I'm writing the book. Now will you please leave me be so that I can get back into this? My writing process usually begins with me rolling around on the floor for several hours and bemoaning that I have to write anything in the first place. If I lose momentum I'll have to do that all over again."

Trudi nodded in vague understanding before a thought crossed her mind. "Why are you writing your novel inside of your novel?"

"Because you can do anything when you're writing, since you're literally just making things up. Don't overthink it, you'll give yourself a nosebleed. The simple fact of the matter is that in this universe I can afford luxury train travel."

I peered past Trudi, down the adjoining corridor, and through its windows into the first-class passenger car. There were no publishing house executives or narrative realism-purists, thankfully. "You know what, kid? Why don't you have a cup of tea while you're here? I've got a minimum word count to hit and this'll be an extra three pages."

She thought for a moment before accepting my offer and allowing me to usher her further into the suite.

"Come on, come on," I said. "The fourth wall can go to hell."

The inside of my presidential suite was luxurious, of course. Priceless fine art adorned the walls of an entire train car dedicated to one man's traveling quarters. The large, vaulted windowpanes allowed me to stare lazily off into the distance whenever writing seemed to become a little too much. Which was often.

She sat down on a custom-made sofa. My presidential suite came with that, as well as a mahogany coffee table and several other sitting apparatuses. I walked around an entire bookshelf filled with copies of *Cerberus, From On High* to a kettle that had been boiling on the stove. A range stove, actually. Priceless antique. I mostly use it to boil water.

"Did you like the Ring Around the Rose puzzle?" I asked, placing tea bags into two teacups. "It's not actually an old Cordelian riddle, you know. It was a game a friend taught me all the way back in high school, when I was on the cross-country team. It popped into my head recently, but when I researched it I couldn't find anything about it. So I guess I put it in here as a way to memorialize a very vivid memory from my past."

I poured hot water into the two teacups and walked them over to Trudi, handing her one. "Hell, Cordelia and Neutral Moldevik don't even exist. Did you know that? I just wanted to do a little more world building so that I can plant seeds for later novels if everything goes right and I can keep making money off of these. J.J. not knowing about either country and needing it explained to him is a narrative device used to create a better frame of reference for the reader."

Trudi looked at her teacup, then back to me. "What kind of tea is this?"

"Whatever you want it to be," I said.

She looked at her teacup again before setting it down. "I don't think this is a productive usage of my time."

"Fine, fine, I get it. You don't like the metaphysical aspects of my storytelling. Neither do my critics." I took a sip of my tea before setting the cup down on the mahogany table. On a coaster, obviously. "So how can I help you?"

"My friends and I are into some deep trouble and if I don't figure out a way to help, I think something bad might happen."

"And you're smart enough to remember that I'm not going to give you any hints?"

"I wouldn't, because I also remember that you're making all of this up as you go."

"Outlines are for cowards."

"So I've heard," said Trudi. "I'm not looking for handouts. I just want to better understand the place. Maybe you're the wrong person to ask."

"All right, all right. What do you want to know?"

"What's in front of this train car?"

"Oh, you don't want to go that way," I said.

"And why wouldn't I want to go that way?"

"Because it's just the train engine."

"The train engine sounds pretty important. Why shouldn't I go there?" Trudi asked. "There could be plenty of information to gather in there that could help me and the brothers out."

"I promise you, Trudi, wholeheartedly, that there is nothing of value and no clues in the train engine. It is simply there, narratively, to propel this train forward. That is its one duty."

Trudi folded her arms and put on a look of determination that I found to be surprising. "I think I should be able to see the train engine. I don't see why you're so against this."

"Look," I groaned, getting up and walking around the room. "You want to know the real answer? Here it is: Do you understand just how much train research I had to do to start this novel in the first place? Do you ever wonder how many hardbound books I have on my desk, right now, about the history, form, and function of trains throughout the centuries? Because I've had to read many."

I groaned again. "Now I don't have anything wrong with train enthusiasts or the very concept of train enthusiasm, but if I have to learn just one more train fact against my will then I will take my typewriter and light it on fire before I shove it off on a boat for a true Viking funeral. It is an absolute terror, Trudi, to be burdened with this information."

I collapsed onto one of the more expensive chairs in my presidential suite in a rage-fueled haze. Then, weakly, I spoke again. "Go on up and check out the train engine. I'm sure I can figure something out by the time you get there. Just don't expect me to get the descriptions perfect."

"Thank you," Trudi said. She got up from her sofa. "I suppose I should be going now. It was very nice to meet you."

"Likewise," I replied. "I guess I built you to be more strong-willed than I had initially realized. Good luck solving the mystery."

Trudi got up and walked to the opposite door on the other end of the suite. I didn't bother with any more pleasantries and sat back down at my typewriter: a much more expensive Hermes Media 3 that I upgraded to from my previous Remington Elitra. This book isn't gonna finish itself.

Trudi paused at the door for a moment. Then she turned to me, speaking over the clicking and clacking of creativity. "Doctor, is it true that you control everything I say and do?"

The clicking and clacking paused momentarily. "It's complicated," I said to her. "Kurt Vonnegut once described it as if he could only control his characters' movements approximately, as if he had inertia to overcome. He said he wasn't connected to them by what should feel like steel wires. It was more like he was connected to them by stale rubber bands.

"Like every other character in this book, you, Trudi, are a product of my fears, experiences, hardships, and triumphs. You are a vessel with which I process this information. Just as my understanding of these bright and dark moments of my life is mercurial, so is my understanding of you. And while you could technically say that I'm running the show, only you have the power to surprise me, and not the other way around."

I punctuated my last sentence by turning back to my typewriter and resuming my work. "The short answer is 'yes.'"

I didn't receive a response. Trudi left, but I didn't hear her leave. I had to work, anyway.

* * *

TRUDI WALKED FORWARD ALONG A steel catwalk that wrapped around the exterior of the engine carriage. For the first time since this trip began, she felt wind travel through her hair. It was misty. The train was traveling deeper and deeper into a fog among the desert landscape.

Reaching the entrance to the engine compartment, she opened the door and walked in.

It looked exactly how you'd expect an engine compartment to look.

"Oh, it's you," Trudi heard.

She looked across the engine compartment toward the sound of the voice.

Turning around in a chair that swivels—which I assume you have in an engine compartment—was the train's engineer. She wore her official Harborville Express uniform. While she was much better put together than the conductor, the lines on her face and straying, frazzled hair suggested a very specific form of world-weariness. As if she were created in a sigh and knew that one day she would disappear in another.

"You're the one who wanted to see the engine compartment so badly, so now I exist specifically so that I can show you around it."

"You what?" asked Trudi.

"You heard me," said the engineer. She got up out of her chair, folded her arms, and then leaned against a panel or something.

"Who are you?" asked Trudi, still befuddled.

"I'm the train's engineer," she said. "My name is…"

She looked down to the name tag on her uniform. Embroidered on a patch on her uniform's breast pocket was the word, "Engineer."

"Aw man, I didn't even get a real name," the engineer said. She looked over to Trudi with disappointment. "Thank you, so much."

"I still don't get it," said Trudi. "Are you trying to tell me that the only reason you exist is because the story needed it?"

"Precisely."

"But then how was this train running before you existed?"

"The reader didn't really need to know how a train worked for this story to unfold, right? They just needed to know that it *went*. The whole thing could've run on bubble gum and happy thoughts for all that it mattered."

The engineer massaged her temples with both of her hands. "And now it's run by me. An entire diesel-electric motor. It's a very stressful job, you know?"

Trudi did not know what to say. This was the first time she had ever confronted the existential concept of solipsism. "I'm…sorry?"

"Oh, *you're* sorry?" The engineer paced around the room as she vividly remembered and relived decades and decades of embarrassing moments in her life. Character motivation.

She shot a glance back to Trudi. "Ask me what not existing feels like."

"What does not existing feel like?"

"I don't know. In fact, I was unburdened by the very concept *of* knowing. I did not know anything until just seconds ago when I was forced into existence in order to show you around here." She pointed. "There's the engine controls. You can make the train go faster and slower. I had to study for a really long time in a vocational school to be able to do this."

"I was wondering if you heard anything about the robbery," Trudi attempted.

"Over there's a picture of me on vacation. I'm alone in the picture because I don't have a significant other and I couldn't work up the courage to ask anyone to go with me. I am so lonely, all of the time."

She collapsed back down at her chair, then after a moment motioned weakly to another corner of the compartment. "And there's my bag of specialized train tools."

Trudi looked over to the compartment that the engineer was motioning toward. It was empty.

"Wait—where's my tools?" the engineer demanded as she shot back out of her chair.

"I don't know," said Trudi, "I just showed up."

"Me too. Man, if the Federal Train Governance Commission finds out about this, I'm really gonna get it handed to me."

The engineer got up out of her chair again and paced around the compartment in heavy thought, muttering to herself about what a hassle it was to exist. She eventually sighed, turning to Trudi. "Hey, I'm sorry, I think we got off on the wrong foot. I was sort of dealing with the sudden burden of mortal thought."

She sat back down in her chair. "Listen kid, I gotta keep running this thing up here. Could you let me know if you see my tools anywhere around the train? I'd really appreciate it because now that I exist, there seem to be consequences for decisions made before I was willed into this world without my consent."

"Yeah, sure," said Trudi in a calm tone. She figured the engineer had some introspection to do. "Take care, I think."

The engineer waved unenthusiastically. "I have anxiety."

Trudi left the engine compartment and reentered by way of the presidential car. Thinking it useless to bother me for more clues,[3] Trudi bypassed the door to my suite and entered the first-class passenger car.

---

[3] Correct.

She was moments away from opening the door to her cabin, her hand on the handle, when she heard a click.

Her head turned to follow the sound of the noise, leading her to the door directly next to hers. Slowly, the door creaked open, revealing the face of Luther Adedeji.

"Trudi de la Rosa," he said.

"What do you want?"

"Just your ear for a moment. This Siobhan business—you and I don't necessarily have skin in the game, do we?"

"I thought you only spoke when you had something to say," Trudi said.

"I have something to say," he replied. "Something's up and I intend to get to the bottom of it. You're a smart person. You could be a valuable ally."

"Good afternoon," replied Trudi, trying to end the conversation as she opened her door further and began to step in.

"I'm not here to convince you," said Luther. "Just to plant the seed of an idea. I think you're meant for more than just playing a lackey to two ghost-hunting idiots." He began closing his door. "But I think the reason things happened the way that they did was because someone else was trying to steal the ruby jewels of the duchess of Cordelia."

He closed the door and was gone as quickly as he appeared. Trudi was left alone, clueless as to what the exchange had truly meant.

CHAPTER 9

The Prisoner's Dilemma

J.J. peered out at the hallway of the second-class passenger car from his team's quarters. Looking toward the front of the train, he spotted Coach Hank step out of his own compartment and walk in the direction of the dining car. Turning his head in the opposite direction, J.J. found the rest of the carriage empty.

"Looks like they're starting the next interview," he said, closing the door and readdressing Valentine and Oliver. The two were sitting knee-to-knee in their cramped cabin. "So back to what I was saying: Inspector Horvath has us in your classic prisoner's dilemma."

"Did you ever figure out what that actually was?" asked Valentine.

"I can wing it," J.J. said. He thought hard. "It's this philosophic thought experiment, I think. I don't remember exactly how it goes but you have these two prisoners who can't talk to each other, right? And there's a detective there and he knows he can get the prisoners to rat each other out. So then the...hmm..." J.J. searched his mind. "Look, I've seen it on a ton of detective shows. They split two people up and neither of them know what the other is saying and...shoot. Something happens and then the perp goes down, followed by a credits sequence."

J.J. looked over to Oliver. "Do you know what a prisoner's dilemma is?"

Oliver's ears perked. He made to say something, stopped, and then thought for a moment. "Wait. I actually don't."

"I miss Trudi," said Valentine.

"Listen," J.J. spoke again. "While I may not know exactly how it goes, what I can surmise is this: A viable way to circumvent the prisoner's dilemma entirely is simple. All we have to do is stage a jailbreak of the prisoner."

Valentine furrowed his eyebrows. "I suppose you're not wrong. But how do we go about doing that?"

"Oliver, that's where you and your front-to-back knowledge of the train come in," J.J. replied.

Oliver nodded. "There's a maintenance shaft running above the hallway outside. It'll lead to an access hatch to the top of the train. From there, it's the lounge car, then the dining car, then your target destination: the first-class passenger car."

J.J. picked the thread up from here. "At that point we establish contact with Ghost Hunters Adventure Club team member Trudi de la Rosa in her first-class accommodations, either rescue her or move our base of operations to said first-class accommodations, and then trade info so that the prisoner's dilemma falls on its face. By that time, we'll be in New Troutstead and dealing with what I hope to be non-train-law-related jurisdiction."

"But how do we get inside the first-class passenger car and how do we know which room Trudi's in?" asked Valentine. "I can't imagine it'd look good for us if we were caught sneaking around the other half of the train."

"That's where things get a little tricky," Oliver replied. "There's a similar access hatch on the first-class car, but it'll be locked."

"Not a problem," said J.J., pulling out his lockpick set from his satchel and placing it in his back pocket.

"Right," said Oliver. "In my earlier inspection of the train, I noted that each first-class passenger compartment was full, with the exception of Inspector Horvath's, which was filled when he boarded the train."

"But he said there was an open room there," replied Valentine. "That's how he split us up in the first place."

"Then it stands to reason that she was placed in the auxiliary cabin reserved for the conductor, or whoever the conductor sees fit to bestow it upon. It's a Federal Train Commission bylaw almost as old as trains itself. That's the last door before the next car up."

"Access the hatch, make it to the first-class train car, enter the hatch, enter the last compartment," Valentine summarized. "We can do that."

J.J. opened the door to their room and peeked out again. "Coast is clear. You all ready?"

Valentine and Oliver nodded. They followed J.J. outside and worked quickly, Valentine giving Oliver a boost to a panel in the ceiling. The train nerd then pulled a screwdriver from his pocket and unscrewed the panel, revealing the maintenance hatch they were looking for.

Valentine helped Oliver down, then jumped up himself, grabbing hold of the entrance to the maintenance shaft and pulling himself in. He then turned and reached down a hand to J.J., pulling him up into the shaft.

J.J. popped his head out of the access panel, looking down toward Oliver. Oliver was busy examining some of the finer elements of the Harborville Express's construction, placing a hand against one of its walls, as if he were feeling its heartbeat. "Such a work of art," he said.

J.J. cleared his throat, catching Oliver's attention. "Good work, I'm really feeling the synergy here."

Oliver gave him a thumbs-up before he went back to admiring the train. J.J. slipped back into the maintenance shaft.

The two present members of the Ghost Hunters Adventure Club shimmied through the small confines of the access tunnel that allowed engineers to maintain mechanical equipment throughout the train car. Sliding along the metal grating, J.J. eventually came to a hatch in the ceiling.

"This is it," said J.J., pointing to a handle in the center of the hatch.

He turned the handle and pushed upward. Immediately he was hit with the pressure of wind roaring past the train. Light shone in through the maintenance shaft. J.J. pulled himself out first and then turned to give his brother a hand up. "Make sure the latch doesn't lock. I don't want to be stuck on the roof of the train with a jailbroken prisoner."

After closing the hatch behind him, Valentine stood up against the wind and took in his surroundings. They were on top of a train, of course. It was moving fast enough for the two to have to crouch down to maintain balance. The fog that had surrounded the train was thick now. They could barely see to the front of the train before the world fell off into grayness. The smell of wet dirt was pungent in the air.

"Second-class car, lounge, dining car, first-class car, right?" shouted J.J. over the gusts of wind.

"Right," responded Valentine as the two began creeping forward.

They came to their first train car transition. Looking down into the gap below, hovering precariously over the fast-moving ground just feet beneath them, J.J. whistled. "Sorry fate lies beneath, dear brother."

Valentine joined him at the end of the roof and had a similar reaction. "Let's try to avoid falling off this train."

* * *

AND. UGH. OKAY. INSTEAD of writing this scene out for you like I usually do, why don't you step behind the curtain with me for a moment to see how the sausage is made. I'd rather write it this way than bore you.

You see, writing is an interesting craft because—in a sense—you build all of the tools that you work with yourself. Since you were decent enough to pay for this book, I figure it'd be the least I could do to throw you a free tool for your toolbox.

Currently we have J.J. and Valentine on top of the second-class car. They are traveling at a considerable speed. Their goal is to get to the first-class compartment, which is three cars up. Between all of these cars exist three gaps of space for these brothers to overcome. This is a great place to be as a writer because you always want to put obstacles in front of your objective so that things can stay entertaining. And here we have three in-universe obstacles that can organically produce entertainment.

The number three is useful here. With three identical obstacles, you're able to set up an expectation with the first, reinforce the expectation with the second, and then provide a reversal on that expectation with the last.

So, for example, this scene could play out with J.J. and Valentine jumping safely over the first gap, jumping safely over the second gap, and then failing to jump across the gap in the third.

Hell, you could even expand on the idea and treat the action of them getting safely over the three gaps as a setup of an expectation. This has the added benefit of three-dimensionally mapping the setting for your reader. The reversal on expectations instead comes when J.J. and Valentine rescue Trudi and their once-simple path to their exit now has an obstacle in it.

But how about we do this instead: Let's just assume that J.J. and Valentine have the basic athletic ability to clear these gaps between train cars safely.

* * *

THEY MADE IT TO THE first-class car without incident.

Or, at least they thought they made it there without incident. And Trudi was there to witness it.

You see, unlike J.J., who only had a passing knowledge of the prisoner's dilemma at best, Trudi knew the whole thing.

* * *

THE PRISONER'S DILEMMA, simplified, is a game theory exercise whereby two prisoners who cannot communicate are both offered their freedom if they rat out the other prisoner. The outcomes are mapped out thusly:

> Prisoner A and Prisoner B rat each other out. Both go to jail.
> Prisoner A rats out Prisoner B. Prisoner A goes free and
>   Prisoner B goes to jail.
> Prisoner B rats out Prisoner A. Prisoner B goes free and
>   Prisoner A goes to jail.

The most favorable outcome is this: If both Prisoner A and Prisoner B stay silent, then they both receive a lesser charge than they would have gotten if they had been ratted out, but will inevitably walk free.

In a scenario where the prisoners have no relationship with one another, the obvious, self-interested answer is to rat out the other prisoner. Because who's to say what the other one will do? However, there exists a human systemic bias whereby two parties who can't communicate with each other will still cooperate with one another in the face of rational self-interest.

I hope you can see this game's relevance to the Ghost Hunters Adventure Club's current predicament.

* * *

TRUDI WAS FAMILIAR WITH THE prisoner's dilemma, yes. She was smart. However, a quality of Trudi's that I feel like I've alluded to but haven't outright mentioned is this: Trudi de la Rosa has a very low opinion on the concept of snitching, and an even lower opinion on snitches themselves. Her decision on the prisoner's dilemma was already shored up.

Inspector Horvath would eventually try to put her in a bind, tell her that the brothers had confessed and were implicating her in the heist. He'd tell the brothers the same about her. Then he'd see who would break first.

And Trudi wouldn't fall for that. So, because Trudi's understanding of this particular game theory exercise was more complete than J.J.'s, she had not come to the same conclusion of jailbreaking as he had.

She was, instead, spying on Inspector Horvath's interviews in the dining car of the Harborville Express. She had slipped in undetected from the first-class compartment and had embedded herself among a pile of potatoes in the kitchen's pantry. She knew that Luther and Siobhan were both in their rooms for the time being, and that Inspector Horvath was conducting these interviews alone.

She could not, however, see any of the action taking place in the dining car, due to the potatoes. Right now, all she could do was hear, and right now she was hearing Inspector Horvath rifling through files and humming a soft song to himself.

Then she heard the door to the lounge open.

"Mister—or should I say—Coach Hank, I presume," greeted Inspector Horvath warmly.

"Howdy, Inspector Horvath!" came an exuberant voice. This was definitely Coach Hank. She could picture the ear-to-ear grin that must've been running along his face, the cowboy hat bouncing up and down as he walked.

"Please, please take a seat," Inspector Horvath said. Trudi heard footsteps shuffling along the carpet among the churn of the train wheels below them.

"Say," said Coach Hank, "what's the deal with that conductor fella always hanging out in the lounge, yelling at me if I get close to anything in there?"

"Oh," replied Inspector Horvath. "He's just minding the crime scene so that no one tampers with it. You know how train laws are. Very stringent."

Trudi assumed that there was some silent nodding in agreement here.

"My files tell me you are a baseball coach," the inspector said.

"American baseball! Yesiree, finest game on the planet."

"I'm actually not familiar with it," sighed Inspector Horvath. "The national sport of Neutral Moldevik is to call a Cordelian telephone number and ask them if their refrigerator is running."

"Oh man, you gotta try out baseball sometime. Finest game on the planet."

Trudi, although a big fan of baseball, and a big believer in its worldwide appeal, would have had trouble being as exuberant about baseball as Coach Hank was currently being right now.

"And you coach this minor league team?"

"That's right, the Harborville Elks. Got the whole team on the train. We're on our way to play against the New Troutstead Skipjacks. Should be a hell of a game."

"You'll excuse my ignorance," began Inspector Horvath, as he read down a list. "But these seem like very unconventional names for your players."

"Oh yeah, they must not do that in Neutral Moldevickian crank-calling sports," replied coach Hank. "Y'see, we all got funny nicknames in baseball. There's Neuro, catcher. Sort of the brains of the team. Smalls, the tiny one; it's one of those ironic nicknames because he's got a big heart. Then there's Not Dave, whose name *is* actually Dave but he likes to confuse the opposing team. Ice, that's how he likes his tea. Dolby, real quiet. Ro Ro on first, not to be confused with Rilo on second. And then finally there's Rude Luke."

"That's an intimidating nickname, Rude Luke. What did he do to earn that one?"

"He preferred it," said Coach Hank.

Just then, there was a break in the conversation.

"What was that?" asked Coach Hank.

"What was what?" Inspector Horvath asked.

"It sounded like footsteps on the roof of the train."

"I don't hear it."

"Shh…" said Coach Hank.

There was silence for a moment, then Inspector Horvath spoke again. "I still don't hear it, but let me make sure."

Trudi heard one of them get up and walk to the other end of the train car. The door opened, there was silence, and then she heard the door open again. The footsteps found their way back to the table.

"Thank you for the keen ear," he said. "I have informed the conductor and he will look after the matter personally."

"I mean, if you're looking for your jewel thieves, that was probably them right there."

"I should hope the conductor can provide some more information on that, yes," agreed Inspector Horvath.

"Welp, got any more questions for me?"

"Ah yes. Could you tell me where you were the moment the jewels were stolen?"

"I was having an argument with that Oliver fella by the piano. I do apologize for that, by the way. I can get heated when I talk about sports."

"Oh, it's no bother. You should see how we get when we're crank-calling."

There was silence once again. Then, "Did you steal the ruby jewels of the duchess of Cordelia?"

"Nope."

"Then that's all the questions from me!" said Inspector Horvath cheerfully.

Trudi rolled her eyes at the inspector's strange methods. Here was a man who was so obviously feigning ignorance in order to catch people in traps, yet she still could not figure out his angle. She heard Coach Hank get up and walk toward the other end of the dining car. Before exiting, he spoke one last time to Inspector Horvath.

"Say, what's the deal with that Siobhan lady? Isn't her and her partner supposed to be conducting these interviews with you?"

"They've both retired to their rooms in the first-class cabin," said Inspector Horvath. "Siobhan had mentioned wanting to do some research on her own."

Trudi heard the door close and then Inspector Horvath going back to flipping through papers and humming softly to himself.

She extricated herself from the sack of potatoes and made a stealthy exit from the dining room's kitchen. She had an idea of what to do next.

* * *

J.J. MADE QUICK WORK OF the hatch atop the first-class passenger train car, picking the lock with a tensioner and scraping tool from his lockpick set. The two descended into a similar maintenance shaft and found a similar panel. Opening it revealed access to the train car's hallway.

Cautiously, he popped his head below the confines of the panel and surveyed the car.

"Empty," he said with a sigh of relief.

The two dropped down as quietly as they could into the hallway of the first-class passenger car. Immediately Valentine went to locate the final compartment that Oliver had mentioned. The two brothers nodded at each other, then J.J. knocked on the door in the telltale two quick, one slow, two quick fashion meant to signify a friend of the Ghost Hunters Adventure Club.

"One moment!" came a voice in the room.

Valentine's eyes went wide. He immediately grabbed his brother by the collar and dragged him around a corner into a blind spot.

"What are you doing?" J.J. demanded.

"That isn't Trudi's room," Valentine warned.

Peeking around the corner, the two just barely caught a glimpse of Siobhan Sweeney opening the door to her room before Valentine once again grabbed J.J. by the collar and dragged him back to safety.

"Hello?" came her voice.

Silence. After a few seconds they heard the door close. Venturing another peek, Valentine found the hallway empty again.

"So, if that's not Trudi's compartment, then which one is?" asked J.J. in a whisper.

Valentine looked at the hallway full of doors. "I have no idea. But we're naked out here. If anyone spots us in this hallway we're done for."

Then, through the door to her compartment, they heard Siobhan talking to someone.

"Hold on," whispered J.J. as he leaned in closer to the door.

"Nope," Valentine responded. He had already jumped up to grab hold of the open panel in the ceiling.

J.J. listened closer.

"And I'm telling you that we don't have time to deal with that right now," he heard Siobhan say.

"But Siobhan, it could be lucrative," came a voice. From the few times J.J. had heard him talk, he could recognize it as Luther's.

"J.J. come on. It's not safe here," Valentine implored. He was already in the maintenance shaft, looking down at his brother.

J.J. held up a finger. He was gathering intel.

"Luther, this whole ordeal was meticulously cultivated over the course of months. We don't have the capacity to pivot, especially since Inspector Horvath hasn't solved the case yet, like he was supposed to have done by now."

There was silence.

"And you really gotta quit it with this quiet guy routine. If I had known about this sooner, then we could have had a conversation about it. You've really got to be more proactive."

"I really think we're missing out on something big here."

"Enact the backup plan, Luther."

"The backup plan?" J.J. quietly repeated.

More silence. Then, "Consider it done."

There was the sound of movement.

Here's where J.J.'s eyes went wide. Luther was coming.

J.J. scrambled up from his surveillance position and immediately lunged for Valentine's outstretched hand reaching forth from the maintenance shaft. With a hefty pull, Valentine dragged his brother up into the relative safety of the maintenance shaft just as the door to Siobhan's room was opened and Luther walked out.

The two brothers held their breath while they waited for Luther to leave.

"Siobhan said she was enacting a backup plan," said J.J. "Let's get back up to the top of the train. I have an idea."

Atop the train, the two adventurers noticed the fog getting thicker and thicker. They traveled in a slow descent into what seemed like a basin that stretched for miles, leaving only the surrounding landscape barely visible.

"So what's your plan?" asked Valentine, crouching against the force of the wind.

"It's simple. Since we're not safe in the hallway, the absolute easiest way for us to find Trudi is for me to hang you over the edge of the train and for you to peer into the windows."

"Are you kidding?" Valentine cried out. "Your plan is to hang me over the side of a speeding train?"

"Listen if you want to play rock, paper, scissors for who's doing the holding and who's doing the hanging, I could be convinced. But strong teams are built upon the concept of taking risks and what I'm seeing right now is a patent refusal to do this."

But Valentine was not listening.

"Valentine?"

"J.J.," said Valentine. He motioned with his head to the end of the train, over to the very tired, very disheveled, very angry train conductor hopping onto the first-class passenger car and advancing toward them.

"This is in direct violation of train law!" he yelled over the volume of the wind.

J.J. and Valentine each searched around themselves for potential recourse against the new threat.

"No use running," said Valentine.

"No use jumping," replied J.J. He stared at the train conductor walking toward them. "Do we have any other options?"

"Get thrown off of this train in as comical a fashion as possible?"

"Let's put that in the 'maybe' pile," J.J. replied. Time was running out for the Ghost Hunters Adventure Club. J.J. saw the conductor, step by angry step, continue his advance.

Then, an idea hit him.

"Hey!" yelled J.J. to the train conductor. "What does federal train law say about trial by combat?"

The train conductor, upon hearing this, stopped in his tracks. He unbuttoned his vest and cracked his knuckles.

"It's encouraged."

* * *

TRUDI AVOIDED EYE CONTACT with Luther Adedeji as she entered the first-class train car, waiting until he left before she approached Siobhan's room. She paced back and forth in the hallway until she was ready. Taking a deep breath, she knocked on the door in front of her.

Almost instantaneously, the door opened to reveal the small stature of Siobhan Sweeney in the frame of the door.

"Trudi!" shouted Siobhan, in a pleasant tone. "Were you the ding-dong ditcher this whole time?"

"What?" Trudi asked.

"Oh, never mind." She beckoned her inside. "Please, please, I've been dying to talk to you!"

Siobhan ushered Trudi into a chair and sat, ankles crossed, across from her. "This fog certainly is dreary, isn't it?"

Trudi clenched her jaw. If she had a low opinion of snitches, she had an even lower opinion of formally declared enemies of the team.

"I'm not here to talk long," Trudi started. "I'm onto you, I don't trust you, and I promise you that you'll see yourself in a jail by the end of today."

Siobhan raised her eyebrows. "Glad to see that J.J. still teaches proper etiquette to all of his coworkers."

"I just wanted to give you a fair warning," Trudi said.

"I can see why you'd be so mad," Siobhan replied in a very understanding way. "The brothers have a way of doing that to you."

This threw Trudi for a loop. "What are you talking about?"

"Oh dear." Siobhan made the sort of expression one makes when they realize they have to tell someone a hard truth. "Trudi, how long have you been with the Ghost Hunters Adventure Club?"

"Not very long."

"Not very long, indeed," echoed Siobhan. "Listen, I know that J.J. and Valentine can be a lot of fun. They're goofy nitwits who somehow manage to make it through the day with a little bit of charm and a lot of luck."

Trudi folded her arms. "If you're trying to pull some more of your doe-eyed shenanigans, I need you to know that I eat twee hipsters for breakfast."

"Take my advice or don't take it," Siobhan replied. "All tracks lead to the same station. I just need you to know for my own peace of mind that I used to be in the exact same position that you're in now."

Trudi remained stern. "How so?"

"I used to run in a crew with the boys. Led them, really. It was good for a while, but then they betrayed me during the Orlando incident. Dropped me the second it was convenient for them. And Trudi, did they drop me hard."

Trudi had had enough. "All right, I'm not here for manipulative speeches. I don't usually stand around through lectures from people who I have absolutely no trust in."

"Don't trust me, sure, I get that. But I hope you would trust the rap sheets." Siobhan got up from her chair and walked across the cabin to her closet. Opening it, she picked up two sealed, red, plastic file folders. Sitting back at the table, she slid the files across to Trudi.

The labels on the file folders read J.J. Watts and Valentine Watts. They were each packed with documents.

"Maybe do a little research on who you're getting into business with. It might help you out."

Trudi stared at the folders for a little too long. Long enough to show-case a wavering resolve. She picked up the folders carefully and walked to the exit door of the cabin.

"All I'm trying to say is that you're hitching your wagon to something felonious!" Siobhan called out as Trudi was closing the door.

Trudi walked the few doors down to her own cabin in the first-class passenger car of the Harborville Express. Closing the door behind her, she produced the loudest, most pronounced sigh she could muster. She didn't figure it would be so easy. Her working plan was to just steal some-thing from Siobhan's trash, which was less convenient but still viable.

And Siobhan. She just gave it to her.

Trudi placed the two red plastic folders on her own table, paying barely any mind to its contents. She fished through her luggage, pulling out a small plastic container with the Ghost Hunters Adventure Club logo on it. It was a good thing she brought her kit.

Sitting at the table, she opened the container and pulled out a makeup brush, dipping it into a fine black powder. She sprinkled it onto the folders.

Shaking off the excess, she revealed the faint outline of markings. Placing clear tape on the folder, she lifted the markings and transferred them carefully onto a sheet of white paper.

Flipping over the folder, she repeated the process on the other side. Then repeated that for the next file folder. When she was done, she held up the piece of paper and admired her handiwork.

Now she had Siobhan's fingerprints.

* * *

J.J. AND VALENTINE STARED DOWN the conductor across from them on the roof of the first-class passenger car.

Valentine looked over to his brother. "Got any tactical suggestions?"

"Only to unleash the beast," J.J. replied.

The two boys yelled like idiots as they ran at full clip toward the conductor. The conductor, not to be outdone, yelled like an idiot and ran toward the boys.

J.J. and Valentine collided with the conductor in what would appear to be an extremely well-coordinated and practiced dual takedown. This was assuming, of course, that the boys had done this on purpose.

They had not.

"Get to the hatch!" yelled J.J., as the two scrambled to their feet. "We can fight better without the looming threat of being thrown off of something!"

Valentine had cleared the gap to the dining car. When he didn't hear the telltale thud of his brother behind him, he turned to see that the conductor had just managed to catch J.J.'s ankle.

"Go on without me!" yelled J.J. As morbid as the thought was, he had always wanted to die in a fistfight atop a speeding train. He kicked at the conductor's face with his one free leg.

Valentine got another running start and jumped back onto the first-class passenger car, performing another well-timed and luck-ridden tackle against the conductor.

The conductor, used to being tackled by this point, kicked Valentine off of him. He slid across the top of the train car and over the edge, barely grabbing onto a railing as his legs dangled helplessly over the rushing desert landscape below.

It was here that Valentine could see into the train window directly in front of him. Through a slit in the closed shades, he saw Trudi at the desk in her room, admiring a sheet of paper with what looked like fingerprints taped to it.

"Trudi!" he yelled. But he was drowned out by the rushing wind outside. He looked up to see the train conductor standing above him, placing a boot on the set of fingers that attached him to the train.

"Unleash the beast!" J.J. hollered. He grabbed the conductor by the shoulder, spinning him around and delivering an elbow to his jaw.

The conductor staggered and, in a daze, fell back onto the roof of the first-class passenger car.

J.J. immediately crouched down to give his brother a hand up.

By now the commotion atop the first-class passenger car was loud enough to break Trudi's concentration. She ran to the window of her compartment and threw the shades open. If she had done this just moments sooner, she would have seen Valentine's legs levitating directly in front of her as they were pulled upward. Instead, she saw foggy desert.

"I think we need to make haste, gumshoe," said J.J., pulling Valentine up. They both looked over to see the conductor getting up off of his back, slowly.

"Let's go," Valentine said, as they both turned around and hopped back over to the dining car. They picked up speed and made the next hop to the lounge car unperturbed.

The two brothers leaped to the second-class passenger car roof and saw their exit: the small safety hatch that would lead them through a service tunnel and back to their second-class accommodations, unperturbed.

Sliding in to catch hold of the hatch, J.J. pulled the safety lever with all his might.

It didn't budge.

"Valentine, you left this unlocked, right?"

Valentine dropped down to his knees and pulled on the hatch as well. Nothing.

The two looked up and toward the front of the train. Leaping onto the second-class passenger car roof was the conductor. Tired, disheveled, angry, and now determined, he advanced upon the boys with an unrepentant fury.

He stood over the two boys, who were cowering at their access hatch. "The Federal Train Governance Commission sends its regards."

Then, the train came to a screeching halt.

CHAPTER 10

Lake Nowhere

Trudi de la Rosa heard a loud screech and felt a rumble from beneath her before she was thrown across the room. Landing against the wall of her first-class cabin with a thud, she watched on as her luggage fell to the ground in a disheveled mess.

The train took some time coming to a full stop. There was silence, then Trudi slowly rose from her position on the ground. Her heart racing, she took stock of the situation.

Nothing on her was broken. Maybe there would be a few bruises, but all-in-all she was fine. She turned her attention to her now haphazardly decorated passenger berth. Fine. Fine. Fine.

Wait.

Her heart leapt and she dove into the pile of luggage and detritus. Tearing some clothes off of the pile, she sighed in relief as she found the paper with Siobhan's fingerprints intact.

And then she looked to the other end of the room, where two red folders lay on the floor, covered in a light dusting of fingerprint powder.

She could only imagine what was in there. *Could* she trust the brothers?

She shook the thoughts from her mind. There were more important things to deal with right now. Tucking the fingerprints into her pocket, she walked to the window and drew the shades. Outside of her train window, shrouded in fog, was a town.

From what she could tell, it appeared uninhabited. The station which they had come to a stop in front of was decrepit. Paint peeled from all of the surrounding buildings. Everything was in a state of disrepair.

Trudi left her passenger berth to witness a scene of mild chaos in the first-class passenger car hallway. All of the occupants of the Harborville Express were exiting the train in a confused haze, spilling out into the train station's rickety platform. She figured it would be a good idea to gather more info.

Exiting the carriage, Trudi congregated with members of the baseball team and members of the Harborville Train Appreciation Society. She saw Rudith, Siobhan, Luther, and even Inspector Horvath as he stepped out of the dining car and onto the train platform with a quizzical look on his face. He pulled out his revolver and spun the cylinder to make sure that it had not been damaged during the preceding events.

This was a good moment for Trudi. Always dedicated to the mission at hand, unsuffering of snitches or declared enemies of the team, she knew that this was the perfect cloak of confusion to find J.J. and Valentine and combine information. It would circumvent the prisoner's dilemma altogether.

But when she searched through the crowd of confused train passengers, the two other members of the Ghost Hunters Adventure Club were nowhere to be found.

Just then she saw the engineer exit the engine of the train, letting out a pretty animalistic wail toward the heavens before walking toward the group of passengers. She was furiously massaging her temples.

"Excuse me! Excuse me!" Inspector Horvath caught the attention of the engineer. She paused from her furious temple massaging to address the voice that had called out to her, groaned, and approached the inspector.

"Excuse me," Inspector Horvath went on. "Why did we stop so abruptly?"

The engineer threw her hands up. "Beats me! The emergency brake system engaged and there doesn't seem to be any way to get it disengaged."

"But you're the engineer," said the inspector. "Isn't there anything you can do?"

"I have a name, you know," she responded. Then, remembering, she looked down at the embroidery on her uniform to reconfirm that her name was, in fact, "Engineer." She sighed.

"Look, sir," she began. "I'm very brand-new to all of this. Not the train running stuff. From as far as I can surmise I have a pretty rock-solid knowledge of the thing. It's this universe that I'm still trying to figure out. It's sort of like a cross between genre fiction and plot-motivated absurdism. The fact of the matter is that the train is broken and I can't get it fixed because my toolkit is missing."

"Well, where did it go?" demanded the inspector.

The engineer pointed to the heavens above, angrily. "You're asking the wrong person."

"Then what are we to do?" asked the inspector on behalf of the crowd that had now gathered.

"We wait," she said. "I radioed back to Harborville and a train's already on the way to pick us up and take us the rest of the way to New Troutstead."

She looked at the platform and the train tracks next to it. "Stupid crazy luck for us to stop right in front of Lake Nowhere. The train tracks split into two here, so the next train can just pull right past us without having to wait for the Harborville Express to get repaired."

She went back to massaging her temples. "The Federal Train Governance Commission is gonna eat me for breakfast, lunch, and dinner over this. Is everyone okay?"

The crowd of onlookers surveyed one another, each person taking mental stock to see if anyone was injured or missing.

"Wait," said Rudith Espiritu. "Where did the conductor and those two mystery-solving boys go?"

* * *

THE CONDUCTOR AND THOSE TWO mystery-solving boys were a little further back. When the train came to a screeching halt, they were all launched off of the second-class passenger car roof and into the thick fog. All three of them landed with varying degrees of success upon the moist, spongy desert ground below.

J.J. was the first to get up. The sand clung to him in wet clumps that he brushed off. He coughed some out of his mouth.

"Noticeably saltier than regular sand," he said. He looked over to his brother, also unharmed, who was in the process of rousing himself from the sandy crater that his body had formed. The two nodded at each other.

"That could've ended way worse," J.J. said.

Valentine looked past his brother. "It's about to."

Turning, J.J. spotted the conductor, unharmed, approaching them from his own sand crater.

"He's unstoppable," Valentine said.

The conductor stood menacingly over the two once again. However, instead of laying train-law-sanctioned waste to the two delinquents, as was his believed right, he cracked a broad smile. "Now that was a hell of a fight."

Valentine blinked. "What?"

"And what an elbow!" he exclaimed. "Did you two used to fight professionally?"

"On the record, no," said J.J. "Off the record? There were a few underground fight club moments."

"Hold on," said Valentine. "Not that we're unappreciative of the compliment, but why aren't you currently kicking my and my brother's teeth in?"

The conductor stared at Valentine as if there were something wrong with him. He pointed to the train. "Train law."

Then he gestured to the desert enshrouded by fog around them. "Not train law."

"Oh," the brothers said in unison.

"Just remember that train law goes back into effect as soon as you step back aboard the train. Rest assured that I will kick both of your collective teeths in, as soon as we're back on the Express."

J.J. and Valentine shared a look of terror.

"Which is unfortunate, because with your teeth still intact they'd have been able to identify your bodies. J.J., Valentine, the beating I will lay down upon you two will be Old Testament in nature." The conductor spit in the dirt. "We should get back to the rest of the passengers."

* * *

TRUDI'S HEART LEAPT AS SHE spotted the three missing train occupants when they climbed aboard the platform from the tracks below. But before she could push her way through the crowd to reconnect with the brothers, the conductor made an announcement in a commanding tone. "All right, everyone. Please stay calm and we'll get this sorted out as quickly as possible."

He looked toward the engineer. "Did you radio back to the station?"

"You technically already know the answer because everything in this universe comes from one single consciousness."

"Okay dude, sure," said the conductor with a shrug. He began walking up the steps into the lounge car.

"Excuse me," came another voice from the crowd. The conductor paused midway up the steps and turned around. Everybody directed their attention to Coach Hank. "Does anyone know where we are?"

"Oh, I know this one!" Rudith Espiritu spoke up emphatically. "We're in Lake Nowhere! It used to be an enormous salt mine with a town right next to it to support the workers. The area thrived until it became a ghost town in 1933."

She gazed upon the town around her. "It's so interesting! From the way everything was left here, it seems like they must've gotten out of this place in a hurry. I wonder why that is."

"That all sounds about right to me." The conductor resumed his walk up the stairs.

Oliver Path spoke up. "What are we supposed to do?"

"Whatever you want," the conductor replied in an ambivalent tone. "Replacement train won't be here for two hours."

"Hold on a moment!" Trudi called out. "What about the open investigation we have going on?"

"Oh yeah, that," said the conductor. He nodded the question over to Inspector Horvath.

The inspector thought for a moment, stroking his beard. Eventually he shrugged. "I don't see a problem with a little exploration before the next train gets here."

"What?" Trudi demanded.

Inspector Horvath addressed the conductor. "You'll watch over the crime scene, won't you?"

"Oh yeah, sure, no problem." He paired this with a very disheartening wave of his hand before disappearing back into the train.

"But..." Trudi went on. Her mind raced at the possible motivations for Inspector Horvath to do this. What angle was he running? Was he playing dumb on purpose?

"Hey, cool! Look at all of these old houses!" said one of the train nerds in the crowd.

"Historians love old things!" agreed Rudith Espiritu. The terrors of being the victim of a high-profile robbery seemed to be overshadowed by the coolness of old things.

The crowd murmured their agreement and began to slowly disperse from the train platform.

"Don't get lost in the fog!" Inspector Horvath called out cheerfully.

Trudi shook any possibility of understanding the inspector from her mind and saw her chance to join back up with the brothers. She weaved through the crowd toward them. Her heart beating faster and faster in anticipation of reconnecting with her team.

"Excuse me, Trudi," called the voice of Inspector Horvath behind her. She stopped in her tracks and, as politeness dictated, turned to address him.

"Just the woman I wanted to see! It's time for our interview!"

"Oh, I…" Trudi balked. "I was just gonna…"

"Yes?" asked the inspector. He was always so cheerful. Trudi studied him and for the life of her could not tell if the man was a genius putting on the role of a buffoon or a buffoon putting on the role of a genius.

"I was just gonna say hi to my friends."

"Trudi!" called out J.J. as he spotted her. He and Valentine began weaving through the crowd to reach her side.

"Thank Christmas we found you. We've got so much to fill you in on."

"I apologize, young men," interrupted the inspector. "Trudi and I were about to speak privately."

"Well, that's just silly. There's nothing stopping us from congregating here and speaking under the jurisdiction of land law," demanded J.J.

"I'm afraid our speaking wasn't just a polite suggestion," Inspector Horvath said politely. He produced the revolver from his coat pocket and pointed it at the team. "Please."

Trudi's face fell. "I'll see you guys soon," she said to the two brothers. She cast one last forlorn glance at the two brothers as she was ushered up the steps and into the dining car by Inspector Horvath.

And so, the brothers were once again left to their own devices. They began walking aimlessly toward the town along with the rest of the crowd.

"So where does 'emergency stop at a mysterious ghost town' lead us on the solution to the mystery?" Valentine asked.

"Siobhan told Luther to enact some sort of backup plan. This has to be that, right?"

Valentine puzzled over the situation in his head. "We were almost to New Troutstead, so she must have needed more time for something. It's not like the investigation was going to stop if they didn't catch the thief by the end of the ride."

"If it's not about framing us, then it has to be something to do with the jewels," J.J. said.

They both arrived at the same conclusion in unison, saying the same words at the same time.

"She's trying to hide the jewels."

CHAPTER 11

The Salt Mine

"What kind of ghost town doesn't have a saloon?" J.J. asked his brother as the two walked along the empty dirt streets of Lake Nowhere. The two had been wandering aimlessly for some time now, keeping an eye out for any suspicious activity among the other train passengers exploring the town. The two stopped on the wooden steps to a general store.

"Well, Rudith Espiritu said that this place stopped being a town in the 1930s. Wasn't that during prohibition?" Valentine asked. He picked at a splinter on the door frame, unwittingly pulling a large chunk of punky, rotten wood with it.

"Definitely couldn't hold a leadership summit in there," J.J. said.

"The moisture in the air really did a number on this place." Valentine handed the chunk of wood to his brother. "If you were to hide the ruby jewels of the duchess of Cordelia, would you hide them in a building that was liable to collapse in on itself at any moment?"

"Siobhan wouldn't."

The two kept walking. They had spent the beginning of their short stay at Lake Nowhere township, to Valentine's dismay, attempting to put a tail on Siobhan and Luther. Done in accordance with Ghost Hunters

121

Adventure Club Field Manual-specified guidelines, the two maintained reasonable distance from their suspects only to lose them in the surrounding fog after Valentine vehemently decided their "reasonable distance" wasn't reasonable enough. They had not seen their suspects since.

Despite the low visibility, this is what they made out of the town in their exploration: There was the train station, which led to a small main street of decaying buildings. Wooden storefronts bore the graffiti of local youths yet to find a particular direction for their misunderstood and ungovernable rage. Patterning out in blocks, the streets featured a variety of small houses, presumably meant for the workers of the Lake Nowhere mine. Each house looked like a carbon copy of the last as each succumbed, in its own way, to the decrepitude brought on from wet, salty air.

Every once in a while, the two boys would catch the silhouette of a train nerd or the telltale baseball cap of one of the Harborville Elks just off in the distance. Maybe they were inspecting broken horse hitches or some other half-destroyed something-or-other.

"Wherever you would hide the jewels would have to be a place you could return to later," offered Valentine.

"What about this?" J.J. pointed.

The two came to the edge of the main street of Lake Nowhere. Carved into a wooden sign at the end of the road, just barely legible past the years and years of wear were the words, "MINE." Below the word, a painted arrow pointed into the fog.

J.J. and Valentine could see the outline of a great entrance to a cave just off in the distance. Situated in what seemed to be the foothills of a large mountain, the lip appeared to curve deeper and deeper into the underbelly of the lake.

The two walked the short distance in the fog, turning around periodically to watch Lake Nowhere township disappear as it faded into the mist. Inevitably, they came to the entrance. Before them stood a gargantuan opening to the salt mineshaft. Its wide-open mouth sheltered a dirt path that led down into a deep, dark abyss.

"You could drive a battleship through this thing," remarked J.J. in awe.

"This look like a good hiding spot?"

"Most assuredly."

The boys were surrounded by a vast tunnel of rock salt as they traveled further in. The air was dry down here and everything inside of the mine seemed well-preserved. The conveyor belts and machinery that ran along the vast hallway looked as if they could be turned on tomorrow.

"So, hypothetically, Siobhan hides the jewels somewhere down here because her first plan went wrong." Valentine began. "Then what?"

"Having seen a vast swath of Siobhan's plans, my bet would be that she would find a way for the train investigation to continue into the coming weeks and months until she inevitably pins something on us that sticks. Wouldn't even put it past her to fund the prosecutors through dark, untraceable money sent through valid fundraising pathways. Whatever happens to us, she gets to come back here at her leisure to retrieve the jewels."

Valentine checked his memory of Siobhan's past plans against J.J.'s theory. "That tracks."

The two continued on the path as it dipped down into the salt bed, the light around them quickly dimming to a low shadow. J.J. produced two flashlights with the Grande Chateau logo printed upon their sides, handing one to Valentine.

They swung the beams of their flashlights to the end of the path, illuminating a hallway that grew larger and wider in size. Following it, they found themselves on a great precipice looking down levels and levels of interconnected stairways hewn into the rock salt.

"This must go back miles," remarked Valentine.

"You're telling me," J.J. replied. "Where would we even begin looking for hiding spots here?"

His flashlight beam traced the stone-hewn steps all the way down to the bottom of the cavern. There, on the ground floor, was a shack. Made out of wooden slats, it gave the impression of an administrative building. J.J. looked at his brother. The two nodded, deciding silently that this was as good a place to start as any. They began following the path down to the bottom of the cavern.

"You know, I've been thinking about something," said Valentine as the two reached the final step down to the bottom of the cavern, stopping in front of the wooden shack. Like the machinery in the mine, this too had been preserved by the dry air.

"Everywhere else in Lake Nowhere has already been worked over by taggers. This place is close to New Troutstead, and there's a fire access road that runs along the tracks and leads right to the town, so it makes sense. But why isn't there any graffiti in the mine?"

"You know how local youths are," J.J. replied. He grabbed the handle of the door to the shack and opened it. "Probably think it's haunted or something."

Pushing the door open, J.J. felt tension, then a snap. He screamed and ducked reflexively just in time to dodge a spring-loaded fire ax swinging toward his head. It lodged itself into the door frame with a resounding crack.

"Or it's heavily booby trapped," he said.

When the shock had worn off, the two examined the ax trap that had almost separated J.J.'s head from his body. The contraption had been rigged to swing the moment someone opened the door. A thin, silver string of wire hung loosely from the ax.

"That was close," Valentine sighed. He opened the door the rest of the way and the two ducked under the trap to enter the room.

"At least we already found the trap," said J.J.

Then a bunch of snakes fell on their heads.

Valentine screamed. J.J. screamed. The entire subterranean hollow of the salt mine that they were in was a cacophonous echoing of screams. It took several moments of unbridled terror before the two had the good sense to realize that the snakes were already dead.

Each stifling a panic attack, they shone their flashlights on the ground, revealing a variety of dead snakes at differing levels of decay.

"That doesn't make me feel any better about them being on my head," said Valentine.

"The old snake box above the door trick," J.J. whistled. "Whoever left this place really didn't want anyone to come in here."

"Well, whoever that was should've realized that there's a finite amount of existence that snakes can have as a booby trap," said Valentine.

"And unfortunately that means that, unless our jewel thief had the sort of sense of humor to reset a decades-old booby trap, there probably aren't jewels hidden here. What is this place?"

"Must've been an office," said Valentine. "Foreman-type thing." He walked through to the other side of the shack, making sure to look out for any other sneaky tricks that the shack had in store for them.

Thankfully, there were none.

"Here's something." Valentine opened a well-preserved drawer from a desk at the opposite end of the room. Pulling a file from it, he spoke: "Lake Nowhere Mine, established 1920, mine closed down when it lost government funding in 1930."

"Guess that's how you make a ghost town," J.J. replied.

They were interrupted by a crash outside. The two boys looked at each other before running out of the shack at top speed. They swung their flashlights about wildly, searching for the source of the commotion.

What their flashlights fell on was Oliver Path, hanging upside down by a very old-looking rope near the shack.

"Help!" he called out.

"Hang on!" Valentine called back. The two brothers sprang into action, running up a small slope to Oliver. The rope he hung from was attached by a quick release pulley mechanism on the wall.

Valentine held onto him as J.J. pulled out a pocketknife from his satchel and cut him down. He landed on the ground with a thud.

While he was getting up, J.J. pulled Valentine aside. "What do you think? You be good cop and I'll be bad cop?"

"Aw man," Valentine said. "I'm always good cop."

"We could do bad cop/bad cop if you want," J.J. suggested.

"Have we ever tried good cop/good cop?"

J.J. raised his eyebrows. This was not an idea that had occurred to him before. The two turned back to Oliver Path, who was massaging a bump on his head.

"Oliver!" J.J. started. "Buddy! What brings you to our neck of the woods?"

J.J. and Valentine both aided in brushing the dust off of Oliver.

"Kinda strange of you to be down here in the spooky salt mine alone," he went on. "What were you up to down here, friendo?"

Oliver straightened up. The smell of rubbing alcohol was once again present in the air. "I wanted to check out this historic salt mine. I didn't realize there were traps."

"Yeah," said Valentine consolingly. "That'll happen in places like this."

"Never know when you're gonna run into a booby trap," J.J. added. "That's something you gotta watch out for when you're a junior investigator. The Ghost Hunters Adventure Club takes pride in its understanding of anti-investigative measures."

Oliver looked to J.J. and Valentine. He cracked a sheepish smile.

Then J.J. and Valentine laughed a hearty laugh. They each slapped Oliver Path across the back, pairing the boisterous gesture with a Ghost Hunters Adventure Club-branded covert pat down. This was an advanced maneuver that Oliver did not know about, being a junior detective and all.

The two completed the covert pat down and shared a look. No jewels.

"Oliver," said J.J. "You're a smart man, aren't you?"

"I'm…uh, yeah…I'm smart," stammered Oliver. He gave the impression that he didn't understand this line of questioning.

"Smart enough not to stumble around in the dark and set off a bunch of potentially dangerous booby traps, right?"

Oliver nodded, confused.

"Great. But just in case, I want you to have this." J.J. pressed his own Grande Chateau-branded flashlight into Oliver's hand.

"This is a really sentimental flashlight to me, Oliver," said J.J. "It would mean a lot to me if you were to use it to keep yourself safe."

Oliver blinked several times. "Um, thank you."

"Awesome!" said Valentine cheerfully. "We'll see ourselves out, then. Watch out for anything that might kill you. This place gives me the heebie jeebies."

The two brothers walked toward the entrance to the Lake Nowhere salt mine. A couple steps away, J.J. turned around. "Say, Oliver," he said.

"…yeah?"

"That was a really good idea to use the maintenance hatch to get on the roof of the train."

"Oh, thank you," he replied.

J.J. let the silence hang heavily, maintaining eye contact with Oliver.

"Well, I'm gonna go check out the rest of the salt mine," the young nerd said. He made a slow, mechanical turn away from the brothers.

"There's just one thing," J.J. said, stopping Oliver's turn. "The security latch was locked on our way back. It was a real dangerous scenario up there. Conductor found us. Fella almost kicked my and my dear brother's teeth in."

"It was most unfortunate," Valentine said, crossing his arms.

"Oh, um. I don't know how that could have happened," said Oliver. He seemed nervous.

J.J., a master of the oral art of awkward silences, let this response hang in the air longer than the last. His facial expression gave Oliver nothing to work with by way of response.

Then J.J. willingly broke the tension. "Oh! You know what, Valentine must've let the dang thing lock when he closed it. Valentine does that sometimes. Don't you, Valentine?"

"I can be a real yutz when it comes to things like that," said Valentine. He sneered at Oliver, very pointedly.

"Oh, that…that must've been it," said Oliver.

"Welp, happy trails!" said J.J. He and Valentine whirled around and walked up an incline toward the faint light of the outside world.

Out of earshot from Oliver, Valentine turned to his brother. "He wasn't carrying the jewels."

"Although I can't stop a man from practicing his right to explore creepy mines, I still don't trust him. I just want to say, for the record, since we're still technically here at the Ghost Hunters Adventure Club First Inaugural Leadership Summit, that I made a mistake in trusting that man and his train organization."

"Don't let it get you down. I trusted the guy too. I just wish I could figure out his angle in all of this."

The two kept walking. J.J. spoke. "Got any ideas about a mission statement yet?"

"Don't trust train nerds?" suggested Valentine.

"While I agree and am tempted, I also think we should figure out something that's more all-encompassing."

J.J. and Valentine reentered the town, coming across a large building, the only one they had seen so far that had two floors to it. That, they surmised, was the town hall. Their hypothesis was confirmed by the sign hung over the door to the building. "Town Hall," it said.

Approaching the building, J.J. held up his clenched fist. As per their training, the two dropped down to a crouch in order to decrease their profile.

Valentine looked to his brother, who motioned toward the building. There, just beyond the thick fog, they saw a shadowy figure pause just before the entrance to the town hall. The figure looked left, looked right, and then entered the dilapidated building.

"That look suspicious to you?" asked J.J.

"It looks suspicious to me," replied Valentine.

The two cautiously approached the town hall. They entered through the same door that the shadowy figure had, revealing another decrepit room, long-since picked over and defaced by angry, malcontented youths.

This one was large, though. The walls were crumbling, but they could still make out the semblance of an administrative area behind a counter. A set of rickety stairs led to a second floor. Their mystery figure was nowhere to be seen.

The mystery figure could be heard, though.

Just beyond the administrative area was a back room. The door was closed. The sound of searching and overturning could be heard.

The two crept further, working their way silently around the counter toward the noise. And they were doing great at it too, until Valentine accidentally kicked a piece of debris across the room. It skittered across the floor and landed against a crumbling wall.

"Yutz!" Valentine muttered under his breath.

J.J. thought quickly. "Wow! This is such an interesting, decrepit old building!" he exclaimed with feigned wonder.

His brother picked up on it immediately. A testament to the worth of even basic structured learning as it pertained to improvisational comedy.

"It sure is!" said Valentine, matching intensity. "Look at all these old documents!"

He picked up a piece of paper off of one of the picked-over tables. "Lake Nowhere Township. Established 1920. The town records go all the way to 1933! Cool!"

"Well, this sure is a hoot!" J.J. replied. "But no time to dawdle! We gotta get back to the train!"

J.J. and Valentine made exaggerated stomps toward the exit. J.J. opened the door and closed it again with a dramatic slam.

Then the two waited in silence.

It was a few moments before the back door opened. Who they saw come out surprised them very much.

CHAPTER 12

The Prisoner's Dilemma (Conclusion)

Trudi stood in front of the door to the dining car, smoothing out any perceived wrinkles in her already wrinkleless business casual blazer. She was nervous.

In an effort to calm herself, she practiced the square breathing technique she had read about in the Ghost Hunters Adventure Club Field Manual. Inhale for four seconds. Exhale for four seconds. Focus on the breathing. The goal was to peacefully bring yourself back into the current moment rather than focusing on oftentimes-overexaggerated anxieties. This technique was listed as a footnote in the "Psy Ops" chapter, under a section for resisting prolonged torture.

Readying herself, she walked through the door.

"Miss de la Rosa!" came a voice. Scanning the dining car, she found Inspector Sandor Horvath sitting in the same dining booth that he had been in earlier today. He was flipping through files at a hurried pace, paying little mind to her, adjusting and readjusting the small spectacles at the end of his nose. Placed at his side on the dining table was his revolver.

Trudi walked to the table and waited patiently for him to finish whatever he was working on. He eventually placed the files to the side and looked over to Trudi. "Please, join me. You know how it is with inspecting. One has to inspect everything, right?"

Trudi took her seat. "Where's Siobhan and Luther?" she asked.

"Oh! They wanted to take a look around Lake Nowhere. They said there might be some clues out there. Clues or not, I can't say I blame them. How nice it must be to not be burdened by a mystery right now. To laugh and frolic with your friends in a fun and historically interesting ghost town."

Inspector Horvath cast his gaze out of the closest window and into the gray fog. He sighed whimsically.

"Right," said Trudi. She thought about the evidence folded in the pocket of her business casual blazer, ready to strike with the truth at a moment's notice.

"Trudi," the inspector started, "I bet you're wondering why I called you here for another interview."

Here it is, she thought. Exactly what she expected: the culmination of the prisoner's dilemma. First Inspector Horvath would tell Trudi that he had spoken to the brothers, and that they had told him the whole story. They confessed to the jewel theft and had implicated her in everything.

This, of course, wasn't true. It was simply a detective's trick to lead Trudi into a trap. What he expected her to do was crack under the pressure and confess herself, implicating the brothers in exchange for a reduced sentence. It was not something that she planned on doing.

Inspector Horvath threw up his hands. "I'm stumped!"

This threw Trudi for a loop.

"I have no idea who stole the jewels. I've interviewed every possible suspect on this train and I have nothing! Nothing!"

"I...uh..."

"And what's the deal with train law!?" He picked up the revolver on the table and waved it around wildly. "They gave me a gun! That seems like a little much, don't you think? I'm more likely to give it away than actually use it!"

He placed the gun back down and slumped onto the table. "I haven't an idea what to do to catch whoever did this, and I was wondering if you had any leads I could work with."

Trudi closed her jaw, which she hadn't realized was hanging open since about halfway through the inspector's confession. "You…need my help?"

"You're one of those investigators, aren't you? The Ghost Hunters Adventure Club?"

"Yes, but…"

"So you'll help me? Please?" Inspector Horvath clasped his hands together in a show of sincerity.

"Well," started Trudi, trying hard to figure out where her initial "prisoner's dilemma" defense could be altered on the intellectual battlefield to account for this unexpected line of questioning. "I suppose it would help if we went over everything from the beginning."

"Oh, could we?" asked the inspector with a sense of relief. "That would just be grand."

Trudi remained tense. Her mind visualized the three-dimensional chess battleground, laying out her responses and counterresponses alongside attack success rate models.

She gave up on all that when she noticed that Inspector Horvath was crying a little.

"Okay, fine," she said. "Let's start at the beginning. Earlier today, my friends and I boarded the Harborville Express. I think most everyone had boarded at that station, right?"

"With the exception of myself, yes," said the inspector. "I boarded in Maple Bay."

"And when was the crime committed?"

"After brunch, in the lounge. Miss Sweeney and her friends were treating us to that lovely rendition of 'I Get a Kick out of You' during her recital."

"There was a specific moment when it happened, wasn't there?"

"Well, yes," said Inspector Horvath. By this point he had fully transitioned into the interviewee role in the conversation. "When we went through that tunnel and the train compartment was plunged into darkness."

"That's right. Now we're getting somewhere," said Trudi. She was once again developing anxieties about the concept of leading a horse to water.

"Oh!" yelled the inspector. He buried his face into his hands again. "But when daylight returned, there was chaos. Everything was in disarray! Anyone could have taken the jewels in that moment!"

"I think this is the moment that we need to examine if we want to figure out who did it, right?"

He sniffled for a bit. "You're right. Just moments after, I stood up and announced that it was a crime scene. We ushered everyone out of the lounge and I had the conductor keep watch to make sure that it went unperturbed."

"That's what I was hoping," replied Trudi. "Inspector, what if I told you that not only do I think I know who did it, but I'm certain of the location of the missing jewels?"

Inspector Horvath's eyes widened. "How could this be possible?"

"Come with me." Trudi got out of her chair and walked toward the entrance to the lounge car. Inspector Horvath followed dutifully behind her with a glimmer of hope in his eyes.

Opening the door to the lounge, Trudi found it just as all of them had left it earlier. There remained detritus on the floor of the car: spilled drinks and overturned chairs. Signifiers of a previous chaos. They politely dismissed the conductor so that they could conduct their investigation in private.

"And no one's touched the crime scene since we all left it this morning?"

"Not a soul," said the inspector with conviction. "I had the conductor watch over it all day."

"Inspector, I need you to visualize the crime scene as it existed in the exact moment before the jewels were stolen. Can you point out for me where everyone was?"

"Well, I was sitting down and simply observing from this table over here," said the inspector, motioning to a table close to the piano. "I could see the entire performance while Miss Sweeney was singing that delightful song of hers."

He pointed to the piano. "There were Mrs. Espiritu, Miss Sweeney, and Mr. Adedeji in the moments before the train was bathed in darkness. There was a crowd of people watching the performance in a variety of chairs, some standing, between where I was sitting and where they were performing. There were quite a few people crammed into the train car, what with the baseball team and train appreciation society in attendance."

"Okay, that's great," said Trudi. "We can work with that." Being careful not to disturb the crime scene, she walked over to the piano and beckoned the inspector to join her. "Rudith Espiritu had the ruby jewels in a briefcase, attached to her wrist. What was she doing as the train went through the tunnel?"

"She was in the middle of a sustained note. It was very impressive."

"Precisely. So we have a moment where Rudith Espiritu is distracted, and then the entire train was distracted as we went through the tunnel. When the lights went out, there was a large scuffle, and by the time the lights had come back on, the jewels were stolen."

"Yes," said the inspector. "I follow you."

"All right, Inspector, here comes the big question." Trudi readied herself. "Who on this train could have controlled every variable of the situation to the point where this all happened at the exact right moment? Who had the ability to steal the jewels under the cover of darkness and during the solo portion of 'I Get a Kick out of You'?"

The inspector furrowed his brows. "I don't follow you."

Trudi let out as polite of an exaggerated exhale as she could. "Who on this train could have such intimate knowledge of the train's location, its direction, and everything down to the exact moment of that sustained note portion of the song? How could this all have happened so..."

She looked over to the inspector and saw that his eyes were glazing over. It was at this moment that she gave up on the horse, the water, and the whole damned concept of leading anything anywhere.

"All right," she started over. She pulled out the piece of paper that she had clear taped the fingerprints onto. "These are Siobhan Sweeney's fingerprints."

She pointed again at the piano. "There was enough time to steal the briefcase during our time in the tunnel, but even if there wasn't a scuffle, I doubt there would have been enough time to remove the jewels and replace the briefcase back onto Rudith's handcuffs."

She looked, once again, over to inspector Horvath. She could at the very least tell that he was trying his hardest to understand. Walking over to the piano, she knelt next to the stool that Luther had been sitting on while playing the accompaniment.

Being careful not to disturb any potential fingerprints, she pulled a pen from her pocket and used it to open the stool opposite its hinges. Lifting it up revealed the compartment where one would normally store sheet music for later retrieval.

There was the briefcase.

"My word!" shouted Inspector Horvath.

"Remember," Trudi went on, "there wasn't enough time to get away with the jewels, but there was enough time to hide them. Rudith was singing her solo and Luther remained playing piano accompaniment while Rudith sang. So the only person who had the knowledge of exactly when this would happen, and the only one who could have performed the action of stealing the briefcase, stowing it away, and replacing it with a fake one was none other than Siobhan Sweeney."

She held up the fingerprints again. "If what I think is true, then not only will Siobhan's fingerprints be all over this briefcase, but they'll be all over the piano stool in a pattern that would suggest her opening it and closing it; something she had no business doing at any regular moment throughout her performance. Does that make sense?"

Inspector Horvath stroked his big, well-kept beard in thought. "Well, young adventurer, let's test your theory."

Pulling a handkerchief from his breast pocket, he delicately removed the briefcase from the compartment in the stool. He placed it on the floor between where the two were kneeling.

The lock was already broken.

"What?" asked Trudi. This didn't conform to her theory.

Inspector Horvath used his handkerchief to open the briefcase with a slow, dramatic reveal.

It was empty.

"This...doesn't make any sense," Trudi said.

"No jewels," the inspector said with a heavy sigh. "It would appear that there's an excess of the exact same briefcase here on the Harborville Express." He got up from his kneeling position on the floor. "Well, if your hypothesis is false, then where does that leave us?"

"It can't be!" said Trudi in disbelief. "If I had a little more time I could figure out how Siobhan did it. If I could just dust this for prints then—"

"Unless..." the inspector interrupted. He began stroking his beard and adjusting his spectacles in rapid succession, showcasing a masterful display of the Ghost Hunters Adventure Club Field Manual's suggestion of having props to work with while investigating.

"If not your theory, then who *could* have the precise ability to know where the jewelry was and exactly when to steal it? Who could possibly have the resources and drive to pull off a heist with this complicated of a solution in order to make me, Inspector Horvath, Neutral Moldevik's premier investigator, look like an absolute fool?"

Trudi had thought that Inspector Horvath was doing a great job of making himself look like a fool all on his own.

"Siobhan?"

"The Cordelians!" he shouted triumphantly.

Trudi looked at him quizzically. "I don't think that anything points to there being a great Cordelian conspiracy at the center of this."

"Nonsense," said the inspector. "The clues are all there." He spent a few moments pacing back and forth in the lounge car while ideas fired inside of his head.

Finally, he turned to Trudi. "That will be all, Miss de la Rosa. I can take the investigation from here."

"But…" Trudi began.

"That will be all," Inspector Horvath repeated firmly. "It's time for Neutral Moldevik's premier investigator to do what he does best."

Trudi stood there a moment longer, trying to figure out if there was a way she could salvage this. Inevitably, she gave up. She walked, dejected, back through the dining car and into the first-class passenger car, where she shut the door to her compartment. She placed her back against the door and slid down to the floor in defeat.

She had missed something in her thought process. The disappointment was immeasurable. She fought the urge to scream.

That's when her eyes fell on the red file folders again. Unassuming in their placement on the floor, they demanded her attention.

Trudi walked over and knelt down next to the two sealed folders. She grabbed one, reading J.J.'s name written on the front of it. Undoing its clasp, she picked a file out at random.

On it was a mugshot of a much younger J.J. No red sweater, cheesing for the camera. He didn't have the scar on his nose.

"Rex Sawyer," she read aloud. "Aiding and abetting."

Immediately she placed the paper face down. Siobhan wanted her to read that. She wanted her to doubt her friends. It didn't feel right.

Could she trust them? When this was all over, would she be just another mugshot in a file?

But it wasn't over. Not while her and her friends' lives were at stake. So instead of sulking, as many people would do at a moment like this, she did what she did best. She thought.

Trudi worked the case around in her head, remembering each and every passenger on the train, placing them in a timeline of movement that led to them being at the lounge in the exact moment that the jewels were stolen.

What had she missed? It had to be Siobhan, but why were the jewels gone?

Was Luther right? Could someone else have taken the jewels? But why would he have told her if he was on Siobhan's side? And how could the jewels have been taken from the lounge if the conductor was there the whole time?

Then it hit her. Everything made sense. She had heard the exact moment when the conductor had left the lounge unattended.

She shot up from the floor, overwhelmed with thoughts. The brothers. She needed to find them as soon as possible.

Opening her door in a huff, she darted through the hallway and out of the Harborville Express, making a direct beeline at full sprint for the foggy outline of the Lake Nowhere township. The whole time there was only one person's name on her mind.

Coach Hank.

CHAPTER 13

Rumble in Lake Nowhere

Trudi had been running through Lake Nowhere's sparse main street for only a short amount of time before she spotted footprints in the damp, spongy sand that matched the shoe soles of each brother. This was something she kept on mental file for specifically such a situation as this. You see, Trudi planned ahead for the future and when the future finally came, her plan paid dividends. What I'm trying to say, kid, is that it's never too early to start up a Roth IRA account. You should look into that.

She followed the footsteps at a full sprint to where they ended: the door to what appeared to be the town hall. Bursting through the entrance, she saw Valentine and J.J. standing at a table in the center of the room.

"Oh man, I thought I'd never see you guys again!" she said with great relief. Her mind was running a mile a minute. She unloaded on them.

"It's Coach Hank! Coach Hank stole the rubies! I had to go through this whole ordeal with Inspector Horvath who is an *absolute* idiot by the way, but I almost convinced him that Siobhan stole the jewels and I used, like, legitimate forensic science to prove it and everything was so airtight but when we found the briefcase the jewels were still missing and I was stumped! Stumped!"

She smacked her forehead, going on: "But I had missed one thing and it was so obvious! Siobhan stole the jewels! And then someone stole them after that! Inspector Horvath assured me that there was no point when the lounge car was left alone but I heard for myself when I snuck in there and hid under a pile of potatoes! He was wrong! When Inspector Horvath was interviewing Coach Hank there was a noise on the roof! Was that you guys? Anyway, he sent the conductor to go check it out and that gave Coach Hank a perfect window to steal the jewels from where Siobhan stashed them when the interview was over! But why? I don't know why! But he's the only one who had the time to do it!"

She ended her speech huffing and puffing. J.J. and Valentine blinked vacantly at her a few times.

"Man, that was some great deductive reasoning," said J.J. "But… um…we know."

Trudi's shoulders deflated. "What? How?"

"Because he told us," said Valentine, motioning over to Coach Hank standing at the other end of the table. Between them were the ruby jewels of the duchess of Cordelia, sitting upon an unwrapped handkerchief.

"Howdy!" said Coach Hank, giving her a friendly wave.

Trudi's mouth fell open. "…oh."

"We're really glad to see you," Valentine said, as she joined them around the table. "J.J. and I were exploring the area and we came across Coach Hank here trying to stash the jewels for later retrieval. We caught him in the act."

"That's me," Coach Hank said with a sheepish look.

"And this is where we need your help, Trudes," said J.J. He leaned forward, resting his elbows on the table. "It's about the Ghost Hunters Adventure Club mission statement."

Valentine groaned. "It's *not* about the Ghost Hunters Adventure Club mission statement!"

"Hear me out," said J.J. "What you see before you is a man who has committed a crime. By all accounts he can and should be held to task for his transgressions in the eyes of justice." He paused for dramatic effect. "And yet, were it not for Coach Hank, we would have been framed by Siobhan Sweeney."

"What do you mean?" asked Trudi.

"Coach Hank here had the same idea that Siobhan had," said Valentine. "Wait for the tunnel, shim the handcuffs, swap the briefcase. Only in the chaos, he did his swap *after* Siobhan did her swap. The designated hitter situation we created worked right into his plan."

This made everything snap into place for Trudi. "So that's why the key Siobhan planted on us didn't work on the briefcase! It was the wrong one!"

"I would assume so, partner," Coach Hank said.

"Which leads us into our predicament," J.J. said. "This sure is an ethical quandary, isn't it? Us out here, trying to figure out the morality of turning someone in to save our skins but owing our skins to him in the first place. Wouldn't you agree that that's really something to chew on?"

"Well, yeah," Trudi responded.

"And then there's the wider questions about it all, right? Do we have to solve every case we come across, or is it only the ones that keep us out of jail? Are Neutral Moldevik's business dealings any of our concern? What's Ghost Hunters Adventure Club's position on inserting itself into geopolitical discourse?"

"Okay, but—" Valentine interjected.

"Wouldn't it be so great," J.J. interrupted, "to have a shared pillar of beliefs that we can refer to in times of moral crisis? A list of core values, written and ratified by a cohesive and understanding team? And in that shared set of beliefs we move forward as a unified front in order to excel in both business and in life?"

There hung a heavy silence at the table.

"It's not about the mission statement," Valentine grumbled.

"It's *absolutely* about the mission statement!" J.J. shouted in exasperation.

"I'll make it easier for everyone," Coach Hank said. "I'm gonna turn myself in."

"What? But why?" asked Trudi.

"You know, partners, it's in weak moments like these where I like to sit back and think about what it truly means to be an American. Y'see, it's about our belief and hope for a better tomorrow, and what we do to fight for that better tomorrow."

J.J. nodded.

"And I realize now that I lost my way. I need to do what's right and accept whatever justice has in store for me. Because I, Coach Hank, stole the ruby jewels of the duchess of Cordelia all on my own."

"Well then," J.J. said with relief. "So that means we just have to get you to Inspector Horvath so that you can confess, then this nightmare on rails is over. That seems easy enough."

But it didn't seem easy enough. At least not for Trudi. Something didn't make sense in the coach's story. He didn't have a motivation to steal the jewels in the first place.

Her train of thought was broken when a small knife flew through the air and stuck into the wall behind the team with a loud thunk. Everyone jumped back in shock.

"Guess now I know why things didn't go according to plan," came a voice from the entrance. There, standing in the doorway, were Siobhan Sweeney and Luther Adedeji.

"Easy fix," she said with a certain lightness, "Luther and I caught the Ghost Hunters Adventure Club in the act, attempting to hide the stolen goods. Aiding and abetting, as per usual."

She twirled another knife between her fingertips. "Next one won't miss. Hand over the jewels."

What happened next happened very quickly. In one fluid motion, J.J. snatched the jewels from the table and grabbed hold of the table itself, flipping it forward toward Siobhan and Luther.

"Table!" he yelled, as Siobhan launched the knife into the table with another thunk.

J.J. dove forward and tackled the table further, sending Siobhan and Luther stumbling backward through the door.

"Do you think I only carry two knives on my person?" shouted Siobhan from the other side of the table.

J.J. formed as quick of a plan as he could. He threw the ruby jewels to Valentine, who stared at them the same way someone would stare at a live hand grenade.

"Jump out of the window!" yelled J.J. "We'll distract them, then get Coach Hank over to the inspector to let him squawk!"

Luther shoved the table back, knocking J.J. over onto the floor of the town hall.

"Valentine! Go!" J.J. yelled as he scrambled back to his feet.

Siobhan stepped back into the room with the same grace and poise she normally would. But on her face was a familiar look that Valentine remembered all too well.

Wrath.

Surveying the room, she spotted the jewels in the hands of a very terrified-looking Valentine. She began walking toward him.

Valentine tried to do something. Anything. But there he remained, vibrating in place. His knees locked together in a form of subconscious protest. Again.

"Valentine, hand over the jewels," Siobhan said as she drew closer and closer. "Come on."

He was overwhelmed by an all-consuming terror. He couldn't act.

And then Trudi snatched the ruby jewels, tossing them underhanded across the room to J.J.

J.J., with his path blocked by Luther and the table, ran in the only direction he could: upstairs.

Siobhan paused. Everyone in the room looked up, following the sound of panicked footfalls running back and forth on the only other floor of the two-story town hall.

"Does he know that second floors don't have any exits?" asked Siobhan.

More footfalls, then pattering, then the sound of a wooden window-pane, long since devoid of glass thanks to the actions of misunderstood youths, being crashed through. Everyone looked outside of the door to see J.J. fly through the air and land with a squishy thud on the damp earth below.

He got up just as quickly as he landed and began running down the Lake Nowhere main street, toward the train.

"The jewels!" Siobhan cried out.

But before they could react, everyone inside of the town hall was distracted by the distinct sound of crumbling.

Looking back up, Trudi could see portions of rotten, punky wood separating and crumbling away from more rotten, punky wood. It started near the upstairs window that J.J. had jumped out of and quickly began a chain reaction of destruction.

The house was coming down.

"Everybody get out!" Trudi roared, as the ceiling above them began disintegrating.

It was a mad dash out of the door, with Siobhan and Luther tripping over debris, then having to squeeze three-abreast as Coach Hank tried to exit at the same time as them.

Trudi grabbed a shell-shocked Valentine by the collar and dragged him outside. They both dove into the dirt with Siobhan, Luther, and Coach Hank in time to turn around and see the town hall fold into itself in a shower of splinters.

"That wasn't cool!" Siobhan shouted.

Not realizing that he had demolished an entire building and believing himself to have gotten a race-ending head start, J.J. jogged backward, laughing in triumph. He yelled into the dense fog. "Sorry Siobhan! We win! We got the jewels and we got the confession. Ghost Hunters Adventure Club is back on track!"

He turned around with a smug look on his face and picked up the pace, only to slow down to a jog, then a walk. Then he stood still.

In front of him were the Harborville Elks. The entire team stood in J.J.'s path between him and the Harborville Express. They were all brandishing baseball bats.

J.J. looked at them with dismay. The smallest on the team, Smalls, stepped forward.

"Hand over the jewels," the tiny baseball player demanded.

"What?" asked J.J.

"Hand over the jewels!" echoed Siobhan. She came to a stop a few steps away from J.J. with Luther, Trudi, Valentine, and Coach Hank joining shortly thereafter. They and the Harborville Elks created two semi-circles around J.J. and the jewels.

"The jewels," Smalls said again. The Harborville Elks gripped up on their baseball bats menacingly.

"You don't have to do this, Smalls!" Coach Hank shouted.

"What?" J.J. asked again. He looked over to his teammates. "Trudes, V, you got any idea what's going on?"

Valentine and Trudi looked at each other and then back at J.J. "Nothing's really coming to mind," Trudi said.

The Harborville Elks, Siobhan, and Luther began advancing upon the lone adventurer in the center of the circle.

"Wait! Wait!" J.J. shouted, stopping the advance if only for a moment. "Here's something."

He cocked his arm back and threw the ruby jewels directly up into the air as hard as he could. "Jump ball!" he screamed.

The semi-circles of advancing assailants followed the flying jewels with their eyes, watching it land on the sand just a few yards away.

Then, chaos.

J.J. dove away from the quickly developing dogpile of baseball players and former partners in crime. Coach Hank pushed past Valentine and Trudi to jump into the fray.

Luther was the first to grab the jewels, launching himself up and over the shoulders of a baseball player as if he were playing rugby. The tiny baseball player, Smalls, knocked it out of his hands and over to another baseball player. Then Siobhan threw a well-placed elbow into that baseball player's nose before Coach Hank snuck up and snatched the jewels out of her hands.

It would go on like this in some variation or another for a short while. Away from the scrum, Trudi and Valentine ran over to J.J.

"Jump ball is a basketball term," Trudi said. "I don't know if you were trying to go for baseball-specific gags."

"It was mostly a general sports motif," J.J. replied.

Valentine gave him a hand up. "Your idea was to throw the jewels into the air?"

"Yep."

"But why?"

"Because the jewels don't concern us," J.J. said. "Let 'em pull each other's tonsils out. It'll be enough to show Inspector Horvath that we weren't involved with stealing the thing in the first place."

A body was tossed from the fracas. Smalls. He landed face first in the dirt in front of the trio. Picking his head up, he locked eyes with the adventurers.

"Keep your dukes up, kiddo," said J.J. He mimed a few shadowboxing punches to further clarify the message.

"I hope you choke, you boner," said the baseball player. He got up and ran back into the whirlwind of fists and baseball bats.

"What's eating you, dude?" J.J. said incredulously.

"I never like giving you credit for things like this," said Valentine, "but that was actually a very good idea."

"Making quick decisions under duress was something I wanted us all to dive into more this weekend at the summit. But I think it's good that, in any case, we're learning these lessons on the job."

"So what happens next?" asked Valentine.

"Hold it!" came a voice from just beyond the fog. "Hold it!" the voice screamed louder.

"That," J.J. said.

The ruby jewels launched out of Coach Hank's hand after a pretty decent kick from Luther. It flew through the air once again, landing in a small crater of sand in front of an impressive pair of dress shoes. The baseball team, Coach Hank, Siobhan, and Luther paused momentarily from their royal rumble to look toward the sound of the voice.

Siobhan, one hand wrapped around Coach Hank's collar and the other ready to break his jaw, looked from the jewels to the shoes to the figure that the shoes were attached to. First the short stature, then the bushy beard, then the spectacles.

Inspector Horvath reached down to pick up the ruby jewels of the duchess of Cordelia, then approached the melee. He carried his revolver in his hand.

"Hold it right there, everyone," Inspector Horvath said politely.

Siobhan sprang up and immediately joined Inspector Horvath at his side. "I'm so glad you're here. Look who we found trying to steal the jewels."

"That won't be necessary," said the inspector.

"What?" Siobhan demanded. "Why?"

"Because I've solved the mystery."

CHAPTER 14

The Train Platform Accusation Scene

The crew and passengers of the Harborville Express had been gathered into a crowd on the train platform of Lake Nowhere township. There, set against the backdrop of the dormant Harborville Express, his beard finely waxed for the occasion, his revolver in hand, was Inspector Sandor Horvath.

"Thank you all for assembling on such short notice," the inspector began, gesturing to the crowd of onlookers. "Before we get started, I'd like to check the status of our rescue."

He caught the attention of the engineer, who was pacing rapidly just beyond the crowd of train passengers. "Have we any updates?"

"I dunno, dude!" shouted an exasperated train engineer to the heavens. "Literally every moment of my existence has been packed to the brim with conflict. I was born into this world screaming and I will continue to scream until some merciless higher power wills me out of existence. And he'll probably do it to further someone else's character arc!"

Amongst the crowd, J.J. leaned over to Valentine and Trudi. "What's her deal?"

"That's the engineer," replied Trudi. "She's aware that we're all characters in an imaginary universe and that her role is, rather depressingly, only to further the plot and nothing else."

"Wow," said Valentine.

"Try not to think about it too hard," said Trudi to the brothers. "I get the feeling that if we knew what she knew then we'd be screaming too." She studied the crowd and spotted Rudith, the conductor, and the crew of the Harborville Express. She saw the train nerds, Coach Hank, and the baseball team. She had no idea what the next few minutes had in store for them.

Suspiciously to Valentine, Siobhan and Luther were intermixed among the crowd. They weren't standing by Inspector Horvath. In his mind, this could only be a good thing.

"I'll skip a majority of the setup since I believe we all have an intimate and lived experience with the case," the inspector went on. "But to review, there was a heist of very precious jewelry that is of utmost importance to my people, the Neutral Moldevickians." Reaching into his pocket, he produced the ruby jewels of the duchess of Cordelia, showcasing them to his enraptured audience.

Placing the jewels back into his pocket, he continued. "Naturally I took it upon myself, Inspector Sandor Horvath, Neutral Moldevik's premier sleuth, to capture this thief—or thieves—in the name of my great country."

He made a sweeping gesture to the crowd. "Everyone, please look around you, to your friends, your coworkers, your passengers." He paused for dramatic effect, letting the people take their time to gaze amongst each other.

"Standing here among you…are the thieves."

The crowd gasped. J.J. had to commend Inspector Horvath for his practiced showmanship and was taking notes for speeches he would make in the mirror later. If there was a later.

"Now hold on a second—" Coach Hank stepped out from the crowd.

"Yes, yes, I know," the inspector cut him off. "You'd like to confess for the theft of the jewels. And that would definitely tie things up in a little bow. But please, indulge me for a moment."

The coach stood back, clenching his jaw.

"Now, before I get to the accusation, allow me to explain how exactly I came to my conclusion. It was a conclusion that I came to myself, with no help from any outside parties."

Valentine looked over to Siobhan and Luther to gauge their reactions. It was odd that they weren't being mentioned by the inspector, despite deputizing them at the beginning of this whole fiasco. They remained stone-faced.

Trudi, however, boiled inwardly over all the help she had given to Inspector Horvath, to which he had just thrown the credit for having done so out of the window.

"It began," Inspector Horvath started, "with a hunch."

And then he went on. I'll personally spare you from the unabridged version since the inspector seemed to relish in attention even more so than J.J. So out of respect for everyone's time, here's the gist of it:

Inspector Horvath interviewed everyone on the train who he deemed pertinent to the robbery investigation. Despite painstakingly doing this, he still could not establish a convincing enough motive for the likes of him, Inspector Horvath.

This bothered him for some time, as he assured the crowd was a completely natural thing to have happen for a sleuth and that it's only a part of the detecting process, something he also assured the crowd that they knew nothing about. He was dumbfounded. That was until he discovered, completely alone, the missing briefcase in the seat of the piano inside of the lounge car.

Trudi chose not to speak up here, as he had already been droning on for a solid ten minutes.

In any case, this led him down a path of thinking to ask the following question: Who on earth could be crafty enough to engage in such high conspiracy? Only one word came to his mind. Cordelia.

And this was where the visual aids came out.

"The names, please," the inspector asked. On cue, the conductor stepped out of the dining car with a chalkboard and hung it off of a bolt on the side of the Harborville Express. On it were the nicknames of the Harborville Elks baseball team:

NEURO

SMALLS

NOT DAVE

ICE

DOLBY

RO RO

RILO

RUDE LUKE

"A Cordelian can't resist a good puzzle, can they?" the inspector said. "Why don't we go ahead and show them what these nicknames are an anagram of?"

The conductor flipped over the chalkboard, revealing the following words:

CORDELIA RULES

NEUTRAL MOLDEVIK DROOLS

YOU BONER

The crowd gasped. Inspector Sandor Horvath, who had been lulling the crowd into a false sense of complacency, was positioned for his final accusation. Having placed himself behind the baseball team, he spoke.

"And that's why the mastermind of this entire plot was none other than Princess Annalise of the nation of Cordelia!"

And the absolute goddamndest thing? He was right.

Before anyone had a chance to respond or even take a moment to check the inspector's anagram work, Inspector Sandor Horvath snatched the baseball cap from Smalls's head. Immediately, strands of long and silky brown hair fell down past the baseball player's shoulders.

The reaction that this achieved from the crowd was something that J.J. hoped he would get to experience from one of his own parlor-room-type accusations in his lifetime.

Inspector Sandor Horvath clutched the baseball cap in his hand as he whirled around back to the semicircle of shocked train passengers. "Ladies and gentlemen, may I present to you, Princess Annalise!"

Immediately the newly discovered princess lunged at the inspector. An international incident was narrowly avoided by Coach Hank grabbing her by the collar of her uniform. She swung wildly and toward the general vicinity of Inspector Horvath.

"Let me at that noodle-brained dickweed!" yelled the princess.

"I should have guessed that it was you from the start."

"Come a little closer and say that so I can rearrange your jawline," she responded.

"Wow!" came a voice from the crowd. "Wow!" the voice repeated.

Everyone turned their heads to watch Luther Adedeji step through to the center of the accusation circle. "I gotta admit, something seemed strange about this operation from the moment that I stepped onto the train."

To J.J., this was shocking because this was the greatest number of words that Luther had said in succession since he met him.

To Valentine, it was suspicious. He shot a glance over to Siobhan, who looked just as shocked as everyone else was. This wasn't planned.

"I mean, it was supposed to be a simple frame-up gig," Luther went on. "But *something* was up. So you know what I did? I waited. I watched. I listened. And it turns out that there was a princess to be held hostage for ransom! Wow!"

"What are you getting at here?" Trudi asked from the crowd.

"One minute," replied Luther. He looked over to Inspector Horvath and gestured to the weapon in his hand. "Hey, can I see that for a second?"

"What, this?" replied the inspector, flipping the revolver around in his hand before giving it to Luther.

"It was that easy! I didn't even have to try hard!" Luther replied before immediately training the revolver back on to the inspector. The crowd gasped again as Inspector Horvath reflexively shot his hands up in the air.

"Can he do this?" the frightened inspector asked aloud. He looked over to the conductor for confirmation.

It took the man a moment to come to his conclusion, speaking with resigned sadness. "This is beyond train law."

Off in the distance, a train's horn could be heard cutting through the dense fog. It sounded a second time.

Luther looked at his watch. "And not a minute too soon, too! Man, everything's just working out perfectly."

He looked down to the front of the train. "Oliver!"

Popping his head out of the window to the train engine, now wearing a train engineer's hat, was Oliver Path. "Whaddya need?"

"That engine all fixed and ready to go?"

Oliver sounded the train's horn a few times to confirm.

"Perfect. Now we're gonna take this train and make ourselves a getaway." He addressed the inspector. "The rubies, please."

Inspector Horvath slowly reached into his pocket and produced the ruby jewels of the duchess of Cordelia. He tossed them over to Luther.

"Now, the princess. Jewels are nice, but ransom is so much more lucrative."

Coach Hank stepped forward. He spoke solemnly. "My name is Coach Hank of the Cordelian Royal Guard. I will not allow you to take Princess Annalise. My team, they are not just the Cordelian national baseball team fronting itself as the Harborville Elks, but also, due to the size of my country, they are members of the royal guard. We will not allow you to take our princess. We have more players than you have bullets."

"Wow, I had figured something like this may be the case," said Luther, looking as if he were stifling a smile. He looked once again to the shocked crowd. "Members of the Harborville Train Appreciation Society?"

The crowd looked to the small group of train nerds. Once unsuspecting fans of large-scale mechanical engineering, completely innocuous, each of them in turn pulled out a variety of train-specific tools, now repurposed as bludgeoning weapons. They looked menacing.

"My train tools!" cried out the engineer. "That's where they went! My train tools were used to facilitate an armed uprising aboard my train!" She stifled a scream. "The Federal Train Governance Commission! They're gonna be so mad!"

"Hand over the royalty," Luther repeated.

"No," Coach Hank said resolutely.

"It's okay," Princess Annalise said as she put a hand on the coach's shoulder.

"But princess..."

"Take care of your men. I'll figure out what to do with this thin-dicked ass hat."

"She...has such an imaginative mind," said Luther.

"I am going to eat your remains, leaving no evidence of your crime," she responded.

Coach Hank released Princess Annalise to Luther, who immediately grabbed hold of her arm. The train was slowly rolling forward now. As it pulled away from the station, he led the princess up the steps to the final car in the procession.

"Siobhan, you coming or what?"

Without saying a word, Siobhan broke from the crowd and joined Luther and his prisoner at the back of the train.

"Oliver," J.J. shouted out. "Why'd you do it? Why'd you betray us like this?"

Oliver Path once again popped his head out of the window of the engine compartment. The train nerds were filing toward the train now.

He shrugged. "Free train."

All of the members of the train appreciation society shared looks and murmurs of agreement with each other as they boarded the open doors of the train car.

"Hey J.J.," Luther cut in once again. "Two things. First, this is what we in the business-management and teambuilding world call 'leveraging an opportunity.'"

J.J. clenched his fists. He hated being beaten at team development.

"Second," Luther said, hanging out of the door and waving his revolver in the air. "I had you and everyone else played this whole time. I actually talk the normal amount that a regular person does. Wow!"

And with that, Luther stepped back into the Harborville Express with the princess and Siobhan, leaving the Ghost Hunters Adventure Club and the rest of the previous passengers of the Harborville Express stranded on the platform as they disappeared into the fog.

J.J. was the first to break the silence. "That jerk Oliver never gave me back my flashlight."

Then he turned to his teammates. "What exactly just happened?"

"Train mutiny?" Valentine offered.

"International conspiracy?" Trudi offered as well.

"An absolute travesty!" howled Inspector Horvath. He slumped to the floor emphatically and burst into tears. "I've been duped!"

Then they heard a horn again. First were the bright orange headlights cutting through the dense fog, then an entire train with just as many train cars as the Harborville Express took shape. Along the side was its name: Maple Bay Delight.

When the engine reached the platform, an engineer stuck his head out of the compartment window. "What's going on?"

This was enough to break everyone from their spell. J.J. dashed into action.

"Val, Trudi, help everyone aboard! I'll talk to the engineer!"

Trudi and Valentine sprang forward, running to separate train cars, opening doors and ushering passengers through with great haste.

J.J. climbed the metal-runged ladder at the front of the train to where the engineer was. "There's been a great political incident!" J.J. yelled as he burst through the compartment doors. This one, much like the engine compartment of the Harborville Express, looked exactly how you'd expect an engine compartment to look.

The engineer, dressed in a Maple Bay Delight uniform and cap, swung around in his chair slowly. He took a long slurp from a large gas station mug of cola, processing what he had just heard.

"What?" he asked.

The next person to burst through the door was the engineer. "We got a runaway on the—"

Her train of thought was broken when she saw the name tag sewed onto the lapel of the new engineer's uniform. "Phil."

"You got to have a name!?" the engineer cried out. "What cruel god would taunt me like this?"

"What?" Phil asked again.

Then the conductor barged through the door. "You gotta get the engine—"

His train of thought was broken when he spotted J.J. in the increasingly cramped train compartment. He raised his fist in anger. "Why I oughta…"

J.J. flinched and yelped, embarrassingly. The conductor caught himself before he swung.

"Sorry, sorry. This isn't my train to govern unless appointed by the current conductor or in the event of a presidential assassination."

Phil took another slurp of his comically sized cup of soft drink. The engineer, the conductor, and J.J. all turned to Phil.

"Follow that train!" J.J. shouted, pointing out of the front windshield and down the tracks, into the fog. "And step on it!"

Phil looked to the conductor and engineer, who nodded their approval and, potentially, in the doctrine of train law, gave some sort of nonverbal command recognizing their authority structure.

He immediately slammed a lever forward in response. The train began to crawl forward.

It continued to crawl forward.

"This is 'step on it'?" asked J.J.

"Sir, this is a train," said Phil.

"Oh." J.J. awkwardly shuffled around while the train began to pick up speed. "I guess to explain everything to you, Phil, someone tried to steal the Harborville Express. Well, they actually stole it. And now we're trying to get this engineer's train back. Isn't that right?"

J.J. looked over to the engineer, who instead of focusing on the situation at hand was staring hatefully at Phil.

"Are you ever depressed, Phil?" she asked.

Phil thought for a moment. "Sometimes, I guess."

"Sometimes, you guess," repeated the engineer in a wry tone.

The train picked up speed. Before long, it was traveling at above full clip and J.J. had briefed Phil on all of the pertinents. Soon enough, through all of the thick fog that lay before them, they saw the blurry outline of the Harborville Express.

"Don't lose them!" J.J. exclaimed.

"Sir, this continues to be a train," Phil replied, "we are on the same train tracks."

Another shadow made itself clear. Looming over them like a cloud, as if it stood guard over Lake Nowhere, was a great mountain. At the base of that mountain was a tunnel. It was rapidly approaching.

"Just past this tunnel and over the bridge is New Troutstead," said the conductor. "There's no way they can get away now."

J.J. peered further into the fog. "That doesn't sound like such a well-thought-out plan of Luther's, does it? What's he gonna do when the stolen train gets to New Troutstead?"

The cabin grew louder now, the sound of their roaring engines echoing back at them from both the mountain and the tunnel. J.J. saw the Harborville Express slowly begin to pull away from their pursuing train.

Darkness again. First the Harborville Express disappeared in the shadows of the tunnel, then moments later the pursuit train followed. Their engines screamed against the claustrophobic stone walls surrounding them.

It took an entire minute to run the length of the tunnel. With the tracks curving around a bend and the Harborville Express pulling away, the crew in the engine department of the Maple Bay Delight lost sight of the Harborville Express, just beyond the reach of its headlights, for only a moment.

Then there was light. The Maple Bay Delight burst through the end of the tunnel. The fog kept at bay by the massive expanse of mountains left them bathed in midafternoon sunlight.

J.J. stared out of the windshield of the Maple Bay Delight in disbelief. Just beyond them was a great bridge looming high above an even greater river. Following the river, he could see the lines converge off in the distance, toward New Troutstead, now visible in the distance. He then focused on the tracks ahead of them.

The Harborville Express was gone.

CHAPTER 15

Interlude

I used to only see him in the shadows.

The man at the edge of the woods, that is. You remember him, don't you? At the cabin. The last novel. I would always see him late at night, saddled deep enough in the darkness so that I couldn't quite make out the shape of him. He was holding something. A flash of steel in the moonlight.

He wouldn't move. No, of course he wouldn't. Why would he give me the relief of knowing he was human? Even if I called out to him, even if I shined a flashlight upon him, even if I took the cautious few steps away from my cabin. He stood still.

That was, until I went to sleep.

First there was the tapping on the windowsill just above my bed. Then there was the scratching. Then there was the voice. Sick and raspy. "Cecil, come outside. Come outside and pay for your sins."

I did not have the courage to tell you this in the last novel, but there were some nights that I almost obeyed. Each and every godforsaken time he spoke to me I could feel the compulsion in every molecule of my body. My muscles ached to rise from my bed, to walk to my door, to accept my fate for what it was: something my body and mind agreed was a simple consequence for my actions. It was a tab coming due.

One night—and I may be divulging too much information at this point—but one night I awoke from my slumber, fully dressed, with my hand wrapped around the handle to my front door.

The mind is a vessel in a great ocean. It moves slowly, turns slowly, through an infinite expanse of fog. Up until now I had believed that I was in control. But what had I decided to do when I was no longer at the helm of my own ship? Am I the commander of this vessel?

I thought I had left that wretched creature at the cabin in the woods. Perhaps I was foolish to be so optimistic. Perhaps this should be a reminder to me.

From the moment I sat down in my presidential suite here on the Harborville Express, I have been plagued by this mysterious man in the shadows. There he was on the platform, out of the corner of my eye in Harborville. When I looked again he was gone.

I spent those first tense moments convincing myself it was just a trick of the light. Something I had imagined. But then there was Maple Bay, where I had Inspector Horvath board the train. There he was again, sitting in the ticket booth, looking right at me.

It felt like television static. A million prickles of electric shock slamming into my chest at supersonic velocity, radiating outward into my extremities. The buzzing in my ears grew louder and louder the longer I looked at him. I smelled sulphur. I tasted copper.

I had to turn away.

The times when I'm not writing on this trip are spent scribbling on a map. I would mark the time on my watch whenever I saw him. Then I'd take that time and compare it to roads following the Harborville Express's route.

There was no way that I could have spotted him at that barn by the river, only to have him run down the steps once I was out of eyeshot, hop into a car, and then drive at ninety miles an hour down a dirt service road.

There's no way he had enough time to be there at the edge of the fog, outside of my window, just as the train came to a screeching halt in Lake Nowhere. It just doesn't make sense.

At least I'm safe here. Or at least I *feel* safe.

Let's move on.

Hello, dear reader! It's your old pal, Dr. Cecil H.H. Mills, noted fiction scribe and self-described hobbyist pugilist. I'm still at it, as you know, tapping away at the manuscript here on the Harborville Express. No, I won't tell you where the train is now. That would spoil the story. How dare you even think that.

I will, however, tell you that wherever this is, it's very dark. The emergency lights of the Harborville Express are on, so we're not totally without our bearings. If you'd like to imagine me cast in a dramatic, stark glow, I'd appreciate it. Maybe a strong rim light to separate me from the background. It's your imagination, kid. Build the scene in your mind.

You know, I wouldn't even be entertaining that sort of question if this were one of my adult novels. Adults know that stories aren't always mystery and intrigue and affordable action set pieces for the hopeful movie adaptation. They can understand conflict in subtle ways. I mused with this idea in *That Which Waits Beyond the Veil*, my novel where I famously induced medical death for twenty-two minutes so that I could befriend a cool ghost.

I'll stop complaining, I promise. However, lastly, I will say that publishing house Bradford and Bradford can suck an egg. They couldn't spot a quality, contemporary adult novel if it died for twenty-two minutes to befriend them.

In any case, while I still have you here and while I'm still contractually obligated to a minimum word count, let me at least try to be useful to the sorts of people who read interludes in YA mystery novels.

Hey bud, how's it going? How are the bootleg shirts coming along? Remember that if you don't have access to a screen printer, you can use fabric paint and a stencil on heavier cardstock paper to create a really effective look. Just print out your image in two-tone, cut out the design with a pen knife, and then use a foam roller to evenly spread the paint over the stencil and onto the T-shirt. You can even let that layer dry and then stencil different colors on top of that to create a multicolor print. Just make sure that you set the paint into the fabric by ironing over it with a towel.

You must be overwhelmed. Hey, listen, I get it. I super get it. This world you found yourself in, the *grift*, is a brand new one for you. It can be scary setting out on your own and I'm sure you have a lot of questions. I'm taking this deal we've made seriously, as I hope you are, so let me try to give you some advice. Here's two pieces of it:

One: Work hard. You have to learn from your failures and challenge yourself to be the best version of you, every day. That's nonnegotiable. That's necessary to survive. But you're hungry and ambitious, I can tell. Not everybody reads interludes. So keep at it. Keep working hard. You're gonna be fine, kiddo.

Two: You don't even need to work that hard. I'm writing a Young Adult mystery novel, for crying out loud. Every single trick under the sun has been meticulously cataloged and peer reviewed, over literal millennia, by people much smarter than you. And it's all just one research session away.

Here's one for free. Something you should watch out for.

Let's say you're working at a bar, right? A quiet little pub. Real quaint. It's the middle of the day, you're polishing mugs or whatever, and a man walks in with a dog. He's quiet at first, but eventually he starts going on and on about how he's down on his luck. His wife left him, he lost his job, all that. And to top it all off he forgot his wallet and needs to go get it before he pays the bill. As collateral, he leaves the dog, his last worldly possession, in your care.

There's another guy at the bar. He's been there longer than the first. Friendly guy, strikes up a conversation every now and then. Once the first man leaves, he'll lean over and tell you that that dog is a rare breed. An expensive breed. A red-eared hunting spaniel or some similar sort of fine pedigree. He'll maybe even offer you money for it. One thousand dollars. Since it's not yours, you'll politely turn him down.

That man will settle his tab and leave, then a couple minutes later the first man will walk in again. Things have gotten worse. He's not gonna make rent and he doesn't know how he's gonna make up the difference.

Whatever you do, *do not* offer that man $200 for his dog. He'll haggle it up to $250, everyone will walk away happy, and when you try to sell the dog you'll find out that it was just recently snagged from a local dog park.

The second man at the bar is the first man's patsy. He's cut in at 40 percent on the $250. His job was to convince you that this was a random happenstance when, in actuality, every piece of this puzzle was put together in order to let your greed get the better of you.

This is called the fiddle game. The fiddle is metaphorical; it can be anything. It was popularized in the 2006 song, "Can't Con an Honest John" by The Streets.

Hold on, my phone's ringing.

I stepped away from my typewriter and took a seat on one of the several chaise lounges I had created for myself in my presidential suite. There was a rotary phone on an accent table, ringing. I picked it up.

"Don't ask me how a landline telephone works on a train," I said.

"Dr. Mills," I heard the voice on the other end of the line say. "It's Trudi."

"Is this what you're using your one phone call on? You children will never cease to amaze me."

"Hear me out..."

"Listen, of course you're in big trouble. You just actively aided in a geopolitical scandal. Don't you think that's something that some people would consider to be a pretty big deal?"

"It's not about that," her voice came in from the other line after a short pause.

"Then what is it?"

"How come you keep giving me whiffs, Doctor?"

I raised an eyebrow. "What do you mean by that?"

"I laid out everything perfectly for Rudith Espiritu, but she didn't get it. I did the same for Inspector Horvath and he didn't get it either. Even when I figured everything out about Coach Hank, by the time I got to the brothers they had magically come to the same conclusion by luck. I did legitimate investigation work, Doctor. This isn't fair."

"But the point is that it isn't fair, don't you see? It's supposed to be a metaphor about the unfairness of life. It's a very complex one that I don't expect you to understand. Just know that you can't expect easy wins, kid."

"It's a pretty weak metaphor," Trudi said glibly.

"Listen, I really don't want to rehash this bit from the last novel. Something something triumph of the human spirit something something with the power of friendship you can overcome anything or whatever."

There was silence on the line. Trudi waited before she spoke again. "Is this really why you do it, Dr. Cecil? The money?"

This put me a little on the back foot. Sure, I can have my characters challenge me on a philosophical level. It's what she would say anyway, isn't it? I decided to let this play out.

"This is one hundred percent specifically about the money."

"That's the thing," she said. "There's just so many other ways to earn a living. Easier ways. Honest ways. You always talk about the past lives you've had. The jobs you've done. So I ask you this again, why writing?"

"What are you getting at here?"

"I think it's about you wanting the acceptance of people who you claim to not even care about in the first place. I think it's a deep-down desire to be understood. To find people who hurt in the same way you do."

I thought about this for a second, formulating a calculated response. "That sounds dumb as hell."

"Fine," Trudi said. "I only have one more question, then."

"What is it?"

"You're still making this all up as you go, right?"

"Yes, obviously."

"I can work with that."

The line on the other end clicked. She was gone. I held the receiver away from my ear and looked at it as if it had personally wronged me. That was strange.

Hmm...

Well. I stood up from the lounge chair and walked over to the other end of the presidential car, sitting back down at my typewriter and read-dressing you, the reader.

Never mind what just happened there.

Say, you're not developing an emotional attachment to these characters, are you? I know, I know, I wrote them very well. They each have their independent wants and needs, and the way that they handle situations—yes, I admit—can be humorous at times; even endearing.

But that isn't part of the Yacht Plan, dear reader. That's the point of what I'm trying to get through to you during this chapter. If you're going to survive in the real world, you gotta have what it takes to make hard decisions.

I need you to remember again that they are not real. The members of the Ghost Hunters Adventure Club are simply words on a page designed specifically to sell merchandise to unsuspecting dimwits. They were designed in a laboratory to be likeable—to then have that likability leveraged for capitalistic gains.

In reality, their actions continue to be an abhorrent affront to rationalism. They continually and willingly put themselves in harm's way, uncaring of any laws set forth that would discourage such recklessness. Their actions should not be emulated unless one is looking to lead a sad, sorrowful life on the run from higher powers of authority.

It isn't right.

This was the deal we had made in the first place, remember. So harden your heart, forget about these idiots, and let me give you one more parting grift.

This one's for writers. Yes, a grift can be applied to a variety of mediums as well as a variety of career paths. All the tools already exist. You don't need to recreate a hammer. You just need to find the tool and put it into your toolbox.

And this tool, my dear reader, is called Chekhov's gun. Elucidated by famed 19th century Russian author Anton Chekhov in many of his letters to colleagues, this rule suggests that there should be no unnecessary element within your story. A promise made is a promise kept. Like, for example, when you're telling a story and you show a gun in the first act, the gun has to go off by the end of the third act.

Hitchcock used it, Christie used it, Hammett used it. All the greats have utilized this device at one time or another. Hell, I'm even using this tool *right now*. Why do you think I gave Inspector Horvath a gun at the beginning of this story? Did you think that was no longer in play? Luther has it now. Wouldn't you think that this has foreshadowed implications for the final pages of this book?

Let me remind you, once again, that I will do whatever it takes to make as much money off of this intellectual property as possible. And I need to make sure you're still with the program.

This story needs to go out with a bang. There needs to be controversy to drive sales. Fans need to be arguing with one another, and their arguments need to be so loud that it convinces other people to buy the book. That's the only way we can take off on this rocket ship and land anywhere in the vicinity of a yacht-shaped object. If the early reviewers come in and call the plot weak, then my Yacht Plan, *our* Yacht Plan, is as good as sunk.

But worry not, because I have a plan. Something that will create such a groundswell of dispute that we cannot be ignored. Fans will rage against each other, we'll be on all the bestseller lists, Ghost Hunters Adventure Club will become an internationally recognized brand, and every single ancillary revenue stream will be ours. But most important of all: We'll all get our yachts.

My dear reader, if this grift is going to work, then one of our main characters has to die.

CHAPTER 16

New Troutstead

Trudi placed the phone back on its hook on the desk in front of her. She was sitting with J.J. and Valentine of the Ghost Hunters Adventure Club inside of the New Troutstead police station. They were at the desk of a young police officer, his workstation cordoned off by cubicle walls. It was a busy day at the precinct, what with the train incident that just rolled into town.

"I got what I needed," she said.

The young police officer seated across the table from them stared confusedly at the small notepad in his hand. "All right, one more time, could you start from the top?"

"Of course," J.J. replied, leaning back in the chair. "I was thinking of ways to increase team synergy and I realized, hey, why don't we have a mission statement? That's where the idea of the Ghost Hunters Adventure Club First Inaugural Leadership Summit came up—"

"Let's skip that again," the police officer interrupted. "Where were you when the jewels were stolen?"

"We were all in the lounge car with everybody else," said Valentine. "But we weren't trying to steal the jewels, we were trying to stop Siobhan from stealing them."

"Right, Siobhan. Your…" the police officer flipped a few pages back in his pocket notebook, "'nemesis hell bent on your annihilation and the annihilation of everyone and everything you hold dear.'"

"Correct," said Valentine.

"And where does that baseball team come in?"

"Well, they're not actually baseball players," Trudi said. "At least not in this context. They're the Cordelian royal guard."

"The what?" asked the police officer.

J.J. spoke up. "It's a postage stamp-sized country bordering another postage stamp-sized country in Europe. Don't worry, I didn't know either."

"They were trying to steal their jewels back from their rival country—" said Valentine.

"Neutral Moldevik," J.J. cut him off. "Also a new one."

"Neutral Moldevik," Valentine repeated. "The Cordelians' attempt to steal the jewels interfered with Siobhan's original plan to frame us for stealing the jewels."

"One of them was a princess," said Trudi. "She was kidnapped by Siobhan's second-in-command and they all got away on the Harborville Express."

The young police officer seemed overwhelmed.

"Did we mention that the train disappeared?" added J.J. in a very unhelpful way.

The police officer squinted at his notes one last time, trying his best to make heads or tails out of them. He looked at the Ghost Hunters Adventure Club again, studying their faces.

"Wait, are you two actually brothers?"

"An ironclad nondisclosure agreement prevents me from answering that," J.J. said with a tone of indignation. "Our turn to ask a question. What's up with your name tag?"

The police officer clenched his jaw and looked down at the name tag written across his dark blue uniform. It read, "Ofc. Hot Dog."

The man they were speaking to was Buster Tibbits. Now, an eagle-eyed reader would remember that the name "Tibbits" was used earlier in this saga, in book one, to describe a sixteen-year-old receptionist character named Rusty Tibbits. Rusty was an idiot, an annoying child born of wealth, stuck at the Grande Chateau ski resort in the care of his parents, the well-to-do sorts of people who could afford expensive ski resort vacations. His idiocy only served to be a hindrance to the Ghost Hunters Adventure Club's quest to do whatever it was they did in the last novel.

This Buster Tibbits was the older brother of *that* Rusty Tibbits. Not content to live a life of excess for excess's sake, Buster set out on his own to make a name for himself aside from his self-described cursed familial lineage. So far things were going alright for him, having landed a job as the newest officer of the New Troutstead Police Department.

But despite the decent job and the life on his own, there was always a quiet voice way deep down inside of him. It said the same thing to him, over and over again: *There must be something more. There must be something more.*

Buster Tibbits was not an idiot like his brother was. But he was still young, so he might as well have been. You see, on top of being the sort of naive you get when you're old enough to buy alcohol but still too young to rent a car, Buster was an idealist. He believed in the core tenets of good will, in helping your fellow man. He believed that ideas could change the world, that evil men triumphed when good men did nothing. He believed in honor, integrity, and the moralistic values of the greater good. He was a lover of arts and sciences, consuming knowledge voraciously in an effort not only to benefit himself, but to enrich the lives of those around him. He enjoyed intellectual conversations and liked reading in his spare time.

All of these ideals, while important to the story later, will eventually be beaten out of him by the cruel and crushing realities of daily existence over the next couple of years.

"This department likes to razz the new guys," he said, forcing a curt smile.

"So why Officer Hot Dog?" asked Trudi.

"I ate a hot dog weird once."

An empty soda can flew through the air, knocking Officer Hot Dog on the side of his regulation crew cut. He was redheaded, like his brother, like the rest of his family.

"Hey Officer Hot Dog!" called out one of his superiors from the other end of the police bullpen. "Having fun with the train case?"

Officer Hot Dog raised his hand and smiled as if to say, *Good one, buddy. That was a really fun joke you just did.* He was trying very hard to show that this wasn't getting to him.

"Don't forget to pick up the school bus," his superior officer said.

The young officer turned back to the three members of the Ghost Hunters Adventure Club. "Look, obviously this is a complicated situation. We haven't even dug into how that man you just called…" he flipped his notebook a few more pages back, "controls everything we say and do as if he were the god king of our universe."

"He said it was more like he was attached to us with stale rubber bands," Trudi tried to clarify.

Officer Hot Dog massaged the portion of his head that had connected with the soda can. "Look, we're gonna have to hold you for further questioning. I don't know what to charge anyone with here yet, but there has to be something that strictly prohibits geopolitical conflict on American soil."

"What?" J.J. shouted as he jumped up from his chair. "You can't arrest us without just cause!"

* * *

AND SO THE JAIL DOORS closed on J.J., Trudi, and Valentine in the holding cell of the New Troutstead police department.

"This is a gross overreach of power!" J.J. shouted through the bars, as the young police officer walked up the stairs back to his bullpen. "You'll be hearing from my lawyer!"

His protestations fell on deaf ears. He sighed, then turned to the rest of his cellmates.

Valentine leaned against the bars on the other end of the cell. "You know that when you say they'll be hearing from your lawyer, your lawyer is just you calling them back and using a fake accent, right?"

J.J. probably shot back with a fun retort here. But if he did, Valentine didn't hear it. He was busy examining the events that occurred earlier in the day. He didn't feel good about them.

"I couldn't move when Siobhan came at me in the town hall," Valentine said. "I was paralyzed with fear, and because of that I endangered my friends." He stared idly at his hands for a while. "I need to grow up."

"It's okay, Valentine," Trudi said sympathetically. "We got out of it safely enough. You didn't know how you were gonna react in the moment."

She rested with her chin in her hands on the bottom cot of a bunk bed. She knew Siobhan had suggested it to her, sure. But she was right. Trudi was technically hitching her wagon to something felonious.

"Rough time?" asked a voice in a separate holding cell across from theirs. The team looked over to see Rudith Espiritu sitting on a bench.

"Rudith," Trudi spoke up. "What are you doing here?"

"Held for questioning," the old lady replied politely. "What's the Harborville Museum of Fine Art gonna think when they find me here? Still, it could be worse." She motioned with a sympathetic nod of her head over to the entire baseball team of people next to her. Coach Hank and the rest of the Harborville Elks, minus Smalls. They all seemed to carry a heavy weight of defeat.

"Oh great," said J.J. "You guys. Hey Coach Hank, got any other last-minute revelations to drop on us?"

"I'm sorry for being deceitful, partner," said Coach Hank with a sigh, "but above all else, above the very concept of baseball, I serve the princess."

"Well I'm appreciative of the apology, but that still leaves us stuck in this jail cell."

"She wanted to go alone, you know?" the coach went on. "But I wouldn't have it. I was able to convince her to try the baseball team plan. Maybe things would've turned out differently if we weren't here. I don't know. But that's what you get for taking pride in virtue, honesty, and steadfastness."

"But why did she do it?" Trudi asked. "Why did she want to steal the jewels?"

The coach looked at her. He spoke solemnly. "She's the princess of Cordelia. The duchess was her mom."

"Was?" asked Valentine.

The coach nodded. He didn't need to say anything more for the team to get it.

"What's gonna happen to you guys?" Trudi asked.

"Inspector Horvath is sending an envoy to take us back to his mother country for sentencing. We'll probably be launched out of a catapult," he said bluntly. "It's an old Neutral Moldevickian tradition for high crimes against the state. The moment we reach Neutral Moldevickian soil it's straight into the catapult. The only real say we have in the matter is what the catapult gets launched at."

He went on. "Heck, we'll be lucky if that's all that happens. With a missing princess and stolen jewels, this could be the thing that finally pushes our two nations to war."

Coach Hank sank back into his cell and sat amongst his team. All of them seemed to carry the same weight of honor, truth, courage, and, now, failure.

J.J. disengaged from the conversation with the baseball team and took a seat next to Trudi on the bottom cot of the bunk. He too buried his head in his hands. "This is the worst First Inaugural Ghost Hunters Adventure Club Leadership Summit ever."

"What are we gonna do?" Trudi asked.

J.J. pulled his head up from between his knees. "We gotta figure out a new plan."

"You're right," said Valentine. "There's no way on earth that a huge train just disappears out of thin air. There has to be another explanation."

"Are you kidding?" J.J. shot back at his brother. "I was talking about figuring out our legal defense. Trudi, that was a good bit you did with the god king stuff. If we can successfully argue an insanity plea then I figure we'll be out of the facility after about five years of ground work."

"Valentine's right," said Trudi. "The puzzle pieces aren't fitting together and it's not making sense. If only we could get back to Lake Nowhere, we could try to stop Luther and Siobhan."

"As much as I love the idea of having a rich princess indebted to us," said J.J., gesturing to the jail cell around them, "We're stuck here until we can find a way out."

Just then, the door to the police officer's bullpen opened and a different officer walked in. He marched to the holding cell of Trudi, J.J., and Valentine, unlocked the door, and slid the jail bars open.

Then he spoke. "Your lawyer is here to see you."

CHAPTER 17

Legal Advice

The Ghost Hunters Adventure Club was placed in a small interrogation room at the back of the police station. Sitting under the watchful eye of a security camera, they all sat handcuffed together on one end of a long metal table.

"Why'd they have to restrain us together?" Trudi asked. She had been placed in the rightmost position of the chain gang. Handcuffed to her left hand was Valentine. Handcuffed to his left hand was J.J.

"You use one less set of handcuffs this way," J.J. replied. This was not his first time handcuffed to multiple people.

The sound of a door opening behind them put a pause on the conversation. Turning their heads, the three spotted Valentine's worst nightmare.

"Oh, come on!" he cried out, his fight-or-flight response spinning into overdrive. "*You're* our lawyer?"

Standing in the door was Siobhan Sweeney. She was dressed in smart business attire, her hair pulled back into a tight knot behind her head. She carried her briefcase in her hand.

Closing the door behind her, she sat down at the table across from J.J., Trudi, and Valentine.

"Really glad to see you, Siobhan," started J.J. "Did you come here to rub your superiority in our faces or were you just going to kill us all right here and now?"

Valentine attempted to hop out of his chair to get away. Realizing that he was handcuffed to his compatriots, he settled on screaming as loud as he could. "Help! We're trapped in here with our nemesis! She'll grind our bones to dust if you don't let us out of here!"

"They can't hear you," Siobhan said in a calm demeanor.

Valentine turned his head to her, his face a combination of fear and confusion. "How come?"

"One, attorney-client privileges. Two…" Siobhan reached into her coat pocket and threw a bundle of electrical wires onto the table. "…because I don't want them to."

J.J. raised his eyebrows. "And why's that?"

"Because I don't want audio-visual evidence of this to exist." Siobhan bowed her head and collected herself for a moment. Looking back up at them, she spoke:

"I need your guys' help."

Siobhan's face flushed red with embarrassment, her sentence hanging heavily in the air for a long while.

J.J. cut the sober moment by bursting into cackling laughter. "Siobhan! Sweeney! Wants our help!"

"I know—" started Siobhan.

"Siobhan Sweeney! Who used to rule over us with titanium fists! Needs the help of the Ghost Hunters Adventure Club!"

"J.J., it's—"

"The help of the Ghost Hunters Adventure Club! She comes groveling to the very crew of people who she just earlier tried to frame for grand theft over international borders!"

"Let her speak her piece," interrupted Trudi. "Siobhan, why aren't you with Luther?"

"He's who I've come to speak to you guys about," she replied. "I need your help bringing him down."

This got J.J. to stop cackling. "Wait, what happened between you and Luther?"

"I tried to stop him. I almost got away with the princess, too. But then that Oliver Path punk and his band of nerds got the jump on me. Next thing I knew I was eating dirt on the side of the tracks in Lake Nowhere. I hopped onto the backup train and hitched a ride into town that way."

"Wait," said Valentine. "You're fine with framing us for the theft of valuable jewelry and then stealing it, too, but you draw the line at whatever Luther pulled?"

"Ransoming a princess between two warring nations isn't in alignment with my mission statement."

J.J. very pointedly looked to Valentine, then to Trudi. "This is a real-world example of the benefit of mission statements."

"Do you know what happened to the train?" asked Trudi.

"No," said Siobhan. "None of this was planned past the Lake Nowhere stop. I was just as surprised as you guys were when I saw the Harborville Express missing, but something has to be up. You can't just make a train disappear like that."

"We were thinking the same thing," said Valentine, not realizing that he was letting his love for solving mysteries get in the way of his intense and sometimes irrational (but in most cases already presented completely rational) fear of Siobhan. "It has to have something to do with that town. Why would the salt mine be booby trapped?"

"So you'll help me?" Siobhan asked, once again showcasing a rarely-before-seen vulnerability.

J.J. slapped his hands on the table. "Well, Siobhan! This certainly has been a delight! You almost had us going there with the rarely-before-seen display of vulnerability. So, you can either stab us all to death with whatever sharp object you have concealed on your person or leave us be in this police station, because I guarantee that either of those situations will be less humiliating than whatever you have planned for us once you trick us into helping you."

Siobhan let out a deep exhale. "Look, I know you guys don't have any reason to trust me. But there's a big difference between what I pulled and what he pulled, and right now I'm letting my personal vendetta against Luther take priority over my personal vendetta with you guys."

This last part was hard for her to say. "So, what I'm trying to propose…is a truce."

J.J., Valentine, and Trudi all looked to one another. Each weighed their options, each realized that it was either this or stay in jail and hope that a for-profit incarceration system would look kindly upon them. Silently confirming their decision amongst one another, J.J. spoke for the group.

"These are billable hours, you know."

"You can certainly say that they are," replied Siobhan. She looked at the watch on her wrist. "And right on time."

"Right on time for what?" asked Trudi.

"My plan. You think I spent this entire time not figuring out an elaborate way to spring you three from jail?"

Siobhan pulled two red file folders out from her briefcase and tossed it onto the table. Trudi's heart leapt. She recognized the file folders on J.J. and Valentine that Siobhan had handed her earlier in the day.

"Managed to pick this up in your room, Trudi, before I got kicked off the Express."

J.J. and Valentine were intimately familiar with these file folders.

"You gave Trudi our rap sheets?" J.J. was shocked.

"Those were supposed to be sealed once we turned eighteen," Valentine added. He was turning red himself.

"Relax, relax, I was just trying to sow discord among the ranks. Had to get Trudi to think you two were felonious and untrustworthy as a tertiary backup."

J.J. and Valentine looked embarrassed.

"I wasn't gonna look at them," Trudi said in her defense.

"But did you?" asked J.J.

Trudi joined the brothers in the feeling of embarrassment. "I…uh…I might have seen a few things."

"Focus, people," Siobhan said. "Let's get you out of the New Troutstead police station before you guys get to bickering."

She let down her hair and took off her coat. Stuffing it into her briefcase, she traded it for a down jacket she had placed there for safekeeping. After donning a Harborville Elks baseball cap on her head along with a police badge around her neck, she now looked nothing like the lawyer who had just walked in a few minutes ago.

"And now, Melissa Chapman of the Harborville Sheriff's Department is transferring you back to Harborville for booking on a couple priors." She pulled a file out at random from one of the folders. "Avian theft. That oughta do it."

She walked over to the door of the interrogation room and opened it, peeling off the tape she had stuck to the door latch to keep it from locking. She then led the team of handcuffed members of the Ghost Hunters Adventure Club out into an empty hallway. "There's an officer stationed around the corner. We gotta get past her first."

"How do we do that?" asked Valentine.

"Like this," she said, confirming the time on her wristwatch as she walked casually through the hallway. Just as she rounded a corner, a man in a button-down shirt and glasses walked through the door leading out into the police bullpen. He carried a toolkit and appeared to work in information technology.

"Heard you had problems with your surveillance system," he said to the officer sitting in front of a row of CCTV monitors.

"Dang thing went out a couple minutes ago." She hit the monitors a couple times on the sides of them. "No idea what happened."

Using the information technology professional as a screen, the four walked out of the door and into the bullpen, unperturbed. "That's one," said Siobhan.

The four were now in the main area of the police department. The room was crowded with police officers walking around the bullpen, going about their police business. J.J.'s skin crawled at the thought of being in such close proximity to so many officers of the law.

One of the police officers looked up and addressed Siobhan. "Hey, where'd you come from?"

"What now?" Valentine whispered to his three compatriots.

Siobhan checked her watch again. "This."

A man in a pinstripe suit and straw boater's hat burst through the doors of the police station. A broad smile stretched its way across his face. He carried an obscene amount of balloons. "Haaaaappy birthday!" he roared in a sing-song manner.

"You remembered!" came a voice from the other side of the room. Everyone turned to see an elated dispatcher jump up from his chair. The man in the pinstripe suit strutted over to him and began leading the station in a rendition of "For He's a Jolly Good Fellow."

The police officers, not wanting to let on that they had, in fact, not remembered this man's birthday, joined in.

Once again, Siobhan walked coolly and calmly through a group of distracted officers of the law. "Glad that worked," she said to J.J., Valentine, and Trudi. "It's always someone's birthday. Nobody ever remembers."

J.J. whistled, impressed.

"Nearly there," she said as she led them to the front entrance of the police station. "We got one last hurdle and we're good to go."

Just as she reached for the handle and their presumptive freedom, a voice called out from behind them. "What do you think you're doing?"

"Immaculately timed," Siobhan said.

The four turned to see the supervising officer who had thrown a can at Officer Hot Dog's head earlier. He sat at a desk in the main lobby, going over papers.

"Man, I've been looking everywhere for you," said Siobhan without missing a beat. She approached the officer, flashing her badge. "Melissa Chapman, Harborville Sheriff's Department."

She handed him the file that she pulled earlier. "These suckers turned up in our system; I'm transferring them back to Harborville."

The senior officer eyed her skeptically. He looked down at the file. "Avian theft?"

"It was across state lines," J.J. piped up. "Very illegal."

"Where's the arresting officer?" the man asked Siobhan. "He's supposed to sign off on this."

"Oh, Officer Hot Dog? Is he not around here?"

The man folded his arms. "I sent him to pick up the school bus for that baseball team. You're gonna have to wait for him to get back before we do anything with you."

Siobhan sat down at the desk in front of the supervising officer. She spoke in a friendly way. "Y'see, the thing is I'm on a pretty tight schedule. It's a long drive to Harborville and I gotta get back on my beat."

"No signature, no transfer," the supervising officer said resolutely.

"Even just this once? Sounds like this Officer Hot Dog made a mistake. We all make mistakes sometimes," Siobhan said with a smile. "Isn't that right, Officer Gym Shorts Boner?"

The officer's eye's bulged. He leaned forward on his desk. "That was thirty years ago. I was a rookie on the force. It took me three transfers to get rid of that nickname."

"And yet it's still publicly searchable on your record. I'd really hate for that one to get around the office."

"Fine, fine," Officer Gym Shorts Boner said. He scribbled his signature on the file. "Just don't let me see you running around here again."

"Your secret's safe with me," Siobhan replied. She mimed closing a zipper across her lips before ushering the three out of the door and into the late afternoon New Troutstead sunlight.

When they were a safe-enough distance away from the police station, J.J. cheered. "Now *that* was a plan."

"Thank you, thank you," Siobhan accepted the adulation.

"Okay Siobhan, where are the keys?" Valentine asked.

"The what?"

"For the handcuffs?" Valentine raised both of his hands, showcasing that he was still restrained to both J.J. and Trudi.

"J.J., aren't you a master lockpick? You were talking a pretty big game about shimming handcuffs earlier. My plan kind of took that into account."

"Do you see a can of soda or a pair of scissors anywhere around here?" J.J. cried out.

Trudi sighed. "I guess we're stuck like this until we can find a way to get ourselves out." She looked to Siobhan. "So what's next?"

"What?"

"You know, your plan," J.J. chimed in.

"Get to Lake Nowhere? I guess? My plan was to spring you guys from the New Troutstead PD. I had to come up with that one while I was hanging onto the back of a luggage car and I had very little time to execute it in the way that I did. So from here on out we're laying the tracks in front of us as the train moves forward."

"Ugh," Valentine replied. "We can figure it out."

"Wait," Siobhan said. "Do you guys think I keep meticulous plans for everything?"

Their argument was cut short when J.J. spotted the school bus.

CHAPTER 18

A Good Deed Indicative of Character Growth

Looking from where they were across the street, J.J., Valentine, Trudi, and Siobhan saw Officer Hot Dog in the driver's seat of a school bus, pulling into the parking lot of the New Troutstead Police Department. Instinctively, everyone but Trudi jumped into a nearby hedgerow. She was, however, immediately dragged along due to her being handcuffed to Valentine.

"What's the deal with that?" asked J.J.

"New Troutstead is a small town," Siobhan replied. "They don't have their own police wagon, so they have to call up New Troutstead Elementary whenever they need to transfer a bunch of prisoners."

"The Cordelians," Trudi said grimly.

Parking the school bus next to a dumpster on the other end of the lot, Officer Hot Dog killed the engine and slid open the door to the entryway. He walked across the empty blacktop, entering the police station through a side door.

Moments later, the side doors opened again and the eight remaining members of the Harborville Elks were ushered outside by several police officers. One by one they were led into the school bus, sat down at a seat, then handcuffed to a bar connected to the seat in front of them.

"They're being taken back to Neutral Moldevik," said Trudi. "Coach Hank told us himself when we were locked up next to them. I bet they're just waiting for Inspector Horvath to arrive."

"We've got to help them," Valentine said, looking to the team.

"Are you kidding?" Siobhan asked. "We've go to get back to Lake Nowhere."

"They're dead men the moment they step on Neutral Moldevickian soil."

"Dead men who knew what they were getting into when they decided to help their princess steal some jewels! Every moment we waste is a moment that Luther could get away."

"Technically, she's right," J.J. interrupted. "Also, technically, there's nothing keeping us here. Technically we could all just run away from Siobhan right now and be done with everything."

Everyone looked at J.J.

"What? Is she gonna be *double* mad at us?"

"I agree with Valentine," Trudi spoke up. "They're the reason we're not being tried for jewel theft right now."

"I'm unsympathetic to that," Siobhan replied.

J.J. chimed in. "And now it's three to one."

"I don't remember our deal involving democratic issue-resolving."

"Should've gotten it in writing then."

Siobhan huffed. "Fine, okay. It's probably a good thing that I don't keep eight catapulted Cordelians on my conscience. But I don't have a plan for this."

"Looks like we're gonna have to get improvisational," said J.J., who specialized in half-baked plans.

They all surveyed the parking lot. Once the Harborville Elks were all ushered into the school bus, the remainder of the officers walked back toward the side entrance to the police station. One of them made sure to knock the police cap off of Officer Hot Dog's head as they traded places at the door. He carried several trash bags. It appeared that taking out departmental trash was another job for the rookies.

He walked the trash bags over to the dumpster on the other side from the school bus, tossing them in and then taking up a sentry position at the doors to the bus.

A spark flashed in J.J.'s mind. He remembered the soda can in Officer Hot Dog's trash bin. "I got an idea. Siobhan, gimme a knife."

"You're not allowed to kill anyone with this," she said as she pulled a small dagger out of the sleeve of her jacket.

J.J. looked at her. "It's weird how fast you produced that from your person."

"So what's your idea?" Siobhan asked.

"Go distract Officer Hot Dog for as long as you can. We're going dumpster diving."

Siobhan nodded and slipped away from the hedges.

"You don't make this sound appealing," said Valentine to his hand-cuffed brother as the three made their way down the street. They crossed back over to the police station parking lot out of eyeshot from Officer Hot Dog, waiting for Siobhan to work her magic.

Now, to the distant observer, it would appear that Officer Hot Dog was laser focused. His stouthearted gaze cut through the late afternoon air, showcasing a resoluteness in his oath to guard the school bus he stood before. He was the image of justice standing stalwart.

This was, in fact, not true. The stalwart sentry look had been hard-practiced during his time at the police academy. Right now Officer Hot Dog's mind was soaring through the clouds, dreaming about art and civics. That little voice inside of him was only growing louder. *There must be something more. There must be something more.*

"Nice bus," came a voice.

This startled the young officer a little, but it wasn't enough to drop his veneer of officiality, of course. Before him stood a small woman in a down jacket and baseball cap. A badge hung on a chain around her neck. He tried to place her in his mind. He couldn't.

"Can I help you?" he asked.

"Melissa Chapman, Harborville Sheriff's," the woman introduced herself. She threw a thumb back to a squad car at the other end of the parking lot that was not hers. "I was just walking back to my squad car. Saw the bus and figured I should say something about it. This what you're shipping that fake baseball team in?"

"Our force isn't anywhere near the size of Harborville's." He motioned over to the school bus. "Pulled it just a couple minutes ago on short notice. Figure there's gotta be a bunch of school supplies or even a kid we forgot about in there."

Siobhan laughed a genuine, kindhearted laugh. Her smile was radiant. "You must be the new guy."

"Is it that obvious?"

"Caught the guys razzing you back there. Also," she indicated the name on his shirt.

The young officer looked down at his nametag again. Through his veneer of rank-and-file professionalism, one could almost see a hint of bashfulness.

"Relax, we've all been there," said "Melissa." "You didn't hear it from me, but your supervising officer was nicknamed Officer Gym Shorts Boner back in his Harborville days."

"You don't say?" A smirk crossed the young officer's face. This considerably brightened his day. The two shared a look.

His practiced defense of professional indifference had been breached.

"Siobhan's got him," Trudi whispered to her two handcuffed compatriots alongside her beneath the school bus. The three shimmied backward to their safe harbor between the bus and the police department's dumpster.

"Time for phase two," J.J. said. "You guys establish contact with the Cordelians while I start my arts and crafts session."

As silently as he could, J.J. slipped open the lid of the dumpster and slid himself in. He grimaced the entire way down. Valentine, handcuffed to his brother, was dragged slowly closer and closer to the edge of the dumpster until his arm hung inside of it.

"What are you guys doing here?" came a loud whisper from the school bus. Turning, Valentine and Trudi saw Coach Hank speaking through the small opening of a partially cracked-open window.

Trudi was closest to the school bus due to her placement in the current chain gang. "Just hang tight, we're gonna try to help you."

"There's an officer over there. You guys should be careful."

"Could you give us a little volume to work with?" she asked.

Coach Hank nodded, then looked to the rest of his team. They all began a conversation about baseball amongst each other at moderate volume.

Officer Hot Dog didn't notice the volume shift. He was engaged in conversation with Melissa Chapman of the Harborville Sheriff's Department. There was something about her that compelled him to tell her everything about himself. To embarrass himself with how forthcoming he was. Looking at her made his mind shoot around the universe.

Siobhan was very good at her job.

The young officer, as happens sometimes at that age, was in love. Or at least he thought he was in love. What was actually happening to the young officer was that someone pretty was paying attention to him, and this forced his brain to focus on the *idea* of love rather than the practicality of it. Officer Hot Dog had fallen for this before in his life, but this seemingly would not stop him from doing so again. He was still young.

"Justice, huh?" said Siobhan, trying to keep the conversation going. "Pretty great thing to dedicate your life to, right?"

But justice didn't interest him right now. His mind soared. He wanted to know everything about her. He wanted her to know everything about him. The voice in his head was deafening. *There must be something more. There must be something more.*

He wanted to ask her a question that was very important to him.

But what if she didn't feel like he did. What if she didn't hurt in the way he did? That was life, wasn't it? You take a chance, you might get hurt.

He shook the thoughts from his mind. It was a goddamn grace from god that he was alive and he didn't care who knew it. He decided to take a chance. Looking Siobhan directly in her eyes, the same way she was looking at him, he spoke.

"What's your favorite movie?"

"My what?" Siobhan responded.

"You know, your favorite movie. Everyone's got a favorite movie, right?"

"Uhhh…" said Siobhan, as if she were trying to mimic the sound of a dial tone.

Trudi saw this unfold from under the school bus. She looked back to Valentine, who she was handcuffed to. "Officer Hot Dog asked Siobhan about movies."

Valentine's face fell. He was sandwiched very uncomfortably between a woman under a bus and a man in a dumpster. He looked over to his brother, who he was also handcuffed to. "Bro."

J.J.'s head popped out of the dumpster as silently as he could. "What?"

"Officer Hot Dog asked Siobhan about movies."

"Oh, that would be so nice to see under different circumstances," he whispered back. "But I'm sure she can handle herself."

Valentine looked over to Trudi. He shrugged.

"I'm so glad you asked," Officer Hot Dog continued the conversation without Siobhan's answer. "My favorite movie is John Carpenter's 1982 classic, *The Thing*."

"Wow!" said Siobhan. She was visibly sweating now. "That's, um, that's my favorite movie too!"

Officer Hot Dog's eyes went wide. "We have so much to talk about."

Trudi turned to Valentine. "She just said *The Thing* was her favorite movie."

Valentine looked to J.J., who was still rummaging. "Either you gotta find a can of soda quick or we're done for. Siobhan said her favorite movie was *The Thing*."

"It's a horror masterpiece," J.J. said, reminiscing.

"Focus," said Valentine.

"If you can get a message to her, have her bring up Rob Bottin. He put himself into the hospital working on the monster effects for that movie. Film buffs love bringing up that bit of trivia." He dove back into the dumpster and continued rummaging.

Valentine looked to Trudi. "Got any ideas?"

Trudi thought quick. She got up from under the bus and addressed Coach Hank at the window, who was continuing a lively conversation about the best right fielders of all time with the baseball player ahead of him.

"Coach Hank," she said. "Have any of you seen *The Thing*?"

"The what?"

"Never mind. Is there any way you can get a message to Siobhan?"

Coach Hank looked over his team inside the school bus, then read-dressed Trudi. "There's a notepad and some markers on the floor here. We're athletic enough to get something written while handcuffed."

"Have her bring up Rob Bottin."

"Bring up Rob Bottin. Got it."

And so Coach Hank passed the message up the length of the bus, from one baseball player to another, like a game of telephone. Eventually the message came to the baseball player at the front of the bus, sitting just outside of the conversation that Siobhan and Officer Hot Dog were having. He wrote down what he heard with a marker in his mouth.

"And that's why I think the paranoia in the movie was so effective," Officer Hot Dog went on. "But I'm so sorry, I've been rambling. It's just, man, is that a good movie. But I'm eager to hear your thoughts on it."

Siobhan's eyes darted back and forth. Up until now she was holding her own in this conversation by nodding excitedly and parroting back everything the officer had said to her as if she knew exactly what he was talking about.

Suddenly she saw something in the school bus. Pressed against the window by the face of one of the baseball players was a notebook. In childlike writing was the following:

Binge on Rad Broman(?)

Siobhan grimaced. She didn't have good faith in that question mark encased in parentheses. Still, it was the only shot she had.

"Rad Broman is bingeworthy," she chanced, feeling that that might not be an actual person's name.

Officer Hot Dog looked at her quizzically. "Who's Rad Broman?"

"Oh," Siobhan caught herself as best as she could. "He's...a director...whose work I love."

"Wow, I've never heard of him." The officer looked down in thought, then back at Siobhan. There was no suspicion in his voice. "But that's so interesting! If you mention him in the same space as John Carpenter then he must be a director worth knowing."

"That isn't gonna work a second time," Trudi said to Valentine. She got out from under the bus again and readdressed Coach Hank. "Coach, get me the notepad."

Coach Hank passed the message up to the front of the bus. What returned was someone's shoe. He shrugged.

"The notepad!" Trudi said as loud as she could without arousing suspicion.

After some negotiation, the notepad and marker finally arrived to Coach Hank. He placed it in his mouth from his handcuffed hands and slid it through the slit in the window.

Trudi scribbled on the notepad as quickly as she could, sliding it back into the school bus.

"They used actual flamethrowers in *The Thing*, which was really uncommon for movies to do in the '80s," the young officer continued.

Siobhan was at her wit's end. She had never had to sustain a conversation for this long about a movie she neither knew nor cared about. Officer Hot Dog, himself, seemed to be running out of fun trivia from the movie to impress her with. To her he was just a moment from realizing that she was trying to fool him. Then the whole operation would blow up.

And then, as if by a miracle of practical special effects magic, she saw the notepad in the window again. This time it read:

BRING UP ROB BOTTIN

She chanced it again. "Rob Bottin sure is interesting."

"Oh man, Rob Bottin?" the young officer asked excitedly.

"Yes!" shouted Siobhan excitedly, for the first time finding a foothold in the conversation. "Rob Bottin!"

"Gosh, I know," said the young officer, feeling understood. "That was his first-ever movie he was leading a team on. He was only twenty-two years old; the poor guy worked himself to the bone on that production. But man if he didn't do a masterwork on that film. I could talk about that guy for hours."

"Please do," Siobhan said as she breathed a sigh of relief.

Trudi breathed her own sigh of relief when she heard the young officer continuing on about the importance of in-camera effects. She shimmied back from under the school bus. "I think we have a little time."

J.J. once again popped his head out of the dumpster, excited. In his hand was an aluminum can of soda. Hopping out of his trash prison, he looked over to Trudi. She gave a thumbs up, confirming that Siobhan was holding her own in a conversation about cinema. This was of great surprise to him.

Working quickly, he carved the top and bottom of the can off, leaving a small strip of aluminum for him to work with.

That was when he saw the familiar blue-and-red flashing lights against the school bus.

Instinctively, J.J. ran to hide behind the dumpster, dragging his brother and Trudi along with him. Peeking out from behind the dumpster, the three saw a lone police car enter the parking lot. Riding in the passenger seat was Inspector Sandor Horvath.

Officer Hot Dog turned his head from the approaching police car that had just pulled into the parking lot. "And another thing about Kurt Russell—"

He stopped mid-sentence. Melissa Chapman was no longer there.

"Horvath's in that police car," Siobhan said, popping up behind the Ghost Hunters Adventure Club team. They all jumped a little in shock. "If he spots us, it's over."

J.J. had just finished folding the aluminum sheet into a small triangle. He inserted it into his own cuff, trying to undo the safety catch and release himself.

"J.J., we gotta get out of here," said Valentine.

Unable to undo his handcuff in time, J.J. grunted in frustration.

"We've gotta scoot," Siobhan urged.

J.J. looked at Siobhan, then at the school bus, then at the hastily-made shim in his hand. Panicking, he flung the small aluminum object like a discus toward the open window of the school bus.

To his credit, the projectile hit its target.

Siobhan grabbed Trudi, who was handcuffed to Valentine, who was handcuffed to J.J. She dragged the chain of adventurers through a row of hedges. They jogged for a little while longer until they found an alleyway that they found suitably safe.

"Well, I hope you're all happy with the good deed you just did," said Siobhan. "Luther's probably halfway around the world by now."

"Do you think we helped them?" asked Trudi.

Valentine shook his head. "I don't know."

"There's no time to think about that now," Siobhan said. "We gotta refocus on the mission."

"Well," J.J. took inventory. "You've got three mystery-solvers hand-cuffed together and no current way for the four of us to get back to Lake Nowhere. If anyone here can figure transport out, I'd like to hear your thoughts."

"Wait," said Trudi. "I know what we can do."

CHAPTER 19

The Whistle Stop

The Whistle Stop was a bar in New Troutstead. It was a train-themed bar. Memorabilia from centuries of train history adorned the walls of the dimly lit establishment as "Midnight Train to Georgia" by Gladys Knight & the Pips played on the jukebox.

It was slow right now, like a Pullman car rolling into the depot after a long haul. Of the few train industry employees mingling in the establishment in the early evening, there was one of utmost importance.

Sitting by herself, tucked away in the corner of the lacquered wooden bar, staring forlornly at a glass of whiskey, was the engineer. She let out a pained groan, slumping forward. She had had a pretty rough day.

"Excuse me," came a voice from behind her. The woman turned to see four young adults, three of whom were handcuffed together.

"You guys again!" the engineer cried out. "How did you even know I was here?"

Trudi made as if she was about to speak, but she caught herself and thought for a moment. "I...don't actually know."

"Oh," said the engineer. "Then I guess I must've been the next plot point." She returned to her drink at the bar table. "Can you just leave me alone? I find myself overburdened with nihilistic thought."

"We're sorry about everything that happened today," Trudi began. "About what happened to your train."

"I got fired," said the engineer, swirling the drink in her hand as she watched the ice cubes clink together uselessly; as if all they were made to do was clink against each other. As if that were their only purpose. "My first day of existence and I lose my job for—get this—having my train stolen in a heist plot between two fictional European nations."

"This has definitely been outlandishly plotted," agreed J.J., popping his head into the conversation. "Say, you don't happen to have a can of soda around here anywhere, do you? I'm trying to get these handcuffs off."

He held up his hand, attached to Valentine's, to illustrate his point.

The engineer looked at J.J. quizzically. "There's something genuinely flawed about your character." She nodded to the bartender, who wore a fun conductor's hat. He dug out a soda can from under the bar and slid it over.

"Oh, it doesn't need to be full," said J.J. "I just need the can. Don't even need the full can. Just need a slip of aluminum, really."

"We need your help getting back to Lake Nowhere," Trudi said bluntly.

"No you don't," the engineer responded.

"But the princess has been kidnapped and we're the only ones who can save her—"

"The princess isn't real."

Trudi was taken aback. "What do you mean? If we don't do something then Luther—"

"Luther isn't real."

"But—"

"Don't you understand?" the engineer interjected, seeming to succumb under the weight of her thoughts. Waving her arms around, she gestured to various effects within the Whistle Stop.

"That's not real. That's not real. That's not real. None of this is real. This is all just a cruel facsimile of existence."

Valentine, who had only shared momentary scenes in proximal location to the engineer and thus did not have a full understanding of the totality of her anguish, stepped forward. "What are you trying to say? That because Dr. Cecil writes us, then we aren't real?"

"That is precisely what I'm trying to say," said the engineer.

"But…" Valentine looked down at his hands. "I *feel* real."

The engineer chortled. "Buddy, wake up and smell the marketable content machine. We're all just imaginary objects floating through the mind of a sad, angry man. This world solely exists so that we can be run through a ringer of misery, over and over again, for as long as we can be profited off of."

She turned back to her tumbler of whiskey, shaking it. She watched the ice clink together in the glass. That's all they'd ever do. "And I'm here to say no. To opt out. To be the one conscientious objector to this fixed train wreck of a reality. The timetable is stacked against all of us, kids. And right now you should all be asking yourselves if you even have to be on the tracks in the first place."

J.J. popped his head back into the conversation. "Again, I'm very sympathetic to your feelings right now. Strange plot, lots of interesting questions about the ethics of storytelling. But, um, Siobhan. Can I borrow a knife? I had to drink the whole can of soda to get it ready to turn into a shim. And uh, I need a knife. Siobhan?"

Siobhan handed him a small blade that she had tucked away in her hair. He disappeared again to do his work.

Trudi put a hand on Valentine's shoulder and stepped in front of him, addressing the engineer. "There's gotta be something we can do to convince you."

"I guarantee you there is not."

Trudi huffed. She had thought the suspension of disbelief inherent within all storytelling would be enough to propel the story forward, but apparently she was wrong. She needed to figure out another way.

The young adventurer thought before speaking again. An idea slowly forming in her mind. "So you believe that because none of this exists, then none of this matters."

"Anybody who thinks about it enough will come to the same terminal station that I did," the engineer said, turning back to the bar and leaving a very cold shoulder between herself and Trudi.

"And you won't lift a finger, despite how real this all feels and how badly we need your help?"

The engineer placed her drink on the bar. She watched the ice. "It's as simple as saying no."

"All right," said Trudi. "Then if I can't convince you on a philosophical level, I'm just gonna beat the shit out of you."

The engineer turned to her with a shocked face. "W-what?"

Trudi pushed her off of the barstool with her free hand. With the other she dragged along an equally shocked Valentine and J.J.

"This matters to me," she said, speaking with an anger and conviction that I had previously thought her incapable of. She pushed the engineer again, sending her backpedaling through the Whistle Stop.

"This matters to my friends." Trudi pushed the engineer again. She fell back onto the leather cushions of a booth at the back of the establishment. She looked around frantically for help, but there was only Trudi's menacing frame towering over her.

"And it matters enough for me to tell you that this stupid ivory tower-ass argument can go to hell before I break your goddamn nose over it!"

Trudi pulled back for the punch. The engineer held her hands up in front of her face, shrieking in fear.

Then, nothing. The blow didn't come. The engineer opened her eyes.

There Trudi still was. She dropped her hand, speaking softer now. "That you fear for your life means you value it. Weird thing to do in a universe that doesn't exist."

Turning around, she dragged her two teammates along with her toward the entrance to the bar, scooping up an awestruck Siobhan along the way.

"Come on," she said, ushering them out of the doors. "We're getting to Lake Nowhere, even if I have to rip through the pages to get there."

And there the engineer was, left alone with her thoughts among the various train memorabilia within the Whistle Stop. She let out a long sigh before returning to her barstool. There was the ice clinking around in the glass again. Yes, that's all it would ever do.

But didn't ice melt and become liquid? the engineer thought. *And then didn't that water have value? Even if it were thrown out. Even if it made its way to a storm drain, to the ocean. Wouldn't that water one day evaporate to the heavens, to be reborn again as blessed, renewing rainfall? And then wouldn't it start anew? Wouldn't that—*

A hand gripped around the tumbler of whiskey, shocking the engineer. The drink flew across the room and shattered against the wall in a shower of glass.

Trudi stood there, her two teammates still in tow. She was heaving in anger. "I've had it up to here with all of these goddamn metaphors!"

She dragged J.J. and Valentine back to the entrance. Stopping at the doors, she turned back to the engineer. "The gift of life isn't just for the living. There. That's the point you were trying to make."

And then she dragged the two the rest of the way out of the Whistle Stop.

"Very cogent points," J.J. said on the sidewalk outside of the establishment. He slid his newly-made shim between the teeth of Trudi's handcuff where they met the locking mechanism, freeing her from the chain gang. "But I don't think we convinced her."

"I wasn't trying to convince her," Trudi said matter-of-factly. She had calmed down a bit by now. "I was trying to convince the person who wrote her."

Valentine, mid-handcuff removal, tilted his head and looked at her. "What do you mean?"

"Dr. Cecil isn't an omnipotent being, you know? Especially since he's making this all up as he goes. He told me himself that only we have the ability to surprise him, and not the other way around. So I decided to do just that, because I know that he'll always and forever be bound by one thing."

"What's that?" asked Siobhan.

"He has to write a good story."

…

Fine.

Just then, the doors to the Whistle Stop shot open. The four young adventurers turned to see that, standing in the doorway, was the engineer. Something was different about her. She was determined.

She didn't wait long before she spoke. "I can get us a train."

* * *

THE LONE ENGINE HURTLED ON the track away from the city against the setting sun. Without the burden of train cars behind it, it moved at a much faster pace than one would expect. Across the cab, in bright cursive writing, was its name: the Spirit of New Troutstead.

At the helm was the engineer, a smile as wide as the Grand Canyon across her face. For the first time in her life she felt hope.

J.J. massaged his wrist, now handcuffless, while he watched New Troutstead disappear in the distance. He turned to address his compatriots in the engine compartment with him.

"As much as I chew it over, I don't think that 'the gift of life isn't just for the living' is the exact mission statement we're looking for."

"It seemed to work for me," said the engineer. She felt a new closeness to everything around her, as if she could feel the edges of her body bleed into the edges of the universe.

"Not that we're unappreciative of the ride and the renewed vigor for life," said Valentine. "But what's the Federal Train Governance Commission gonna say about us stealing a train from their yard?"

The engineer thought this over. "If the letter of train law honors selfless acts of bravery done in the face of danger in the way that I know they do, then everything will turn out for the best."

She thought it over for longer. "Otherwise I could just find something new. I've always wanted to be a pilot."

J.J. brought the conversation back on track. "We're almost there; we need to figure out a plan."

"To stop Luther we're gonna have to find the train first," said Trudi.

"Our best bet right now is the mine," said Siobhan. "If Luther isn't long gone, then the only reasonable place to hide something of that size is the enormous hiding spot next to the train's route."

"The booby-trapped mine," added J.J.

"I didn't say stopping Luther was gonna be easy."

"Easier or harder than watching a two-hour film?"

"They're just so long," Siobhan said with a sigh.

Trudi glanced out of the window at the scenery passing by. There was something that had been bothering her since Lake Nowhere. "Wait, who's Rex Sawyer?"

J.J.'s face flushed red. "It, um, it took a couple tries to come up with J.J."

"Oh, that's just the tip of the iceberg," Siobhan remarked. "You had Warrick Wolf…Flint Steele…Stud Douglas…"

"Siobhan! Those names weren't meant to be associated with my brand!" J.J. shouted in exasperation.

"Kirk Stonefist…Gibson Gold…'Sin Nombre'…that one came with a luchador mask."

"Siobhan!" J.J. shouted even louder before she waved him off with a giggle.

"You all clearly have something you need to work out without me in the room," said the engineer. She stared out at the setting sun. There was so much hope in her.

The four young adventurers looked out the front window of the train engine's passenger compartment. Just beyond the great bridge, beyond the river that snaked all the way back to New Troutstead, was the tunnel to Lake Nowhere.

And sure, let them have their moment of levity. They can have their tiny little victories, that's just fine. They can force my hand and have their silly little arguments against my own strongly held worldview. I'll even let it push the story forward.

I figure it's the least I could do, considering what was about to happen.

You see, none of these fools realized what was in store for them in these waning pages of the story. They were all so blissfully unaware of it; their youthful determination taking the place of reason.

I pity them. I really do. Because by the end of the day, one of these idiots would be dead.

CHAPTER 20

The Great Stone Door Puzzle

The lone train engine braked to a stop inside of the tunnel leading to Lake Nowhere. Fine particles of dust danced in front of its headlights, their beams falling off as the rock salt channel curved away.

Exiting the engine's operation compartment—thankfully, because I'm not even sure if that's what it's called—were J.J., Valentine, and Trudi. Joining just behind them was their former enemy and now begrudging compatriot, Siobhan Sweeney. Each of them carried flashlights.

The four climbed down the service ladder on the side of the Spirit of New Troutstead, down to the small gap of space between the engine and the tunnel walls.

"You sure you wanna get dropped off here?" the engineer asked, popping her head out of the control room window.

"If this is where the Harborville Express disappeared," Trudi replied, "then it couldn't have gone too far."

"I really admire your resolution," the engineer said. "I'm gonna park this engine at the train station just up ahead."

"Can't you stay here?" J.J. pleaded. "Having been in similar situations throughout my admittedly burgeoning career, it's usually bad to put the getaway driver so far away."

"Parking your train engine inside of a dark tunnel on active train tracks is a great way to have someone crash into your train," replied the engineer. "The tracks have a switch up at the station so I can hold there safely for a while."

J.J. nodded in understanding. The engineer released the brakes to the train and began pulling away. In the space of moments, the four adventurers were left in complete darkness, saved only by the glow of their flashlights.

"And we've completely ruled out the ghost train theory, right?" J.J. asked. "As in the Harborville Express and everyone on that train were ghosts the whole time and were simply passing through our reality?"

"I'd be willing to entertain the idea until we can think of anything else," Trudi replied.

And so the four walked along the corridors of the Lake Nowhere tunnel, examining the walls, floor, and ceilings with their flashlights.

Rock salt. Train tracks. Rock salt. In that order. It went on like this for a while. Search as they might, they could not seem to find anything untoward about the tunnel that surrounded them.

"So, hypothetically," J.J. went on, "a temporal ectoplasmic wormhole of sufficient size could facilitate the transference of an entire train, passengers included. It'd feel as real to us as anything. It was a lot like how in *Donnie Darko*…"

He paused. "Siobhan, *Donnie Darko* was a 2001 cult classic film starring Jake Gyllenhaal, directed by Richard Kelly."

"Thank you J.J.," Siobhan said politely.

Valentine was lost in in his own world of thought. "It still doesn't make any sense."

"I mean, yeah," said J.J. "But with how studios released movies in that era, the film would have had to develop a fanbase through home video first before it became popular."

"I meant the Harborville Express. Even if it were in the mine, how could it have gotten there from here?"

"There could be adjoining tracks," Trudi offered. "But why would they be in the middle of a tunnel?"

"If it means anything," J.J. offered, "Val and I found a document in the mine that said it closed down when it lost government funding in 1930. Maybe that's when the wormhole split timelines."

"That's weird," said Trudi. "Rudith told us that the town ran until 1933. Three years is a long while for a mining town to be running without a source of revenue."

A thought popped into Siobhan's head. "Unless the town found a different source of revenue."

Their flashlights rested upon a sheet of rock wall. Flying past it in a train engine, one might easily overlook that it seemed ever so slightly different from the wall of rock salt beside it. But walking on the train tracks seemed to tell a different story.

The four approached the oddly colored cavern wall, examining all around it.

"There's something here," said Trudi, pointing to the grooves in the rock salt. Following the lines, the four could just barely make out an outline in the shape of a small door.

"Something pivotal happened in American history in 1933," Siobhan said. "Something that would explain why the town finally closed down three years after the mine closed." She reached her fingers into the grooves of the wall and swung open a panel behind the veneer of rock salt. There, connected to the ground, was a metal train switch.

"What?" asked J.J.

She gripped the handle with both hands and pulled. Immediately, their portion of the tunnel echoed with the sound of creaking metal. Salt crystals kicked up into the air as behind them the facade of tunnel wall swung backward on hinges. It revealed an offshoot to the tunnel they were currently in.

Siobhan turned to the members of the Ghost Hunters Adventure Club. "The repeal of Prohibition."

Shining their light into the tunnel, they saw split tracks, recently unearthed by movement, now diverting a would-be train toward the innards of the mine.

"If that's the case, then this could have been a secret moonshine running port," said Trudi.

"It makes sense, right?" Valentine replied. "Secret tunnel just before you arrive at New Troutstead."

"It would explain the booby traps we found in the mine, too," added J.J.

The four followed the tracks as they curved down into the mine. The air grew staler the further and deeper they walked.

Eventually, the tunnel widened, their flashlight beams growing wider and weaker before falling off into darkness among the great rock salt cavern they had found themselves in. The tracks led them to the end of the cavern, where they came upon a door.

"Would you look at that," J.J. whistled. He stepped closer to examine the enormous stone door blocking their path. It was, for size comparison purposes, big enough to fit a train through. There was no door handle, or anything that would suggest how to open it. The train tracks beneath the team's feet led directly through the split in the door. A ladder near the door allowed access to a small area above it where the rock salt had been hewn out.

"That doesn't look like rock salt," said Siobhan, indicating the door.

"Whoever built this place must have dragged it all the way in here." Trudi shined her flashlight upon engravings in the door. Parallel and intersecting lines, like train tracks, shot out from the very top of the entryway, leading to the outer edges of the door at their base.

"Hey J.J.," Valentine asked, shining his flashlight upward. "Where does 'moonshiner art installation' fall in relation to your temporal ectoplasmic wormhole theory?"

Following the flashlight's beam, the team saw hundreds and hundreds of clear, glass bottles of all shapes and sizes suspended in the air directly above them. Each was connected by a length of rope to the ceiling of the cavern. In each of the bottles was a clear liquid.

"It doesn't necessarily debunk the theory, but I'd throw it in the 'against' column," J.J. replied. "That's gotta be moonshine, right?"

"But why would anyone put them there?" asked Trudi. Examining their present location further, her flashlight eventually found a small metal contraption bolted into the rock salt where the wall met the floor. Kneeling next to it, she brushed her finger against the metal striker wheel attached to the contraption.

A spark came out.

"It's probably moonshine," she said, shining her flashlight once again around the room. She spotted more of the same metal contraptions dotting along the wall at regular intervals. "If we do something wrong, presumably those bottles will soak us all in high-grade alcohol, and those strikers will light us on fire."

"So now we know what happens if we try to unlock that door wrong," J.J. said. "Unceremonious immolation."

The grimness of his brother's statement didn't seem to deter Valentine's resolve to get through that door. Seeing the ladder again, he walked over and climbed up it, leading him to the area that had been hewn out of the rock face. It was just large enough for him to walk through if he crouched.

"There's a funnel here," he called out to his teammates as he arrived at the top of the entryway. Shining a light into the small channel that led from the small cylindrical opening, he could see the pipe created by laborious chiseling that led down into the door.

Valentine puzzled over this entire conundrum for a bit. Why didn't the door have a handle? Why was there a tube that led into the door? Why would someone want to set someone on fire in such an elaborate way?

Then, it hit him.

"So that's why that jerk always smelled like rubbing alcohol," he said to the three teammates below him.

"Oliver?" asked Trudi.

"We ran into him in the mines back before the train was stolen," Valentine explained. "J.J. and I thought he might be trying to hide the ruby jewels, but it turns out he was down here to open this door. I need one of those bottles of moonshine from the ceiling."

"Knife," said Siobhan. In a move that could be considered "pretty neat," she plucked a dagger clipped inconspicuously in the lapel of her blouse and hurled it in a satisfying arc through a rope that hung above.

"It's important to discuss plans first!" J.J. shouted as he slid to catch a small jar of clear liquid. It remained unbroken. He tossed it up to his brother.

"Liquor has to be fifty percent alcohol by volume or above to be flammable," Valentine said as he caught the jar. "One hundred proof."

He looked down to the team, who seemed surprised by this readily-pulled factoid about spirits.

"You don't make a good whiskey sour just by following a recipe," he said. "Trudi, could you take a look at those engravings on the wall? I think I've figured out how to open this door."

Trudi reexamined the stone entryway, following the engravings with the beam of her flashlight. Upon closer inspection, she saw that the etched lines that formed tracks had shallow grooves running all throughout it.

"Does it look like liquid could flow through that?" Valentine asked.

"Definitely."

"The sorts of guys who'd go this far to smuggle moonshine didn't want to deal with any run of the mill moonshiner," Valentine said. "So why not build a test to see just how good of a brewer you are? I need fire."

Siobhan pulled a lighter from her pocket and tossed it up to Valentine. He paused, looking at it.

"This is Ghost Hunters Adventure Club-branded."

"What?" asked Siobhan. "I can hate you guys and still recognize good branding."

Valentine shook his head. "All right everyone, stand back. If this goes wrong, I want to be the only one immolated."

He unscrewed the mason jar as his three teammates distanced themselves from the stone door. Taking a whiff near the rim of the glass, he drew back in disgust as the fumes burned his nostrils. "That oughta be enough to do it," he coughed.

Tipping the jar over, he poured its contents into the well, watching the moonshine slide down the channel and into the engravings in the door.

"Cross your fingers," he said, holding the lighter to the base of the funnel and flicking the striker. A small blue flame breathed to life immediately at the tip of the well. The three adventurers who could see the door watched with bated breath as the flame slowly traveled down from the top of the well, splitting through the grooves etched into it.

Finally, the flame reached the bottom of the door, disappearing beyond sight into the walls.

There was an audible click. The door unlocked, swinging open by a matter of inches.

"It's pretty poetic that these moonshiners would douse you and set you on fire with their own clearly superior moonshine if yours wasn't good enough," said J.J., as the four congregated in front of the door. Faint light was emanating from the opening. Someone was home.

Siobhan was the first to approach the entryway. She looked to the team and put a finger to her lips, suggesting silence. They nodded and the four of them slipped stealthily through the opening.

They crouched low, following the train tracks as they traveled around another bend, their path lit by dim bulbs that ran along the walls of the tunnel.

After only walking for a short while, they all came to a halt. Parked directly in front of them, on the tracks, was the rear end of the Harborville Express.

CHAPTER 21

Princess Annalise of Cordelia

J.J., Valentine, Trudi, and Siobhan sneaked up to the back side of what they remembered to be the luggage car of the Harborville Express. Peering around the corner toward the front of the train, they saw that the cavern widened out again just a couple yards ahead. Things seemed to be quiet, for now.

"Okay team, I've got an idea," J.J. whispered to the other three. "If we can get up to the front and disable the train, then they're stuck here."

"I can do that," said Siobhan.

"Pick a squad mate. Team two will traverse to Lake Nowhere and get the engineer to radio in backup."

Her response was immediate and jarring. "Valentine."

"Yikes," said J.J.

In testament both to the courage I had written her to have, as well as her willingness to help a bro avoid a bummer situation, Trudi cut the tension by speaking up. "I'll stay with Siobhan."

"It's okay," Valentine said, surprising everyone. Where just earlier in the day he would have been paralyzed by the very notion of Siobhan's presence, now he seemed calm. Determined. "I can handle this."

J.J. looked at his brother. "Are you sure?"

"I'm sure."

"Oh, thank Christmas," J.J. said with a sigh of relief. "It was you or me, man. Or Trudi, technically. You had that one in your pocket, she literally offered to go." He stood up and nodded for Trudi to join him, then looked back to his brother. "You can do this."

The two crept away along the tunnel, back toward the stone door. Just before disappearing around a bend, J.J. whispered loudly to his brother. "Think of a mission statement, if you have the time."

And there Valentine was, left alone with Siobhan.

She broke the silence. "Impressive."

"Let's go," he responded. He crouched low and hugged close to the train cars as he crept forward. Siobhan followed.

Reaching the end of the luggage car, the two saw the cavern widen out into what appeared to be a subterranean warehouse. Dimly lit barrels and dusty bottles of moonshine, stacked atop each other and ordered in rows, lined the expansive space to the side of the Harborville Express.

"I mean it," she said, as Valentine peeked over the barrel toward the front of the train. "I'm impressed."

"Siobhan, if you want to psychologically torture me, could you do it off billable hours? We've got a job to do."

"Listen," she began. "I know we don't get along and I'm intimately aware of what I tried to pull on you earlier today. But you've matured a lot since you left the team. I've seen the change in you, and I think it's for the better."

Valentine stole his gaze away from the front of the train to address Siobhan. "Growth is what happens when you develop a moral compass," he said.

"What do you think I'm trying to do right now?"

If only for the briefest of moments, the two shared a look with one another. It was as if to say, without words, *hey I know that we hate each other but it's sort of impossible to hate someone in their totality. There are pieces of you that will stay with me forever, for better or for worse, and if you and I can't get rid of those pieces then we might as well find a way to appreciate them.*

Shouting from up ahead broke their moment. The two ducked down under a set of barrels and peeked toward the source of the commotion. Several train nerds, all armed with flashlights, spilled out of the various train cars and fanned out around the train.

"This is the third time!" shouted a voice the two could tell was Luther's. Looking toward the front of the train, they saw him step out of the engine compartment with Oliver Path. "Wow! Wow, wow, wow! We were supposed to be long gone as soon as the sun started setting!"

The two climbed down the service ladder on the side of the train. "Oh, I'm *so* sorry we're behind schedule," Oliver said incredulously. He rubbed his wrist. "The only thing worse than that kid's vocabulary is her bite."

"Hold up your end of the deal," Luther responded. "Find wherever that princess ran off to, get her back here, and get us to the bridge."

"And then what? My men and I come back to the mine and just stare lovingly at the stolen train we boosted? How are we gonna get it out of here?"

"The deal was for the train. Not for its safe transport."

"The deal was for the *entire* train," said Oliver. "No missing parts. Don't think I've forgotten about you wanting to detach the luggage car to slow that other train down."

"Just find her," Luther said in a conversation-ending tone.

Oliver snorted loudly, turning away from Luther to join the other train nerds in their search. Luther walked into the door to the first-class passenger car.

"You don't need to go to a leadership summit to call that substandard team synergy," Valentine remarked. There was something Luther said that stuck with him. *Get us to the bridge.* He thought of the great bridge looming over the even greater river, the river that led all the way back to New Troutstead. He looked over to Siobhan. "What did he mean by the bridge?"

"This is our chance," Siobhan interrupted, indicating the empty train engine. She grabbed a bottle of moonshine from beside the barrel they were hiding behind. Nodding to Valentine, the two crept forward through the aisle of barrels, ducking from time to time to avoid the sweeping flashlight from a wandering train nerd.

Before long they reached the front of the train. From their vantage point it appeared that the engine compartment was empty, a faint glow from instrument panels illuminating the interior. Chancing it, the two climbed up the service ladder quickly and slinked across the outer catwalk, opening the door to the control room.

They were alone here. The soft rumble of the idling engine filled the compartment. Before them was a panel of controls and electronic equipment.

"This looks sabotage-able," said Siobhan. "A little bit of fire and they're as good as stuck here."

"That sounds easy," Valentine replied.

And then someone fell from their hiding place on the ceiling.

Valentine and Siobhan both stifled the urge to scream as their unknown assailant landed on top of them, sending all three sprawling on the floor of the Harborville Express.

The two held in another gasp as they realized their assailant was Princess Annalise of Cordelia.

"I swear to god, nobody on this train looks up," said the princess as she dusted off her Harborville Elks uniform. "Hey, Siobhan."

"Told you I'd come back," Siobhan grinned. "Good work with the biting."

Standing up, Valentine got a good look at the princess for the first time since she was revealed by Inspector Sandor Horvath earlier in the day. She was small. She couldn't have been more than thirteen. Her hair, without a baseball cap, was tied in a ponytail behind her head.

"We gotta get you out of here," he said.

"My nuts we do," the princess responded. "Luther's still got my mom's jewels."

"We're a little past that, don't you think?"

"Let's get sabotaging and we can figure that out later," Siobhan said to break the argument. She took the bottle of moonshine in her hands and poured it over the instrument panel, watching the high-proof alcohol seep through cracks and into the inner workings of the train below.

Then she grabbed her Ghost Hunters Adventure Club-branded lighter, placing it close over the drenched electronics. "Hold for chaos."

She was interrupted by a voice. "Hey if you're gonna run the engine, make sure the emergency brake is enga—"

The three turned. Standing in the doorway, thinking he was speaking to one of his lackeys, was Oliver Path. What he saw, instead, was three people trying to light his train on fire.

"My baby!" he wailed. With a shrill scream, he ran forward, flailing his arms in the air and knocking the lighter out of Siobhan's hand. It skittered across the floor of the train compartment.

And then there was a sound, like a snap. Then another snap. Then the noise of high-end electronics frying. Oliver and the three looked over to the instrument panel that had just moments ago been doused in moonshine. Sparks were flying out of it.

The instrument panel set on fire all on its own.

Oliver screamed again.

"We should jam!" Valentine shouted, as he shoved Oliver out of the way. Siobhan and Princess Annalise joined him as the three darted out of the engine compartment, across the catwalk, and down the service ladder to the train tracks below.

"The engine's on fire!" Oliver shouted, sticking his head out of the compartment's window. "Help!"

"What about the jewels?" the princess asked as they ran along the train toward the exit of the cavern. They could see a clear shot through the tunnel, past the end of the train.

"It's sort of a moot point right now." Valentine urged them on. But Princess Annalise had stopped in her tracks next to the dining car of the Harborville Express.

"I'm not leaving without them."

"Princess, come on," Valentine pleaded.

She didn't have a chance to respond. A hand reached out from the door of the dining car and snatched her by the collar, dragging her back into the train.

"Annalise!" shouted Siobhan. She ran to the princess's aid but was stopped by the doors to the dining car abruptly closing.

Standing there, visible through the pane of glass on the door, was Luther Adedeji. He was gripping tightly onto the princess's arm. "Wow!" he yelled through the door before dragging her along with him toward the front of the train.

"We've gotta do something!" Valentine said as he ran up the train tracks, attempting to follow Luther's movement.

Siobhan put her hand on his shoulder. "Wait."

Just ahead, their path was blocked by the sweeping flashlights of train nerds. Advancing forward, they combed over the area beside the train. One of the flashlights rested on the very place where Valentine and Siobhan had been standing.

There was nobody there.

The train nerds disengaged when they heard another yelp from Oliver Path in the engine compartment. They ran to assist him.

"Now what?" Valentine asked. He and Siobhan were lying prone under the train, between it and the tracks. They had rolled under at the last second to avoid detection.

"I don't know," said Siobhan as the two crawled forward.

"The fire's out!" they heard Oliver yell from the engine compartment. "I don't know how bad the damage is, but I think we should be okay!"

Siobhan and Valentine shared a look. This didn't seem like a good development. A few seconds later, they heard the loud clang of machinery.

"Never mind!" Oliver shouted again. "The controls melted into reverse! But everything'll be fine as long as the emergency brake holds!"

Siobhan and Valentine shared another look. They heard another clang.

"The emergency brake snapped!"

The two felt a rumble. The train started inching backward.

"This is bad," Valentine said.

The Harborville Express, once dormant in its secret moonshiner's port, began picking up speed as it moved uncontrollably in reverse. All of the train nerds who had been searching through the area immediately scrambled to jump back aboard.

Faster and faster it went, hurtling backward in the confines of the secret tunnel. It approached the stone door at the end of the tunnel like a great battering ram. With a cacophony of bent steel, the rear of the Harborville Express crashed through the stone door at the end of the port.

If one listened closely, they would have been able to hear a loud twang, as if a guitar string had been plucked. A taut wire shot across the ceiling of the mine in the space of milliseconds. The bottles and bottles of moonshine hanging above the stone door were all simultaneously severed from their ropes, crashing downward and dousing the luggage car of the Harborville Express in a shower of government-unregulated libations.

The small fire-starting contraptions, spaced out at intervals throughout the hall, all sparked in unison.

CHAPTER 22

The Big Train Chase Finale

T hus far, the engineer had spent her time in relative quiet at the Lake Nowhere train station. From the cockpit of the Spirit of New Troutstead, she gazed out into the thick, gray fog as it grew darker and darker in the waning minutes of twilight.

Here she was in the present moment. Mindful. At peace. She took a deep breath and then exhaled. The future was bright.

That's when J.J. started pounding on the window to the engine compartment, shocking her back to alertness. She slid the window open to see the young man standing there with Trudi de la Rosa. Both of them were out of breath.

"What's the situation, big guys?"

"We found the Harborville Express!" J.J. exclaimed between gasps. "If you pull into the tunnel, we can block it off before help arrives!"

"This is great news!" the engineer replied. "I'll call it in." She reached for the radio receiver on her dashboard and held it up to her mouth to speak.

A train's horn blasted in the distance. The engineer paused. It blasted again. She set the receiver back in its cradle and joined J.J. and Trudi on the exterior catwalk. They all stared toward the direction of the sound, toward the tunnel out of Lake Nowhere. The horn began blasting in constant intervals.

First there was an orange glow piercing through the fog. And then the glow kept growing, and growing, and growing, until everybody on the Spirit of New Troutstead could tell that something was very, very wrong.

The Harborville Express was traveling backward. That was fine. Trains do that sometimes. What wasn't fine was that the luggage car was entirely engulfed in flames. Enormous plumes of black smoke billowed from the head of the train procession as the Harborville Express screamed in reverse through the fog.

As the flaming hunk of steel shot past them, the occupants of the Spirit of New Troutstead caught a couple interesting sights. First, they saw Luther and a group of train nerds screaming, running through the train cars with fire extinguishers. Then, they spotted Oliver Path, screaming, pounding frantically on the instrument panel in the engine compartment. Then they saw Valentine and Siobhan.

There they were, clinging for dear life onto the front grille of the Harborville Express's engine.

"Help!" the three observers could hear Valentine yell as the two whooshed past.

J.J., Trudi, and the engineer stood in stunned silence for a moment.

Trudi brought them back to the present moment. "Follow that train!"

The three ran back into the engine compartment of the Spirit of New Troutstead and the engineer threw the train into gear. They began rolling out of the Lake Nowhere station, ratcheting up to the faster speed of an unburdened lone engine. "We gotta figure out how to save them," Trudi said.

J.J. stared out along the tracks as they converged into the fog in front of them. In the distance, further obfuscated by the low visibility, he saw the headlights of the Harborville Express. He had an idea.

"Oliver seemed to be occupied by something else," he said. "We can use the fog to sneak up on them."

The engineer nodded and flipped a switch on her instrument panel, killing the headlights that would give them away in the haze. She turned the throttle further forward and they began closing the distance to their target.

* * *

VALENTINE TRIED HIS HARDEST TO peer through the thick fog that had surrounded him and Siobhan, searching for anything that could help the two out of their current predicament. They hung onto metal slats on the front hood of the train, just above the rushing train tracks below them. All they could see was a thick, gray mist. All they could hear was the rushing of the wind and the chugging of the engine. They were stuck.

"Well, now what?" Siobhan screamed over the wind.

"We don't have many options here!" Valentine yelled back. "Has Oliver fixed the train yet?"

Siobhan climbed up the grille to peek over into the engine compartment. There was Oliver, alone, continuing to work on the instrument panel with various train-specialized tools. He touched two stripped wires together, producing a spark. Smiling with relief, he pulled on the brakes.

It was at this moment—in which he pulled the brakes—that the headlights of the Spirit of New Troutstead flashed into being. Siobhan saw Oliver's expression change instantaneously from one of elation to one of terror.

"This is their plan!?" Valentine shouted as the Spirit of New Troutstead bore down onto them. He looked to the side of the Harborville Express and saw sparks showering from the tracks.

"Braking!" shouted the engineer in the cockpit of the Spirit. She, Trudi, and J.J. all braced themselves as she flipped a lever and the brakes engaged.

"Valentine!" Siobhan shouted, pointing at the train that was about to crash into them.

Valentine heard the screeching of the Spirit of New Troutstead's brakes. He saw it gaining on them. He made a snap decision.

"Bail! Bail! Bail!"

The two jumped away from their hiding place on the hood of the Harborville Express.

"Stick the landing! For the love of Christmas!" they could each hear J.J. yelling from the open window of the Spirit.

Siobhan landed in the moist, clumpy sand to one side of the train tracks, while Valentine hit the ground on the dirt fire road that ran along the tracks on the opposite side. They each got up to watch both trains tear away into the fog.

The Spirit of New Troutstead was inches away from colliding with the Harborville Express before the laws of motion took into effect in any reasonable way. The mass of the Harborville Express made its stopping distance considerably longer than that of a single train engine. They came to a halt some several hundred feet away from each other.

Interestingly enough, the luggage car kept going. The flaming husk of steel shot off from the main procession of train cars and coasted out into the fog until it was barely visible.

"Luther must've jettisoned it," Valentine said to Siobhan. "I'm sure Oliver will love that."

As if to confirm, they both heard Oliver's howl of terror at this development all the way over where they were.

"Let's go," Siobhan said. Valentine nodded and they each began running through the dense sand to rejoin their compatriots.

J.J. pulled his head in from the window to readdress Trudi and the engineer. He had confirmed that Siobhan and Valentine had bailed safely but had since lost them in the fog. "Now what?" he asked.

The two trains were at a standstill. The three occupants of the Spirit of New Troutstead gazed through the fog at the headlights of the Harborville Express just ahead.

With a lurch, the Harborville Express reversed direction and moved toward them.

"Well, this is a pickle," said the engineer. She threw the Spirit of New Troutstead in reverse and pushed the throttle.

Valentine and Siobhan slowed their pace when they saw the two trains headed their way. They took a moment to catch their breath, glad that the direction of the train chase had begun moving in a direction more favorable to them.

Then Siobhan noticed something. "They're speeding up."

Valentine squinted through the fog to confirm that they were, in fact, speeding up. It was by a considerable amount. Before long the familiar red sweater of J.J.'s pierced through the fog. He was out on the catwalk for the Spirit of New Troutstead. His hand was outstretched.

"Oh, here we go," Valentine said. He and Siobhan began running in the direction that the train was headed. By the time the trains had closed the distance, the Spirit of New Troutstead was hard to keep up with.

It was here that Trudi saw something alarming. Up until this point, she had believed only Oliver had occupied the engine compartment of the Harborville Express. But now that the two trains were closer, she saw Luther had since entered, dragging the princess along with him. He and Oliver were having an argument. Against the train nerd's protestations, Luther slammed the throttle forward.

Valentine ran at an all-out sprint toward his brother, outstretching his hand to meet J.J.'s. Siobhan followed closely behind.

"Grab on, you dingus!" J.J. shouted.

And it was in this moment, when Valentine lunged forward to grab his brother's wrist, that the Harborville Express rammed the Spirit of New Troutstead.

There was a loud bang and a crunch of steel. J.J. lost his grip on his brother as he was heaved across the catwalk.

Valentine faltered, tripped, and tumbled through the sand, tripping Siobhan on the way down.

They both looked on helplessly as the two trains sped past them, leaving them stranded in the dust.

* * *

"WE MIGHT HAVE LOST VALENTINE and Siobhan for the remainder of this train chase," J.J. said with a frustrated look as he reentered the engine compartment from the catwalk. "Is everyone okay?"

"I had never before in my life been rammed by another train," the engineer said. "It was a unique human experience, one that I'll cherish for the rest of my life." Then, "It only seems like surface damage. We're still rolling on the tracks."

The Spirit continued traveling backward at high velocity to keep up with the increasing speed of the Harborville Express.

And they're close enough to see each other here, aren't they? Luther from the cockpit of his train, J.J. and Trudi from the cockpit of theirs. Luther could just shoot one of them right now and get the character death over with, couldn't he? Of course he could.

Luther reached into his coat pocket, producing his revolver. He held it level to his eye, aiming directly at J.J.'s heart.

No, no, it doesn't feel right yet.

"Do you have any idea how hard train windshields are to replace?" Oliver demanded, pushing Luther's arm off-target. "You're not damaging *my* train any further!"

Luther groaned in frustration. He exited the cabin and leaned off of the side of the catwalk, aiming once again toward the train ahead of him. But by that time they were too far ahead into the fog. He groaned again.

I'll have to find another way.

"I'm open to ideas," the engineer said to the two present members of the Ghost Hunters Adventure Club.

"I don't suppose you could slam on the brakes and let the Harborville Express crash into us in order to make it stop, could you?" J.J. asked.

"That sounds like a horrible idea," the engineer replied.

Trudi stuck her head out of the engine compartment's window and looked behind them. There among the fog was the faint outline of the Lake Nowhere train station. "Those are electric switches coming up, right?" she asked.

"That's correct."

"Get on the alternate tracks and we can get behind them."

"How's that gonna help?" asked J.J.

"I've got a plan."

By this point, J.J. knew to trust Trudi when she had a plan. Hers seemed to always involve less fire than his. He looked over to the engineer. "Can you make it happen?"

"Hold onto something," the engineer replied. "Our approach is something I would describe as 'screaming.'"

She punched some buttons on her dashboard. The switch in tracks came up beneath them and they felt the Spirit of New Troutstead shift violently, lurching them over to the side of the cabin. She punched some more buttons to return the switch to its original position once they had cleared it.

"Hold onto something again!" yelled the engineer as she slammed the brakes.

Everyone in the compartment braced as they were thrust forward. They looked out of the window again to see the Harborville Express shoot past them on the parallel tracks.

"You're gonna want to hold onto something for a third time!" shouted the engineer, as the Spirit of New Troutstead took another hard turn to merge again with the main tracks.

J.J. could have sworn that he could feel the Spirit of New Troutstead raise up off one side of the rails as the inertia hit. It was as if they were attempting an ill-advised sort of multi-track drift. The Spirit of New Troutstead passed just inches away from the Harborville Express before rocking back to level as it rejoined the main line. A collision would have been catastrophic for all involved.

But now there they were, traveling backward, behind the Harborville Express.

"Punch it!" Trudi yelled.

Right here was where the engineer understood the plan. She pushed the throttle full speed ahead in reverse, gaining ground against the charred end of the train they were chasing. After a few tense moments they felt their cabin jerk violently. The back end of the Spirit of New Troutstead had connected with the second-class passenger compartment of the Harborville Express.

"Can you stop it?" J.J. asked the engineer.

"I can slow it down," she responded, throwing her brake line. Everyone heard a screech as their train car engaged its brakes, and once again they braced themselves against the inertia.

J.J. looked over to Trudi. "Boarding party?"

"Boarding party," she agreed. The two made for the exterior catwalk.

Trudi stopped at the door to the compartment, readdressing the engineer. "I'm sorry for threatening to beat you up. Thanks for everything."

"I needed it," said the engineer with a great gleam of hope in her eyes. She held a closed fist to her heart as a sign of gratitude. "Thank *you*."

The two nodded at each other before Trudi left the compartment. She felt the same hope as the engineer.

J.J. and Trudi traversed over the exterior catwalk to the adjoining corridor, now attached to the second-class passenger car of the Harborville Express. The two hopped across the gap and crouched in front of the door.

"We don't know what's on the other side of that door," J.J. said.

"I don't care," Trudi responded.

"Odds are against us here."

"I still don't care."

J.J. nodded. "All right, then let's go solve the mystery of whose ass we're about to kick." He placed one hand on the handle of the second-class compartment entrance. With the other he held up three fingers, ready to count them down.

Three.

Two.

One.

He paused on one. "I'm really glad you're on the team," he said.

Trudi smiled.

Zero. He opened the door and the two ran into the Harborville Express.

There had been no welcoming party there to greet them in the hallway. Just random effects from passengers knocked loose in the recent train-chase events. They marched forward, sidling around open passenger compartments to circumvent any surprise attack from enemies unknown.

It was at the end of the train car when they saw Oliver Path. He stood in the adjoining corridor to the lounge car. He was carrying a long, iron crowbar. Tears were streaming down his face.

"I cannot describe to you how much I don't want to do this," Oliver said. He jammed the tool downward into the gap between the cars and twisted. Trudi and J.J. heard the sound of screeching metal. Then they saw the lounge car slowly drift away.

"He unhooked the train cars!" Trudi shouted.

The two members of the Ghost Hunters Adventure Club bolted forward toward the widening chasm between the two trains. J.J. jumped first, knocking Oliver back and sending his crowbar skittering across the floor of the lounge. Trudi was next, clearing the gap over the rushing train tracks with great disregard to her own safety. The second-class passenger car disappeared into the fog with the Spirit of New Troutstead in the space of moments. Trudi and J.J. were two *very* angry adventurers on a mission.

"You," J.J. growled, pointing at Oliver. "Come here, you little nerd."

Oliver Path screamed, grabbing his crowbar and stumbling over to the other end of the lounge car. What J.J. saw made his stomach twist in a knot.

There, across from the broken champagne flutes, the spilled drinks, a once plot-relevant piano, and a variety of discarded baseball equipment were the ten other members of the Harborville Train Appreciation Society. Each of them brandished a train-specialized tool in their hands.

Oliver grinned. "You're not going any further."

J.J. worked over the numbers in his head. "Trudes, how many nerds do you think you could take? Conservatively I'd say three myself."

"Definitely not enough to cover the spread," Trudi responded. "We're gonna have to figure something out."

The young man sprang into action, grabbing a baseball that had been rolling across the floor of the lounge. He tossed it to his compatriot.

"What do you want me to do with this?" Trudi asked.

"A well-placed fastball would incapacitate the group's leader, leaving his henchmen directionless and disoriented."

Trudi got it. In one swift and fluid motion, she turned her sights on Oliver Path, wound up her throwing arm, and hurled the meanest four-seamer that she could rally.

The baseball traveled at a strange tangent to where Trudi had initially aimed. It flew across the room and broke one of the windows of the lounge.

Oliver screamed. "My train!"

"Trudi!" shouted J.J.

"What?"

"I thought you knew baseball! You had all of those cool statistics!"

"There's a huge difference between *knowing* baseball and playing baseball."

J.J. gulped. The two turned to face the small army of train nerds marching toward them. They each raised their fists and squared up against their assailants.

"You take the eight on the left," J.J. said.

The group of train nerds halted in their tracks when a horn sounded.

Now, in this situation, a train horn would have been fine. Welcome, even. Any member of the Harborville Train Appreciation Society could have told you exactly what kind of train the sound of that horn belonged to. Some of them could probably even classify it by year and production line number.

However, this wasn't a train horn.

It was a bus horn.

J.J., Trudi, and the group of train nerds all turned their heads to look out of the window. There, on the fire road running parallel to the train tracks, kicking up dirt as it kept pace with the Harborville Express, was a school bus. Across its side read, "New Troutstead Elementary."

"The Cordelians!" J.J. yelled, as he ran to the window to witness the sight for himself. Coach Hank, in his cowboy hat, was driving the school bus. He honked the horn a few more times and waved to J.J.

Just behind him, handcuffed to their seats, were Inspector Sandor Horvath of Neutral Moldevik and Officer Hot Dog of the New Troutstead PD. Neither of them looked happy.

Behind them, and perhaps the most menacing part of the tableau, were the variety of baseball players hanging out of the windows of the school bus. They looked like they were ready for a good scrap.

And then J.J. lit up. Standing in the open entryway to the school bus with determined looks on their faces were none other than Valentine Watts and Siobhan Sweeney.

J.J. couldn't hide the grin forming across his cheeks. He looked over to the train nerds. "Excuse me."

Walking down a set of steps, he opened the doors to the lounge car. Where one would have normally found a train platform to step out onto, J.J. instead found that he was just feet away from the open doors of the moving school bus.

"Virtue, honesty, and steadfastness!" shouted Coach Hank. He honked the horn a few more times to showcase his enthusiasm.

Siobhan jumped aboard first, running up the steps and over to Trudi to face Oliver Path and his band of train-nerd henchmen. Valentine was next, giving a nod to his brother on the way up.

Then came the starting lineup of the Harborville Elks Minor League Baseball Team.

J.J. waved once more to Coach Hank, who honked his horn a few more times before peeling off of the access road. The young adventurer then walked up the stairs and joined his friends.

The two groups stared each other down. The baseball team cracking their knuckles. The train nerds gripping up on their specialized train tools.

And here they are, all of my main characters, on the train now. I'm running out of time. I have to make a decision.

Siobhan broke the silence. "Play ball."

What ensued was violent. Not death-of-a-main-character-violent. But still pretty up there. Siobhan Sweeney, Trudi de la Rosa, Valentine Watts, and a group of athletically talented baseball players/royal guard to a princess all jumped into the melee. They ducked and dodged specialized train tools swung by frantic nerds.

J.J. Watts, however, did not join the fray. He had one person on his mind. He began walking toward Oliver Path, first stepping over a baseball player who had a train nerd on the ground in a headlock. He ducked under a flying train nerd, launched by a baseball player, who soared into the baby grand piano at the other end of the room. It made an extremely satisfying twanging sound.

J.J. walked past Valentine as he threw some impressive uppercuts into the chin of yet another train nerd. He stepped around Trudi, all elbows, real clinical.

Oliver Path saw J.J. on the warpath. Oliver shrieked, dropped his crowbar, and fell over himself running backward. J.J. followed him, at whatever damn pace he felt like, as the nerd stumbled out of the lounge.

Oliver made it a few steps into the aisle between dining tables before he tripped. He crawled forward a few more feet before he felt a hand on the lapel of his dress shirt.

"I can give you your flashlight back!" he yelped.

J.J. pulled him up and spun him around, staring him directly in the face. "It's not about the flashlight."

He then rocked him across the chin with an almighty right cross. A sick crack echoed around the empty dining room.

J.J. held up his fist again, Oliver squirming in his grasp. "Renounce your membership to the Ghost Hunters Adventure Club!" he demanded.

"I renounce my membership to the Ghost Hunters Adventure Club!" Oliver wailed.

"Be more formal about it!"

"What?"

J.J. cocked his fist back again.

"I hereby declare the dissolution of my relationship, both personal and professional, with the entity known as Ghost Hunters Adventure Club! I wish them the best in their future endeavors as I depart to pursue my own!" he rattled.

"Your resignation has been tendered and verbally cosigned," J.J. said.

"J.J.!" Valentine yelled, as he and Trudi ran in from the fracas in the lounge car.

And now here the three are. We're almost to the end of the story. One of them has to get to the front of the train. To where Luther is.

Luther with his gun.

"Now tell us," said J.J. "Where's the princess?"

I can't put it off any longer. I have to choose.

Okay, you know what? Hold on.

CHAPTER 23

Why It's Okay to Kill These Kids, and Which Kid I'm Going to Kill

You're going soft, kid.

Yes, I'm talking to you, dear reader. Here we are, you and me, floating in a gray expanse of nothingness. It's pretty bleak, right? There's not a lot of scenery to chew on. No horizon line to give a sense of depth. It's all just gray. I would describe this as a pretty boring scene, visually.

So here's where you say something to the effect of, "Hey Dr. Cecil, why are we floating out here in the Nothing? Couldn't you have staged this scene literally anywhere other than the liminal space between chapters? Possibly somewhere with a discernible x-axis?"

The answer is no. And it's not because of any sort of limit to my imagination. It's because I'm trying to illustrate a point. Let me be crystal clear right now:

We're floating out here in this gray void because it's all we'll be able to afford if the Yacht Plan fails.

Buddy, we're so close to the end of the book. We have so few pages left. I don't know where you've been for the past indiscernible amount of time, but I've been right here, day after day, hammering at my typewriter.

243

I'm toiling at a breakneck pace to produce fast, quality *Content* for a rapidly growing fanbase with an ever-dwindling patience and an insatiable need to devour.

I am working very, very hard. As hard as I would have worked on an adult novel, even. So I would appreciate it, immensely, if you'd stop letting your feelings about these characters get in the way of me needing to kill one of them.

They're idiots, the Ghost Hunters Adventure Club. All of them. Here they are getting in over their heads yet again. Here they are being driven forward by a naive understanding of justice and an overinflated compulsion to "do what's right."

Listen, I understand how one could get attached to them. I would know as well as anyone. I've spent two entire manuscript production cycles with the Ghost Hunters Adventure Club. There are pieces of me in each and every single character in these books, but most of all within J.J., Valentine, and Trudi. Within those three are fragments of my soul that took decades of sorrow, joy, rage, and anguish to excavate. Their victories are my victories, their pain is my pain. And I would be terrible at my job if you didn't feel that way too.

They are idiots, yes. But they are idiots who learn and grow, who make mistakes, who get knocked down but get back up. They are idiots who care for one another, who protect one another, who see a bright vision of the future and fight their damndest to make that vision a reality. They are mirrors we look into. We can gaze into them, so that we may gaze inward within ourselves, to find those pieces within us that make us special.

But at the very end of the day—and I'm sorry to be the one to tell you this horrible truth—these idiots are nothing more than words on a page. And those words on a page have a primary goal. And that primary goal is to make money.

The point is that it hurts. Can't you see? It's supposed to be as painful as possible to lose a character who means so much to us. We're here to manufacture outrage, to create as deep and as wide a chasm as possible.

We want people to have to shout indignantly over one another to be heard, for journalists to slap together poorly researched articles about fan outrage. Because that's what keeps their attention, that's what sells Content, and that's what puts us on yachts.

This is what separates me from you, dear reader, and this is the reason why our partnership will succeed. I'm willing to make these hard calls for the both of us. I'm willing to circumvent any emotion that might prevent me from success. You don't have to agree with the decisions I make. Hell, sometimes *I* don't even agree with them. But we're past the point of no return. All the foreshadowing is there, and I'm sticking to it.

Be as mad as you want. Go ahead. It makes us both more money that way. But when the dust settles at the end of this book and you feel betrayed, don't blame me. Blame Art's relationship to Capitalism.

* * *

Now, with reactionary emotions completely removed and our commitment to the Yacht Plan reaffirmed, let's figure out who to kill.

J.J. could be an option. That would be a wild left turn, wouldn't it? The plucky and quotable leader of the Ghost Hunters Adventure Club is struck down unceremoniously, leaving Valentine and Trudi to pick up the pieces in the coming sequels.

But his arc doesn't feel complete yet. It wouldn't be satisfying enough. There has to be something else.

Trudi might work. It's starting to bother me how dead to rights she has me, how understanding she's becoming of the metanarrative. I could cut that off right now with a few easy sentences and never have to worry about a character talking back to me ever again.

No, no, that would just be petty. That isn't right either.

Hmm...

I suppose that just leaves us with the young man who has foreshadowed it the most. Yes, that makes sense. Of course that makes sense.

He's the one person whose acceptance of responsibility is at the crux of this very story. He's someone who can pay the worst price that responsibility can ask of someone.

Yes, he'll do.

Valentine.

It has to be Valentine.

CHAPTER 24

Chekhov's Gun

J.J.'s hand hung menacingly in the air, just in front of Oliver Path's nose. "She's in the engine compartment with Luther!" the train nerd volunteered under the fear of being punched again. "But you're too late. Once we get to the bridge they'll be long gone."

"Wow, thanks for all the information," J.J. said. He loosened his grip on Oliver's shirt. "I wouldn't have been able to hit you again, though. My hand is super broken."

He unclenched his punching fist and let out a prolonged groan of pain.

"The bridge?" asked Trudi. "What happens at the bridge?"

The image of the great bridge over the even-greater river flashed through Valentine's mind. The final puzzle piece fell into place. He had to move quickly. He didn't have much time. "Keep an eye on J.J. and help the baseball players close out," he said to Trudi as he sidled around the cowering frame of Oliver Path. "Don't follow me."

"What are you doing?" asked J.J.

"I'm getting to Luther before he gets to the bridge." He kept marching down the aisle of the dining car.

"Valentine!" Trudi called out. "He has a gun."

Valentine stopped. He thought it over. He turned to his two friends. "Well, we do the right thing, even if it isn't the easy thing."

And with that, he left.

J.J., cradling his crumpled hand by the wrist, blinked a few times. He looked back and forth between Trudi and Oliver Path.

"What a great mission statement."

Valentine burst into the hallway of the first-class passenger car, pausing at the window for a moment to see the foggy landscape hurtling by. He took a deep breath, and stared at his fate before him. He ran forward.

But did he really understand where he was running to? Did he really understand the gravity of his situation? He was an idiot. I wrote him to be an idiot. Just a stupid, mystery-solving teen. We all think we're invincible at that age.

So, no. Of course he didn't get it. That's why he was running forward. It was his blinding preoccupation with helping those in need that overrode his own sense of self preservation.

But was that fair to him? Was that fair to what he learned in the past couple hundred pages? Hadn't he grown to understand complex feelings? Wasn't that core to his sacrifice?

So he did get it, actually.

And yet he kept running forward. The damned fool was running to his doom—and he knew it! The end was approaching. I don't know what to do. Dammit I don't know what to do. The train roared on. And just as the Harborville Express screamed into the Lake Nowhere tunnel, he entered...he entered...

He entered the presidential suite!

"Valentine!" I yelled as he burst through the doors of the adjoining corridor. He looked surprised to see me. I was just as surprised to see him.

"I'm so glad you're here," I said. I jumped up from my typewriter and hurried over to place myself between him and the exit at the other end of the train car. "I had a couple story revisions I wanted to run by you."

"I appreciate the invitation into the creative process, Dr. Cecil," Valentine began, "but we're running out of time here."

"There's this coffee shop in New Troutstead. It's just off the main street, tucked away in a cozy little nook. But don't worry, there's still plenty of foot traffic. It, um, it needs a full-time staff to run it."

"Doctor, I need to be going." He attempted to step around me. But there I went, getting in his way again.

"You guys can hop off at the next stop and start brand new lives out there. You'll still experience the day-to-day situational hilarity of working at a small business with your friends, only the stakes will be way, way lower. There'll be sassy clientele and funny comedic back and forths and—"

"Dr. Cecil…"

"And I've already got a great title for it," I said, motioning with my hand to visualize the name in lights. "*Ghost Hunters Adventure Club and the Caper of You Have to Buy Something First Before I Give You the Wifi Code.*"

"Dr. Cecil!" Valentine shouted. "As soon as we get through this tunnel, there's a big bridge over a river that leads to New Troutstead. The smugglers couldn't just roll into the station with all of their illegal moonshine, so what'd they do instead? They floated it down the river, Doc. That's how Luther's gonna get away with the princess and the jewels!"

"Well would you look at that!" I raised my eyebrows in surprise. "You solved the final piece to the mystery! You did it! Why don't you tell me how you figured it out while you relax for a bit on this custom suede loveseat."

"I have to go." Valentine pushed past me. He was determined to make it to the front of the train. To where Luther was.

"You don't wanna go there," I said, unable to stifle the crack in my voice. I didn't know what else to say.

"And why not?"

"You just don't." I could feel a burning in my throat. "Can you just trust me here?"

"I don't have time for this," Valentine said. He turned away from me and began walking away toward the exit of the presidential car. To the end.

"Don't you get that we have all the time in the world?" I blurted out. The words hit Valentine like a speeding train.

"It can take however long I damn well please for us to get to the bridge!" I said, even louder now. I stepped up to the know-nothing idiot who couldn't tell what was good for him, pointing a finger in his stupid idiot face.

"We can sail through this tunnel for all eternity if I want. I could show you the entire universe on the tip of an atom in the space of a nanosecond. I could turn stone to bread. Water into wine. I can make you explode into a thousand tiny little pieces before I reform you, piece by piece, into a character who knows what's good for him! I am the one in control here!"

I was heaving now. The rage blinded me. "You. Do not. Want to go through that door. When are you gonna grow up?"

Here was where the stale rubber bands snapped.

I didn't manage to catch myself as the words came out of my mouth. But there it was. The central theme.

I couldn't hold onto him any longer. I watched him turn away from me. I watched him walk through the exit of my train car. I watched him disappear behind the final door to the engine.

This was it.

Valentine marched through the outer catwalk of the engine compartment as the Harborville Express shot out of the Lake Nowhere tunnel. Where once there was fog, there was now the cloudless night sky over New Troutstead. The bridge was just up ahead. There was nothing I could do now.

The door to the engine compartment slid open. Luther stepped out, one hand gripping the arm of Princess Annalise. The other hand was wrapped around his pistol.

"You shouldn't have come here," he said, extending the gun forward. He held the sights between Valentine's eyes.

Valentine stared down the barrel of the revolver, at the six lead slugs encased in brass, ready to punch as many holes into the poor fool's hopes and dreams. Everything hung helplessly in the balance of this very moment. It wasn't right. Goddammit, it wasn't right.

They're just kids, for Christ's sake!

I threw open the door to the engine compartment and burst forth onto the catwalk, making a mad dash for Valentine and Luther. I didn't care about controversy. I didn't care about yachts. I only cared about what was in front of me.

And just as Luther fired, I dove.

I didn't hear the bang. Only ringing. A loud and all-consuming ringing. There was an unbearable pressure in my chest, as if I was deep underwater.

I turned to face Valentine, my mouth slack. I followed his eyes and looked down. Blood ran in trails through the fingers I clenched around my heart.

I stumbled past him, bracing myself on the railing of the catwalk, catching a glimpse of the dark, glassy rapids way down beneath me. I looked back at them. Then I looked up.

"Stars," I said, pointing up at the night sky…before falling down, down, down into the river below.

* * *

AND…I SUPPOSE THIS MAKES things a little difficult, having a story without a narrator. That's probably bad form, even for me. I suppose…well…I suppose the best thing for me to do now is just butt out of it and tell you the rest of the story as it happens.

Still, if it bothers you, feel free to imagine me shouting the entire rest of the story at you in one last dying breath as I hurtle into the abyss. That might be a little more immersive.

* * *

"DR. CECIL!" VALENTINE SHOUTED OVER the railing, as he watched my body disappear into the inky blackness.

That was where the princess utilized the confusion to her benefit. Shaking loose of Luther's grip, she lunged for his pistoled hand, latching on with her teeth and giving his wrist an excruciating bite.

Luther howled in pain, dropping his revolver. It skittered across the catwalk, falling off the ledge of the train and in an arc toward the river bank below.

In the next motion she reached into his coat pocket and pulled out the ruby jewels of the duchess of Cordelia. The precious stones sparkled in the moonlight as Luther caught hold of them, leaving the two locked in an expensive game of tug-of-war.

"It's over, Luther," Valentine said. "We're past the bridge."

Luther's eyes went wide. He looked across the catwalk. Land surrounded them.

"No!" He shouted. He snatched the jewels back from the princess and hurled her at Valentine. Staggering forward, she tripped, tumbling through the gap in the railing that led to the service ladder.

Valentine dove, catching her at the last second. Her baseball cleats hovered precariously over the rushing terrain beneath her.

Luther stuffed the jewels back into his coat pocket and made a break for the only direction he had left: toward the presidential car. He threw open the door to the adjoining corridor, tore into the suite, and tripped over a long, iron crowbar. He faceplanted into the bookshelf full of copies of *Cerberus, From On High*. Covered in a shower of literature, he turned around, looking in horror at his assailant.

There was Siobhan Sweeney, still in her Harborville Elks hat and undercover cop outfit, crowbar in hand. She picked Luther up by the lapels of his coat, leaned in close, and whispered in his ear. "I'm not to be trifled with."

"Die slow, asshole!" came a shout. And flying in through the open door to the suite was Princess Annalise of Cordelia, kneecap first, delivering a shattering blow to Luther's stomach. He doubled over in pain, falling onto his knees before her.

Valentine ran into the room next, where he saw Luther incapacitated. He saw the princess, now free, getting a couple more choice words over on Luther. Then he saw Siobhan.

"You did it!" he shouted in disbelief.

Siobhan looked at Valentine and smiled. "*We* did it."

Brushing herself off, she picked up the crowbar as she walked past Valentine into the adjoining corridor between the presidential suite and the engine. There was no fear. There was no terror. There were just two people.

"You know," Siobhan turned to him. "I've been meaning to tell you something."

"Yeah?" asked Valentine. The two stood there between the engine and the presidential suite. They were nose to nose, eyes staring deeply into one another's.

"I always thought you were the smart brother," she said.

Valentine was shocked. His face immediately flushed. "Do you...do you mean it?"

She flipped open an access compartment with the long iron crowbar in her hand. Jamming it downward and giving it a twist. There was a lurch and a screech as metal decoupled from metal.

"No," Siobhan snorted. She and the rest of the engine car began slowly drifting away from the presidential suite. Valentine watched in disbelief.

It was a few seconds before he understood what was happening, and even more before he figured out what to say.

"Are we even?" he shouted across the gap.

"I'll think about it," Siobhan shouted back. Then she reached into her own coat pocket and, smiling one last time in the demure way that she did, unfurled the ruby jewels of the duchess of Cordelia.

Valentine watched Siobhan and the engine of the Harborville Express slowly disappear into the distance. He stared at the city lights hanging over New Troutstead for a while before he heard the knocking. Walking back to the other end of the train car, to the opposite adjoining corridor, he saw J.J., Trudi, and several members of the Harborville Elks through the glass windows of the entryway. They were pounding on the door.

Removing the specialty train tool that Siobhan had jammed into the handle, he allowed the cadre of allies into the presidential suite so they could witness the aftermath themselves.

"What happened?" asked Trudi, looking from Princess Annalise to Luther to the engineless front end of the train. They were coasting to a slow, rolling stop miles away from their destination.

Valentine sighed. He sat down on the comfiest custom-made couch he could find. "I think it's over."

CHAPTER 25

The Federal Train Governance Commission

J.J., Valentine, and Trudi sat, unhandcuffed, on three separate chairs across from a desk in a small, nondescript office. Fluorescent lights hung overhead, filling the tiny room with a sterile glow.

The three were covered in lake salt, smoke, and a variety of scuff marks. They had been waiting there for some time. J.J. kept his hand, now bandaged after seeking medical attention, elevated above his head.

"My hand hurts," he said.

The door behind them opened and a man in a gray suit walked in. Remarkable only in his unremarkability, his salt-and-pepper hair was fashioned into an angular flat top. Dark, horn-rimmed glasses sat on his face.

Sitting down at his desk with an air of stern professionalism, he studied the disheveled members of the Ghost Hunters Adventure Club.

"My name is Mr. Union," the man said. "I represent the interests of the Federal Train Governance Commission."

None of the three club members spoke. This was in part because of their distaste for authority figures, but also in part because none of them had any idea what the FTGC wanted from them.

"That was quite an event you three participated in today. Luggage car up in flames. Theft of and damage to the Spirit of New Troutstead. The Harborville Express engine abandoned at the New Troutstead train depot, without the rest of its train…"

Valentine looked up. "Abandoned? Siobhan was on that train engine. What happened to her?"

"The Harborville Express was empty when we found it. I unfortunately have no information on the whereabouts of Miss Sweeney," the man said. "But rest assured that my agents are on the case."

He leaned forward, interlocking his fingers as he rested them on his gray, nondescript desk. "Do you three realize just how much trouble you caused?"

"Oh, if this is where the line of questioning is going," J.J. responded, "then I'm not saying another word until my lawyer gets here. When you see him, never mind that he's a dead ringer for me with a fake mustache and a fun British accent. That's just his personal style."

Mr. Union didn't react. He stared at J.J. "Son, the locomotive industry isn't the most exciting industry in the world, we all understand that. It's not the most high-tech, it's not at the cutting edge of innovation, it's not sexy, it's not cool. And yet locomotion is one of the longest-lasting American industries in the history of our fair nation. Why do you think that is?"

The three adventures looked back and forth between one another. None of them had an answer.

"It's because we're patient," Mr. Union said. "When the world is changing, when the populace is governed by fear and uncertainty, when no one knows what the future will hold, there the trains will be; running on time and to budget. The Federal Train Governance Commission will be—as it always has been—putting one track in front of the other."

He went on, resting his elbows on the desk and leaning further forward. "And in that patience is a perseverance. It is a willingness to wake up every morning from here to eternity in order to do the job we have chosen to do. To uphold train law to the letter with which it has served us since time immemorial."

The three sat up when they heard that word again. Train law.

"What you three did back there was a selfless act of bravery, done in the face of danger for a cause you truly believe in. You displayed courage and conviction the likes of which anyone from the lowliest signalman to the most influential chief mechanical engineer could admire. If that isn't living your life in accordance with train law, then I don't know what is."

The three members of the Ghost Hunters Adventure Club shared looks with one another, trying to confirm if they should be feeling the sense of relief that they were currently feeling.

"What are you trying to say?" asked Trudi.

Mr. Union stood up from his desk and made a slow walk around it. "We're closing the book on this. The Federal Train Commission is burying the story."

"Are you kidding?" Valentine said incredulously. "Train cars were on fire! There was a multi-country conspiracy! Priceless jewels were stolen! How does that not get plastered all over Carly Contreras's WHAB evening broadcast?"

"We all just avoided a horrifying international geopolitical scandal on American soil, Mr. Watts." The man reached the door to his office and gripped the handle. "Let me remind you that Big Locomotive is *big*. We're able to make things like this disappear. You don't want to be on the wrong side of the tracks from us."

"Ha," J.J. let out a little chortle.

"What?" Mr. Union asked sharply.

"It's...uh..." J.J. felt embarrassed. "It was just a funny pun, you know, 'on the wrong side of the tracks?' It was a nice turn of phrase."

"There's nothing funny about Big Locomotive," Mr. Union said.

This silenced J.J. The man went on.

"We're flying the princess and her royal guard back to Cordelia. Sandor Horvath is going back to Neutral Moldevik. Rudith Espiritu keeps her job at the museum. The engineer goes back to work for us. We'll take care of Luther. It's as if the events of today never even happened." Mr. Union opened the door to his office, revealing a gray hallway just beyond it. "You're all free to go as well."

"But what about the rubies?" asked Trudi as the three got up from their chairs.

"Whereabouts unknown," he responded. "It's something the Cordelians and the Neutral Moldevickians will have to work out between each other. But the Federal Train Governance Commission continues to be patient. It can work outside of the bounds of traditional investigation. If this Siobhan Sweeney character is to be found, we'll find her."

"So that's it?" asked J.J. "Everything's back to normal? Everything's fine? We don't see any financial recompense for our troubles?"

"There is one thing," said Mr. Union. "While we can't offer you any remuneration for this event, as per train law doctrine, there is something else. J.J., Valentine, Trudi, I'd like to bestow upon you the highest honor the Federal Train Governance Commission can offer a non-industry civilian."

He reached into his suit pocket and pressed a badge onto the chests of each member of the Ghost Hunters Adventure Club. He stood back and they all looked down. They were now each wearing small pins embossed with the image of a train. Just below it read:

Junior Train Conductor

Mr. Union nodded at them. "Congratulations. These come with novelty conductor hats, if you'd like them."

* * *

J.J., VALENTINE, AND TRUDI SAT on the steps of the Federal Train Governance Commission building under the night sky of New Troutstead.

Beaten down and tired, they were safe for the first time since they stepped onto the Harborville Express this morning.

Each of them had, on their heads, their own novelty conductor's hats.

"What'd he mean by saying, 'We'll be watching you, as Big Locomotive always does?'" asked Trudi.

"I'd take that as a threat," Valentine replied.

J.J. took a deep breath. "Trudi, you deserve to know everything about our past. No more secrets from here on out."

Trudi looked from Valentine to J.J. "I'm fine not knowing."

Valentine raised his eyebrows. "What do you mean?"

"You're allowed to have your past and you're allowed to be as ashamed of it as you want. That you two are actively trying to become better says all I need to hear about your worth as people. I'll find out about anything you want to tell me, whenever you feel ready to tell it to me."

There was a secret handshake performed here.

"Well, said J.J. glumly, "I hope everyone had a fun Ghost Hunters Adventure Club First Inaugural Leadership Summit. Didn't exactly go how we wanted it to."

"Don't be so down," said Trudi. "We've still got two more days of the summit."

"Yeah," said Valentine. "The first day was a bit alternatively-scheduled, but I think we all learned some valuable things about leadership."

J.J.'s eyes lit up. "Y'know, I bet it's still not too late to go check in at the New Troutstead Inn and Suites. We could really get things back into swing."

"It's the right thing to do, even if it isn't the easy thing to do," said Valentine, smiling.

The three got up and walked down into the lamplit city streets of New Troutstead with a certain lightness to them. The air had a chill to it. It was quiet.

J.J. looked over to his two friends. A thought occurred to him.

"That's strange. I feel freer than usual."

THE END

Epilogue

Well, this is awkward.

Hello, dear reader. Dr. Cecil H.H. Mills here. You remember me, right? The author who let his feelings get the better of him and sacrificed himself so that the three main characters of this novel could live? That was an unexpected twist for all of us.

To confirm, yes, I'm still dead. Very dead. And if that was a spoiler for you, I want you to know that I feel no remorse for having written it. Who reads epilogues first? It's unholy.

In any case, here I am doing the "Dear Reader" letter answering section at the end of the book. This might be confusing; sure, I'll concede that. In fact, the only way this epilogue will work, canonically, is if you imagine my mangled corpse floating in knee-deep water on the banks of a river, emitting death rattles in the vague form of answers to reader questions.

Dr. Cecil is dead. Never mind how I'm writing this or whose voice you hear in your head. I get paid to write, not to unpack complex concepts for Young Adult readers.

So right about now seems like a good time to let you—the demographically-relevant, impressionable youth—know a bit more about how the world works. You see, modern society only exists because of one reason. And that reason is contractual obligations. It's as simple as that.

If it weren't for a clause buried deep within a contract filed away in a basement somewhere that expressly forbade it, we'd all be bashing each other's skulls in with rocks for use as a rudimentary form of currency.

When you sign a contract, you are bound by the incongruous and oftentimes contradictory laws of man. And while I have at times leveraged this to my advantage, I will readily admit that sometimes you write yourself into a corner, and sometimes you realize that you have to deliver one final chapter or lose your publishing deal altogether.

So here we are.

First things first: No, I *will not* be answering questions about the damage I did to the concept of narrative storytelling by killing myself off in the finale of this book. However, I *will* say that when I hurl a character off of a cliff, I have never and will never do so lightly. That would be a disservice to the art and the craft of storytelling that I hold so dear. Imagine how cheap it would be for me to think up some completely illogical way for Dr. Cecil to have survived that fall from the bridge. He is not coming back. Wouldn't you prefer to have art that is respectful of your intelligence? Consider reading an adult novel for once.

To wit, by following this thread I come to the bad news: It is with a heavy heart that I say that the novel you hold in your hands is the very last novel of the Ghost Hunters Adventure Club series. Now, far be it from me to cut myself off from a promising revenue stream, but my actions in the last few chapters were weak, embarrassing, and foretelling of questions about the human condition that require deeper self-reflection. I could explore those questions, sure. I could spend more time in this universe to better understand my feelings about these characters and what drove me to sacrifice myself for their safety. That would probably lead me down a road of self-actualization—toward understanding why I'm here on this earth. I would become a better person.

Or—here's an interesting idea—I could just end the series here and avoid that hard work altogether.

The choice seems easy.

Still, I remain here, for the remainder of the chapter, to answer your no-doubt burning questions with an open heart and wizened mind. Have at me, dear reader.

Hi Dr. Cecil,

Do you have any writing advice for aspiring authors? There seems to be so many conflicting opinions about the craft, and I wondered if there were any insights from your long and illustrious career to help me become a great writer?

Tobias, Age 16

Tobias,

Read a lot and write a lot. Anyone who tells you anything different is trying to sell you something.

Dear Dr. Cecil,

What's your favorite color?

Briony, Age 13

Briony,

To be clear, I am trying to sell you something. And any fool who wants to part with their money for a lengthy and heavily-upsold master course filled with basic craft 101 tips, please see how to reach me in the back matter of this book.

Alternatively, you can treat writing like any other craft that takes time to master. Learn what to fix, fix it, and repeat that process until you're the sort of craftsman you want to be.

Briony—it's orange.

Dear Doctor,

Do you have a favorite beverage that you like to consume while writing?

Ian, Age 14

Ian,

Coffee and sparkling water. Listen. I thought about my last two responses for a long time before coming back to this one. Something felt wrong about them. It was like I was missing a gigantic piece of a puzzle.

You see, writing isn't just a craft, despite how much I wish it were. Labeling it as such would be a disservice to why I think we create art in the first place. To me, art is meant to process that which we experience in life, to further understand it and to better ourselves because of it. With that in mind, I think that living a life worth processing is an essential part of the whole game.

Read a lot, write a lot, live a lot. That's how you become a great writer.

Hi Doctor,

You always seem to make a big point of showcasing how much of a recluse you are. I consider myself an introvert, but even I can sometimes be in awe of your shut-in powers. Why are you like this?

Mike, Age 15

Mike,

I am nothing more than a man living a life in accordance with his values. And that value is, very specifically, to only know ten people. Exactly ten. No more, no less. I then take all of the energy that I would have spread too thin amongst multitudes of other people and focus it on those ten people instead. There's a lot less cacophony this way, and the only time things get complicated is when I have to hold ranked, skill-based competitions to see who sits where during dinner parties.

Dear Dr. Cecil,

I know that the fear of failure is prevalent in any industry and that there's always a risk to putting yourself out there. But seeing as you get so many of them, how do you deal with bad reviews?

Safiya, age 17

Safiya,

Whenever you show what you create, you send a signal out into a world of noise. The signal isn't meant for everyone. In fact, no signal can be meant for everyone. That just turns into more noise. The best you can do is hope that you sent your signal in such a way that it gets received by the people it was meant for.

So normally what I do is draw a circle on the ground, about nine feet in diameter. I then invite my critics, one by one, to step into the circle with me. If they can move me out of it, I will concede to their terrible opinion about my work. They may bring a single blunt weapon of their choosing. And while this may be bravado on my part, I will enter the circle unarmed.

Hi Dr. Cecil,

Do you have any advice for people going through a hard time? This last year has been rough on me for so many reasons and right now it feels hard to look out into the world and see any goodness in it.

Theo, Age 15

Theo,

You will survive this hard time, as you have survived every hard time before this. Moreover, you will emerge from this time even stronger than before. Existence is a crucible with which we strengthen the mettle of our being, and with that strength we can search for the goodness in the world. Goodness is hard to find and even harder to defend, but, if defended, and if allowed to grow, then goddammit we all might just stand a chance against the impending robot uprising.

Dr. Cecil,

I'd like to start off by sending my condolences to you for that tragic warehouse fire some years ago. As a voracious reader of your novels, I was very sad to hear that every known copy of your last work for fans of my age had been destroyed.

While the wait was long, I was elated to hear of your return to the literary world with Ghost Hunters Adventure Club and the Secret of the Grande Chateau. *To be truthful, I found the plot hackneyed and the insertion of yourself as a meta-character to be ham-fisted at times. However, in spite of that, there remained this relentless pursuit of triumphant, human moments that I find deeply rooted within everything you create.*

It was a good try.

My question, if it isn't too forward, is regarding the split with your longtime friends and publishers, Bradford & Bradford. I was sorry to see them close their doors, bringing such a legendary collaboration to an end, but I get that warehouse fires can do that sometimes. However, seeing the recent news of Bradford & Bradford's reformation as a publishing house got me to wondering: Will we be seeing a reprint of Cerberus, From On High? *Or perhaps will we see you take on these types of novels again?*

Vernon, Age 33

Vernon,

Wait. Hold on. They did what now?

<<<<>>>>